Tree-
House
comix
Proudly
Presents

CAT KiD
COMIC CLUB
ON PURPOSE

WORDS, ILLUSTRATIONS, AND ARTWORK BY
DAV PILKEY

WITH DIGITAL COLOR BY JOSE GARIBALDI

graphix

AN IMPRINT OF

📖 SCHOLASTIC

TO JEFF, JULIE, WILL, AND GRANT KINNEY

Library of Congress Control Number 2021949401

978-1-338-80194-1 (POB)   978-1-338-80195-8 (Library)

10 9 8 7 6 5 4 3 2 1   22 23 24 25 26

Printed in the U.S.A.   44
First edition, April 2022

Illustrations, 3-D models, photography, and hand lettering by Dav Pilkey.

ALL mini comics colored by Dav Pilkey using pencil, watercolors, acrylic paints, markers, colored pencils, crayons, and gouache. 3-D models built out of recycled plastic lids, clay, paper, wood, wire, tape, glue, broken toys, balloons, and other throwaway items.

Digital Color by Jose Garibaldi | Flatting by Aaron Polk

Editor: Ken Geist | Editorial Team: Megan Peace and Jonah Newman
Book design by Dav Pilkey and Phil Falco
Creative Director: Phil Falco
Publisher: David Saylor

Chapters & Comics

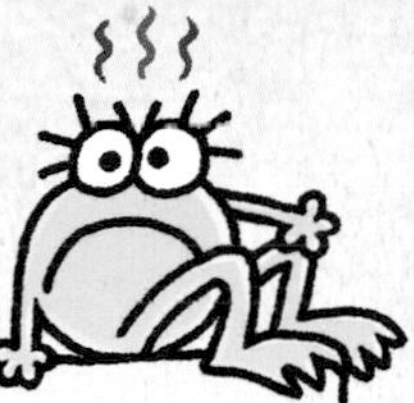

Find out who you are
and do it on purpose.

-Dolly Parton

Chapter 1

Weekend Woes

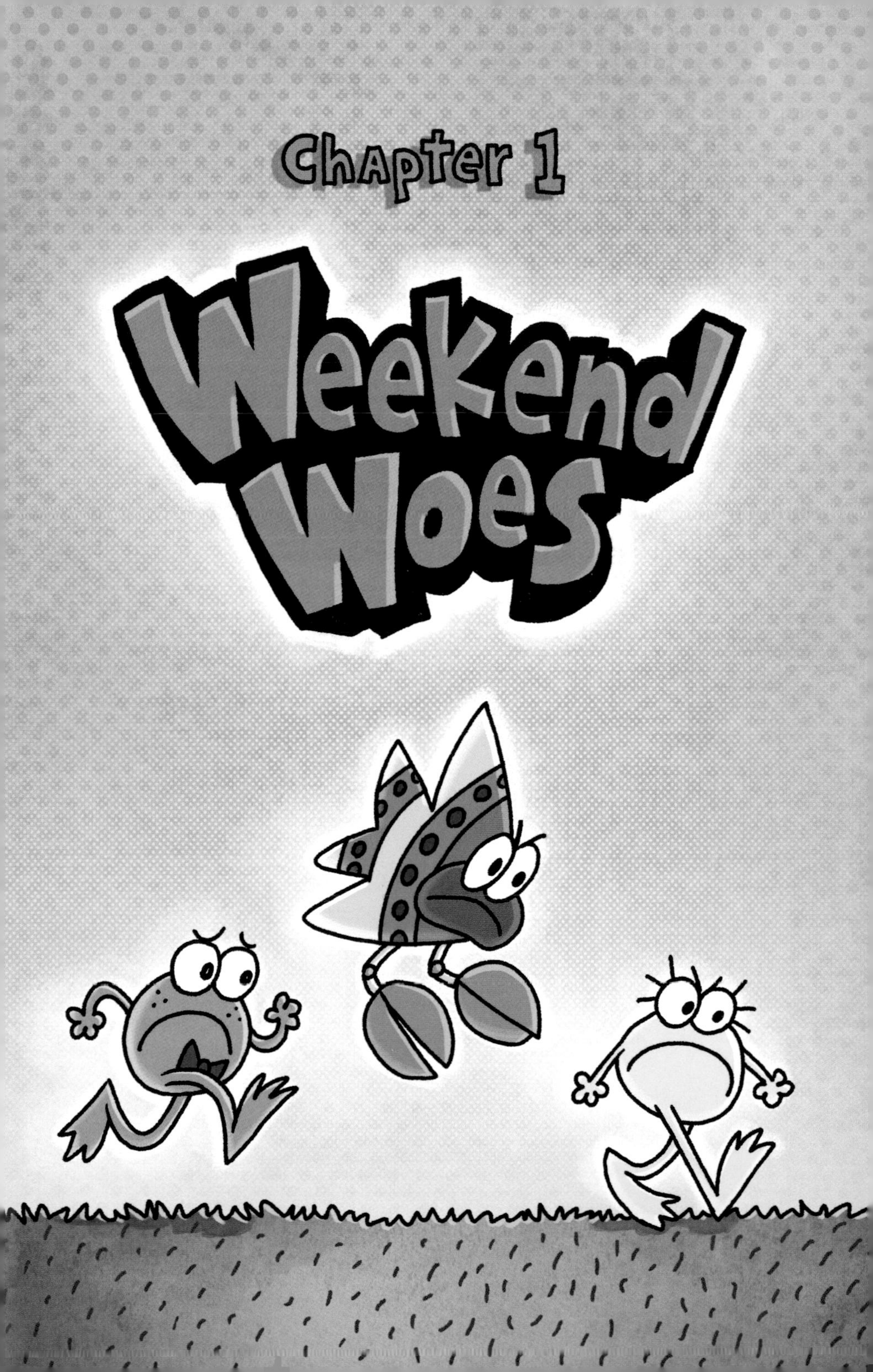

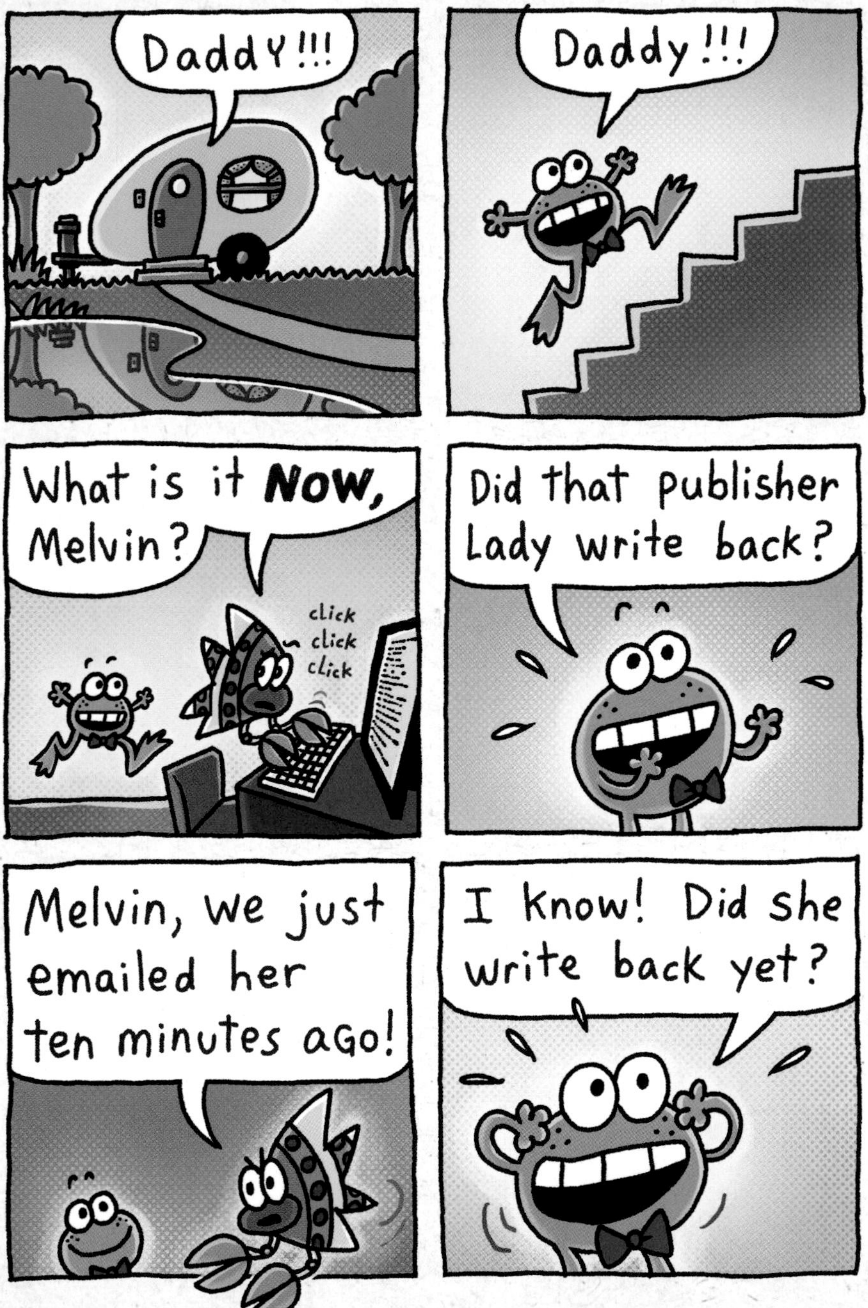
Daddy!!!
Daddy!!!
What is it NOW, Melvin?
click click click
Did that publisher Lady write back?
Melvin, we just emailed her ten minutes ago!
I know! Did she write back yet?

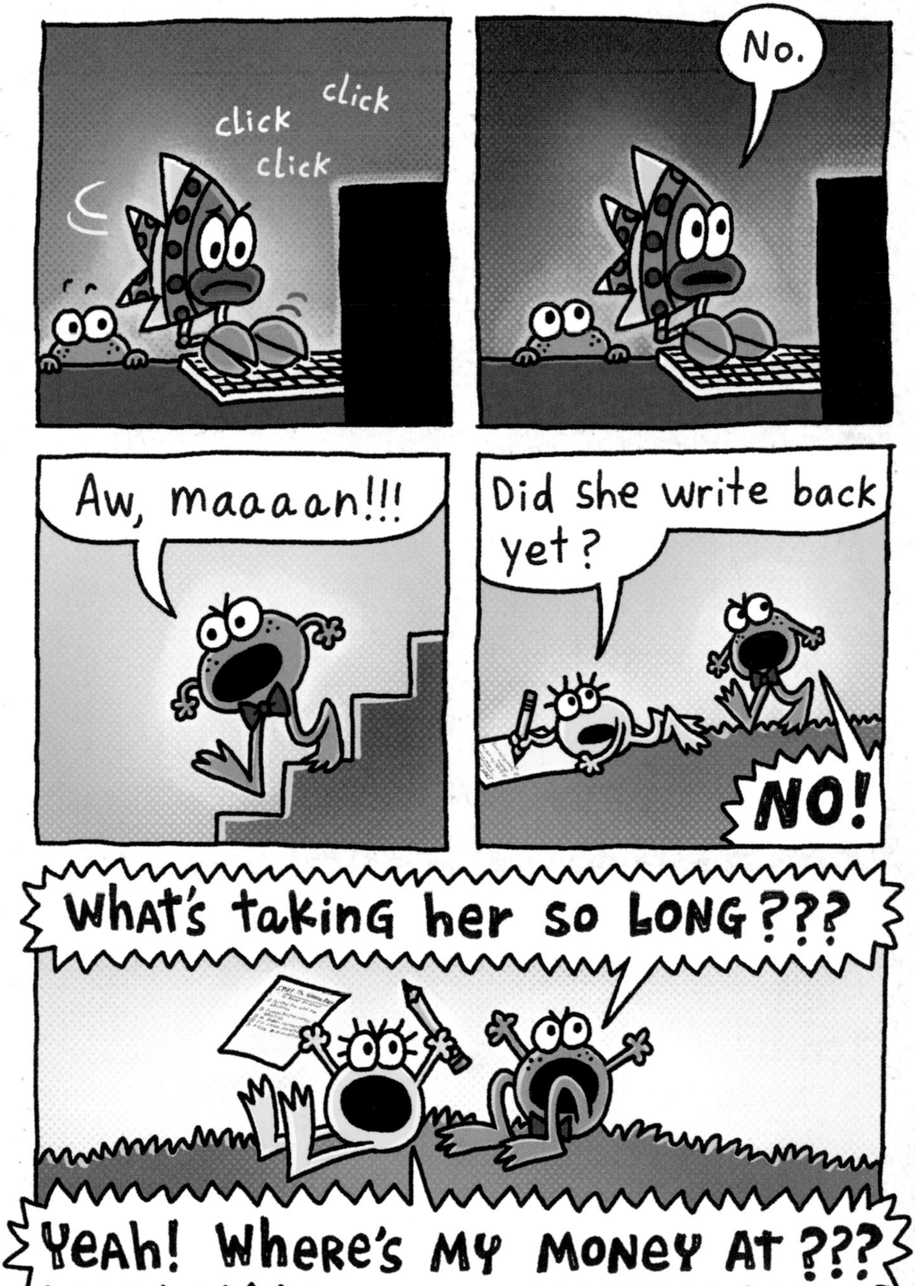
click
click
click
No.
Aw, maaaan!!!
Did she write back yet?
NO!
What's taking her so LONG???
Yeah! Where's MY MONEY AT???

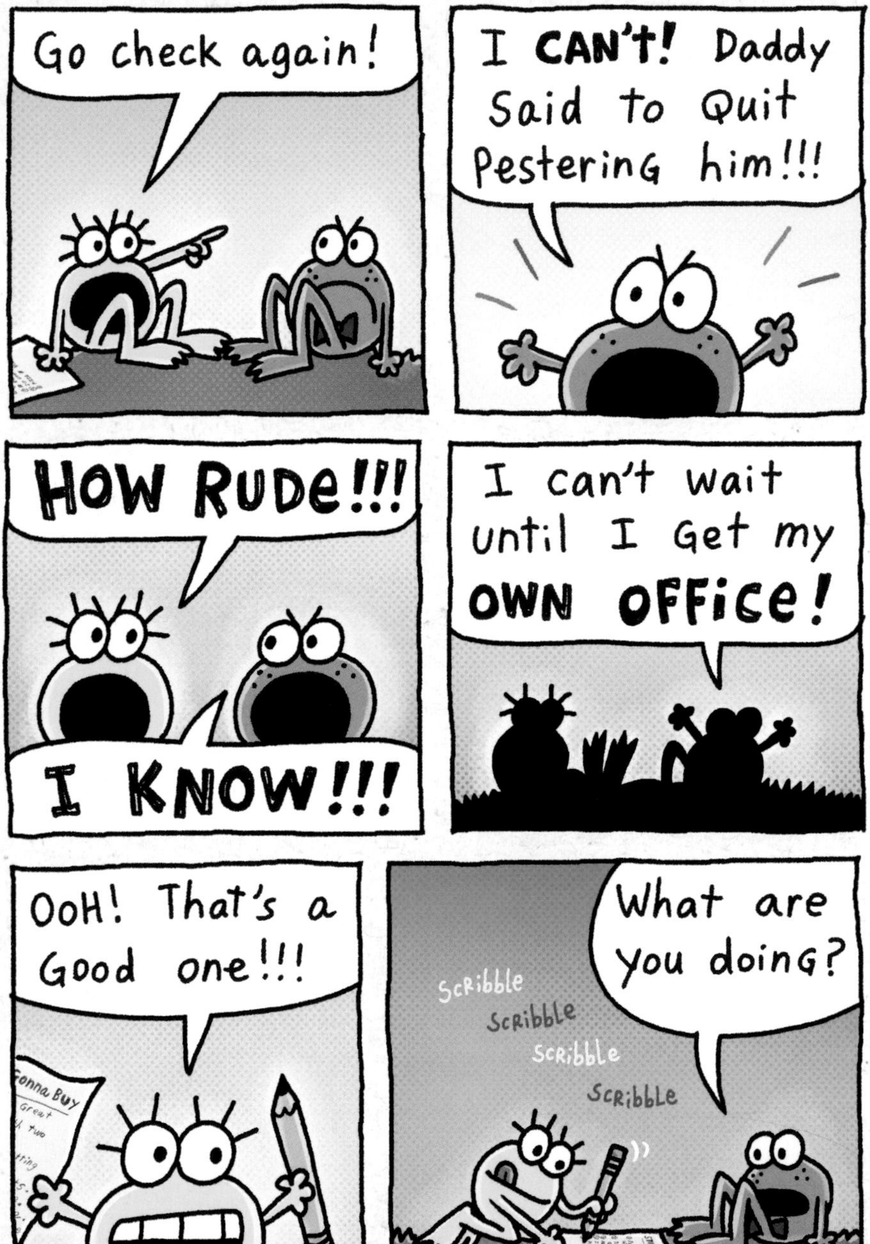
Go check again!
I CAN'T! Daddy Said to Quit Pestering him!!!
HOW RUDE!!!
I KNOW!!!
I can't wait until I Get my OWN OFFICE!
OOH! That's a Good one!!!
Gonna Buy
What are you doinG?
SCRibble
SCRibble
SCRibble
SCRibble

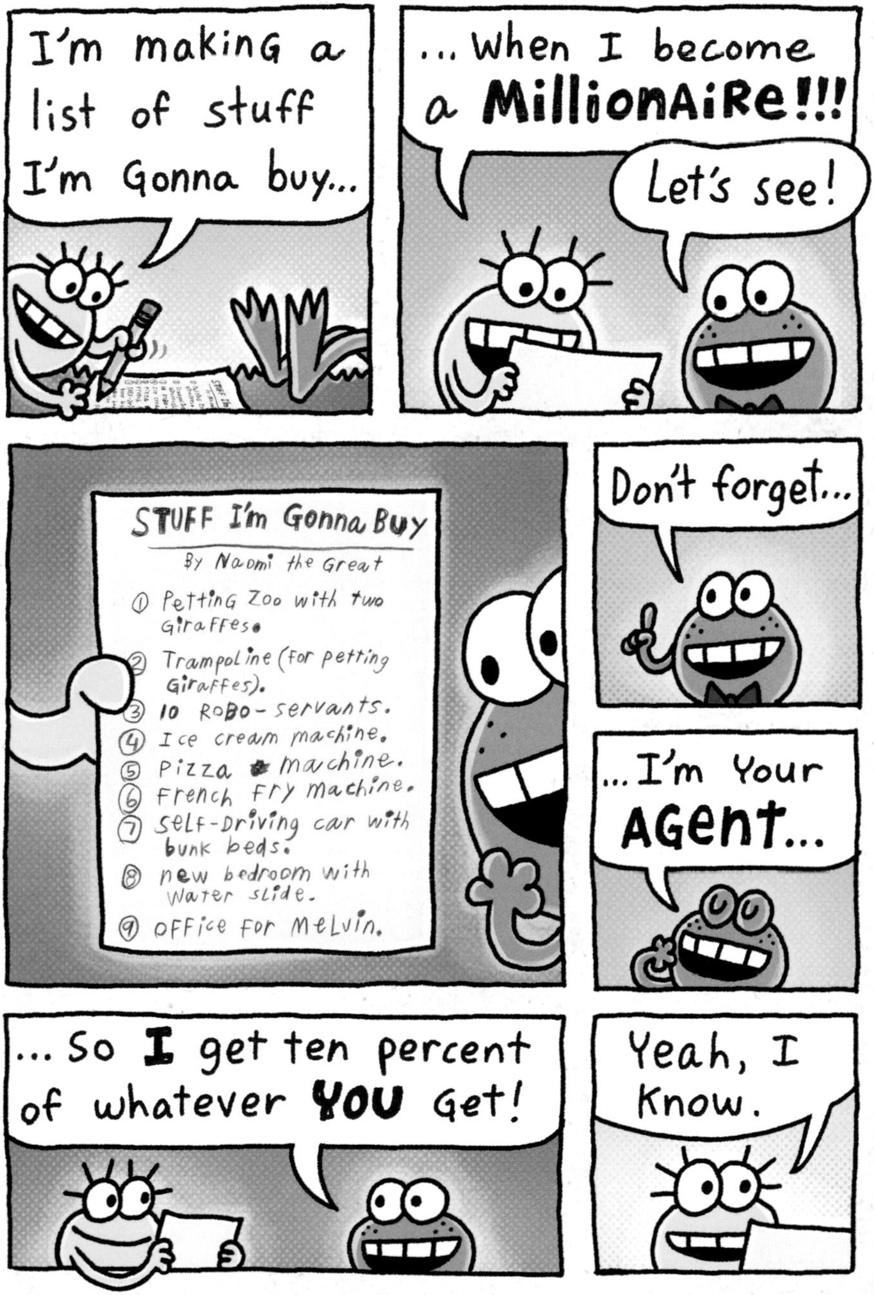
I'm making a list of stuff I'm Gonna buy...
...When I become a MILLIONAIRE!!!
Let's see!
STUFF I'm Gonna Buy
By Naomi the Great
① Petting Zoo with two Giraffes.
② Trampoline (for petting Giraffes).
③ 10 ROBO-servants.
④ Ice cream machine.
⑤ Pizza machine.
⑥ French Fry machine.
⑦ Self-Driving car with bunk beds.
⑧ new bedroom with water slide.
⑨ office for Melvin.
Don't forget...
...I'm your AGENT...
...So I get ten percent of whatever YOU Get!
Yeah, I Know.

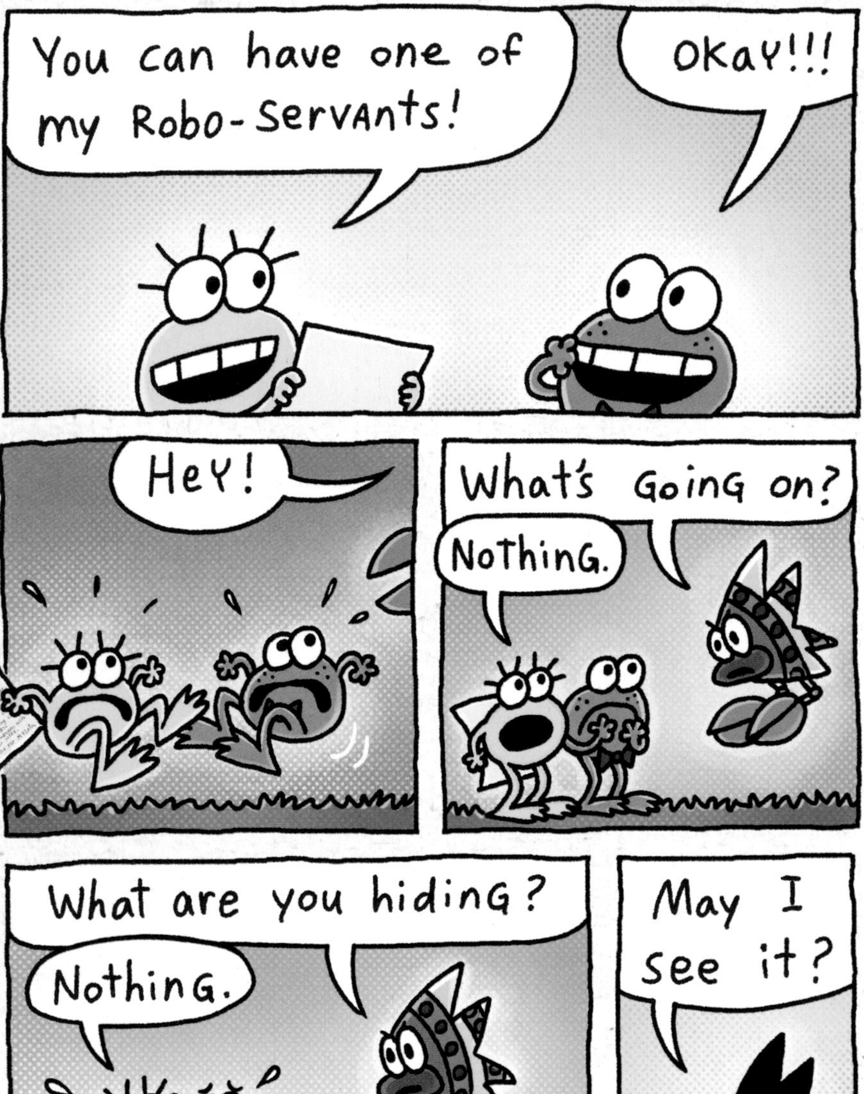
You can have one of my Robo-Servants!
OKAY!!!
HEY!
What's Going on?
Nothing.
What are you hiding?
Nothing.
May I see it?

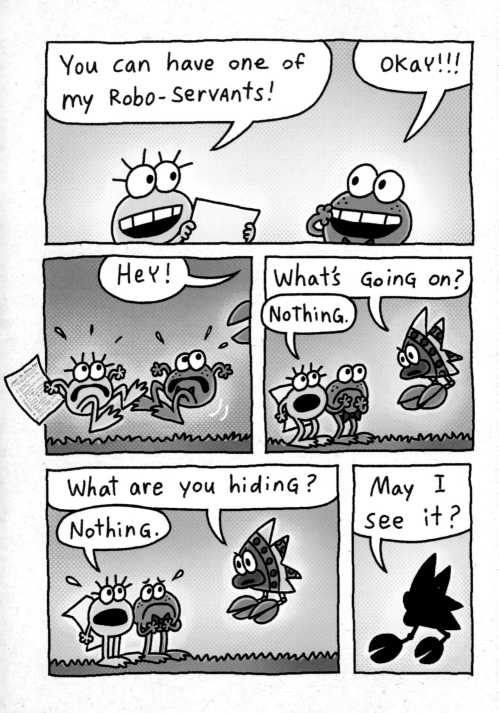

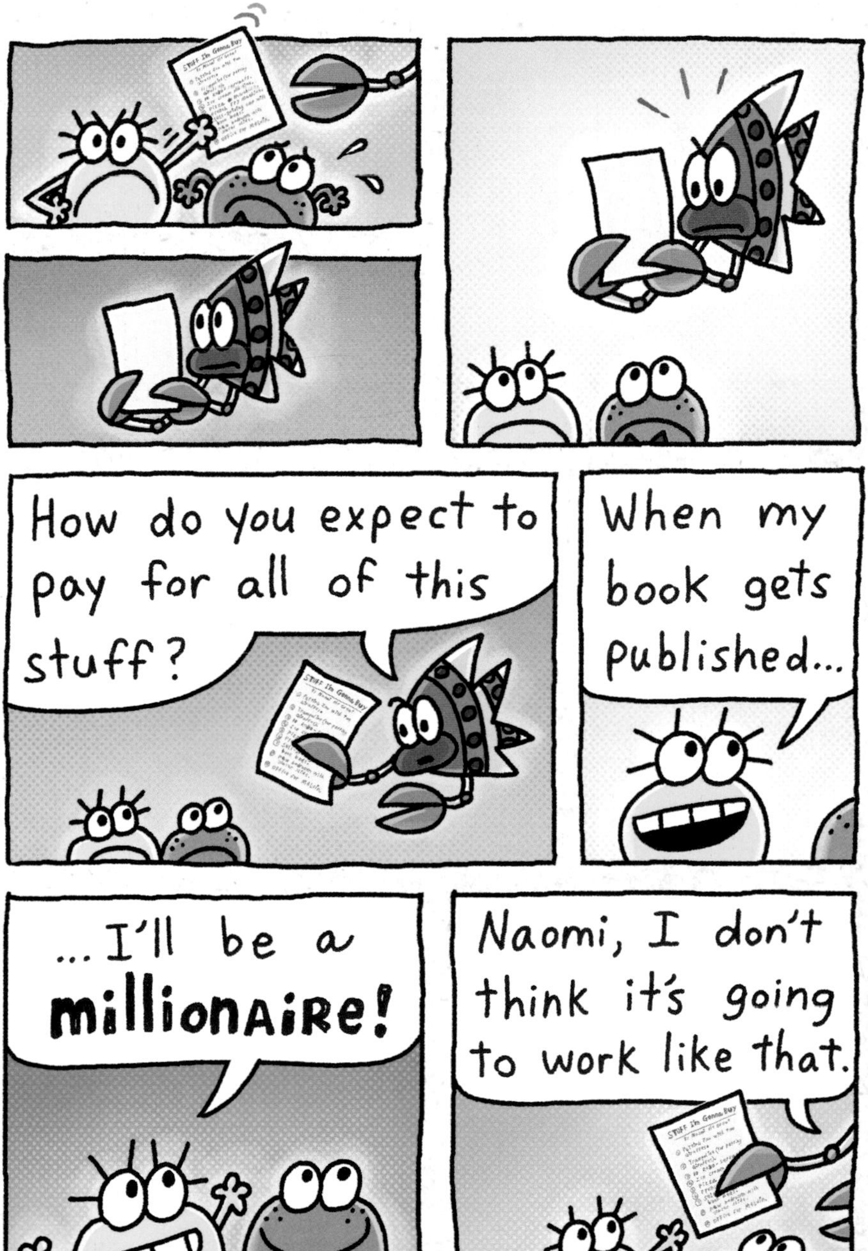
How do you expect to pay for all of this stuff?
When my book gets published...
...I'll be a millionaire!
Naomi, I don't think it's going to work like that.

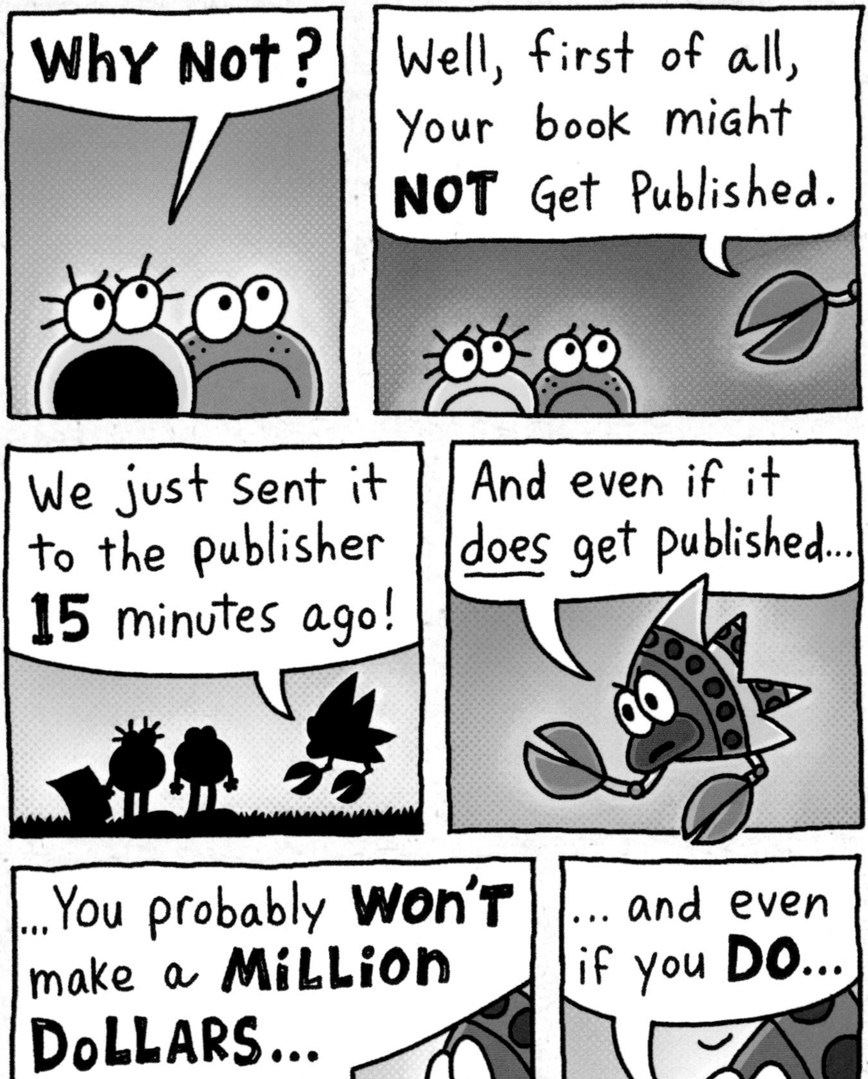
WHY NOT?
Well, first of all, Your book might NOT Get Published.
We just sent it to the publisher 15 minutes ago!
And even if it does get published...
...You probably WON'T make a MILLION DOLLARS...
... and even if you DO...

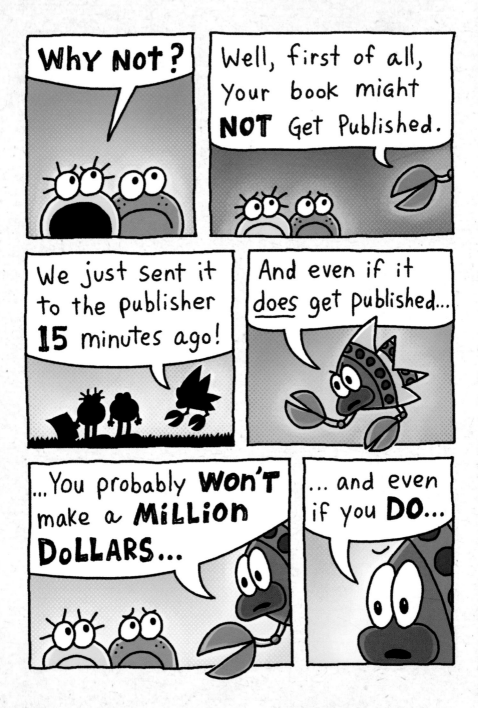

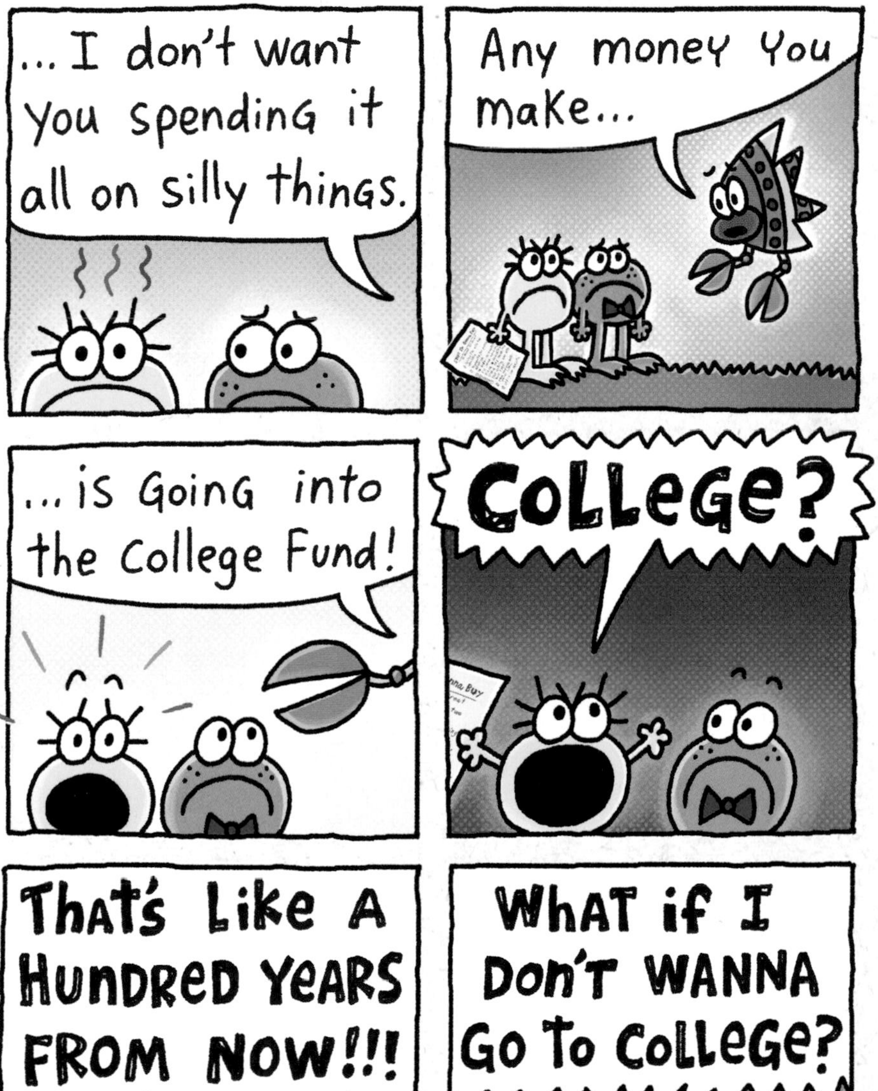
...I don't want you spending it all on silly things.
Any money you make...
...is going into the College Fund!
COLLEGE?
That's like a hundred years from now!!!
What if I don't wanna go to college?

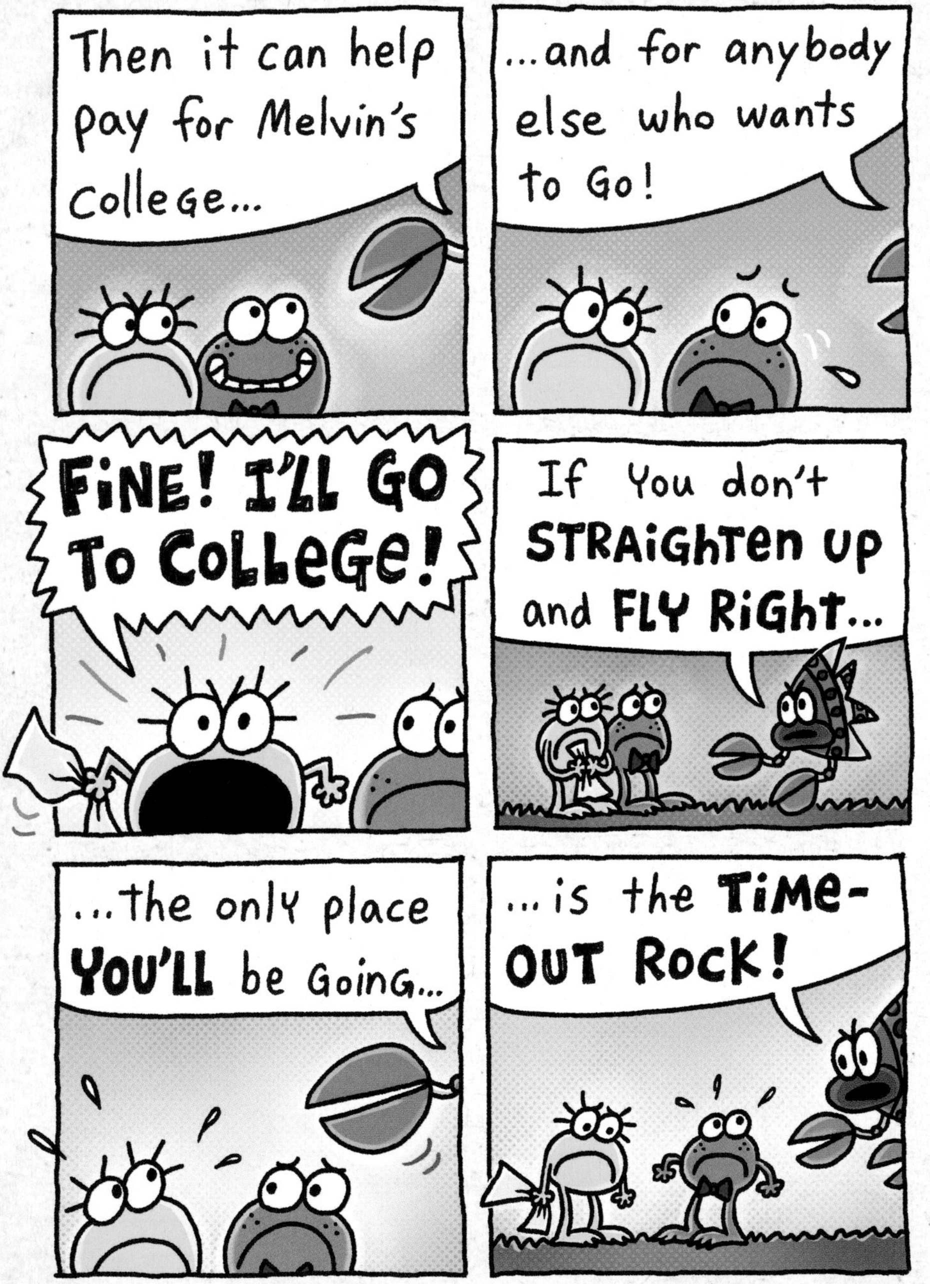
Then it can help pay for Melvin's college...
...and for anybody else who wants to go!
FINE! I'LL GO TO COLLEGE!
If you don't STRAIGHTEN UP and FLY RIGHT...
...the only place YOU'LL be going...
...is the TIME-OUT ROCK!

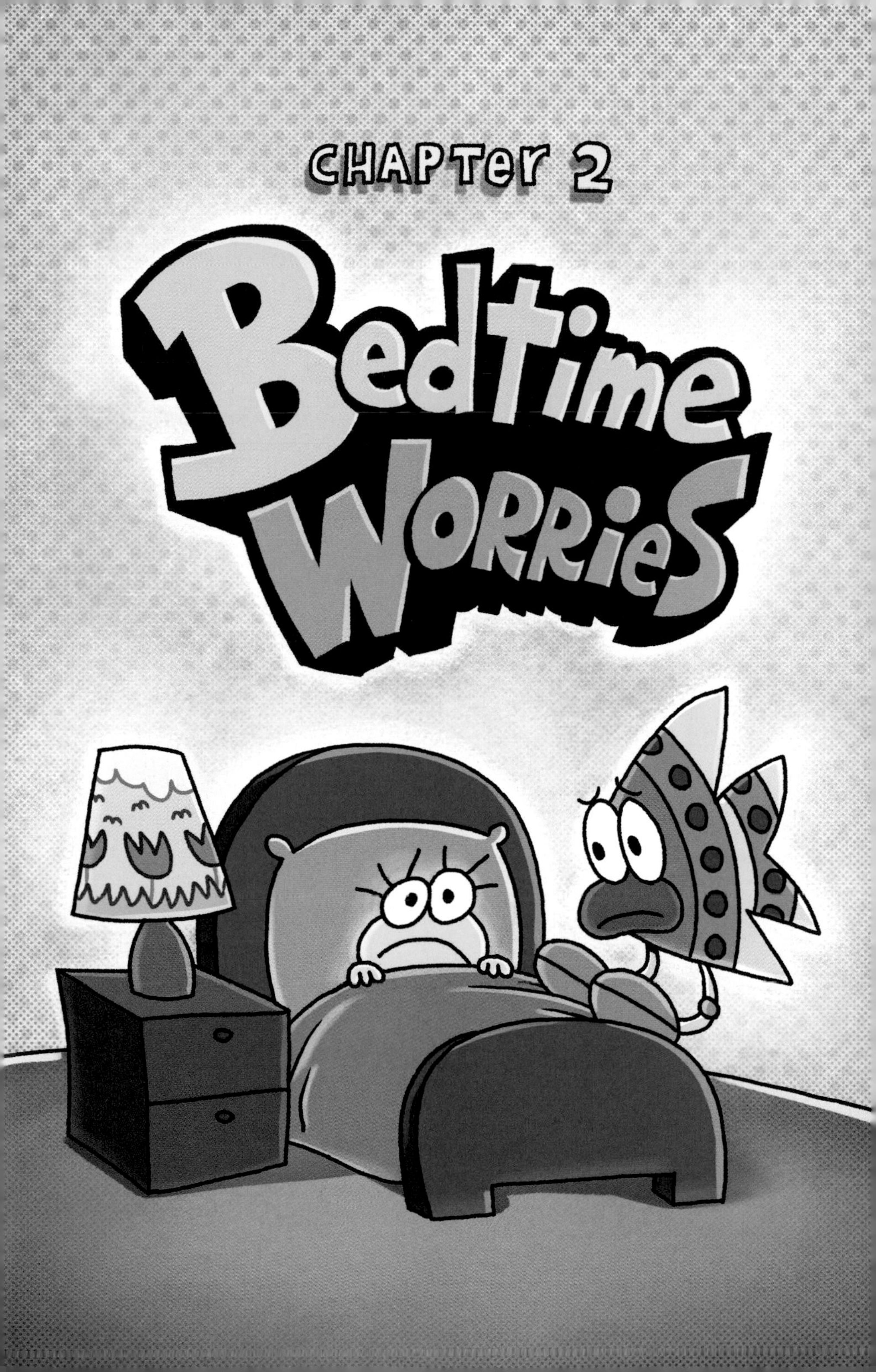
CHAPTER 2
Bedtime Worries

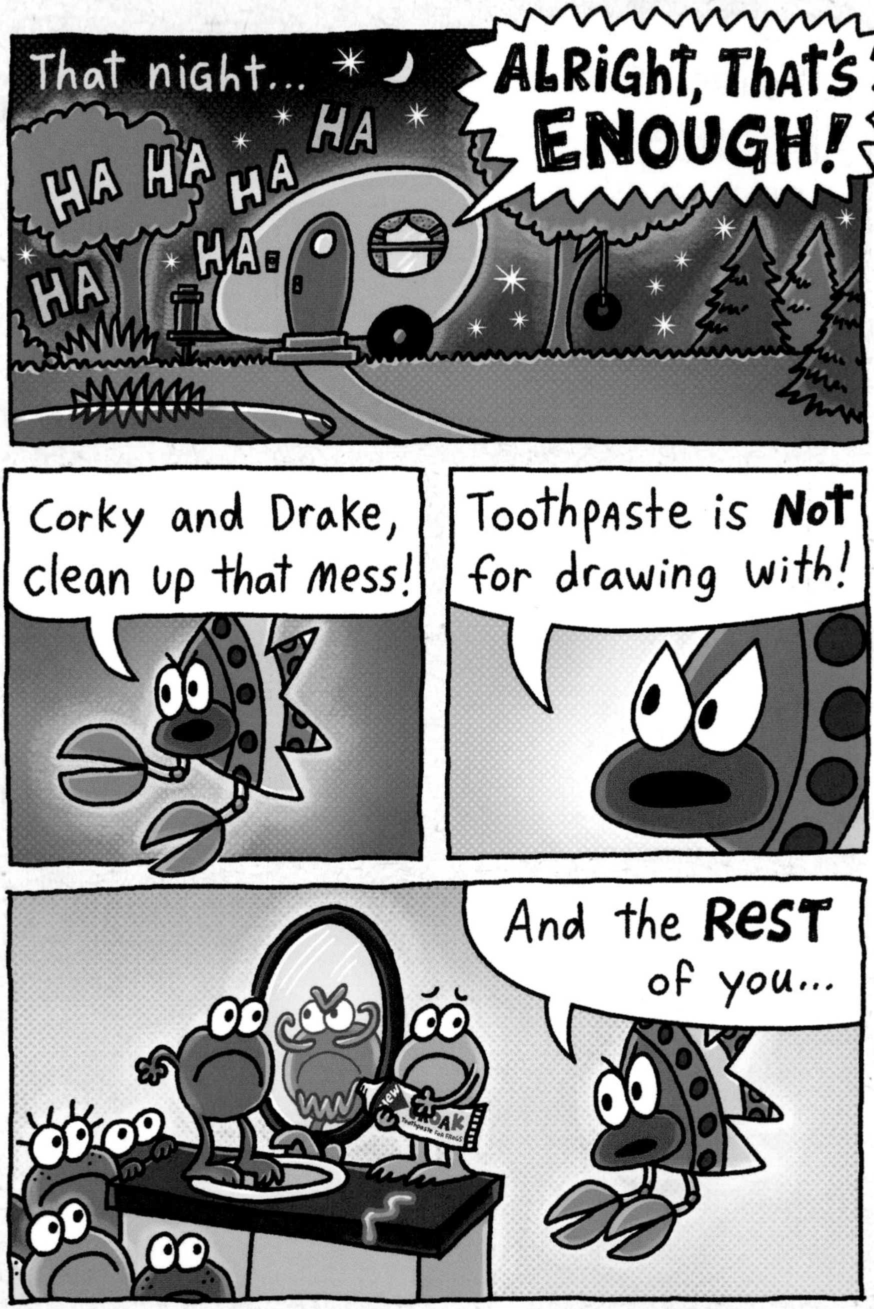
That night...
HA HA HA HA HA HA HA
ALRIGHT, THAT'S ENOUGH!
Corky and Drake, clean up that mess!
Toothpaste is NOT for drawing with!
And the REST of you...
NEW CROAK Toothpaste for FROGS

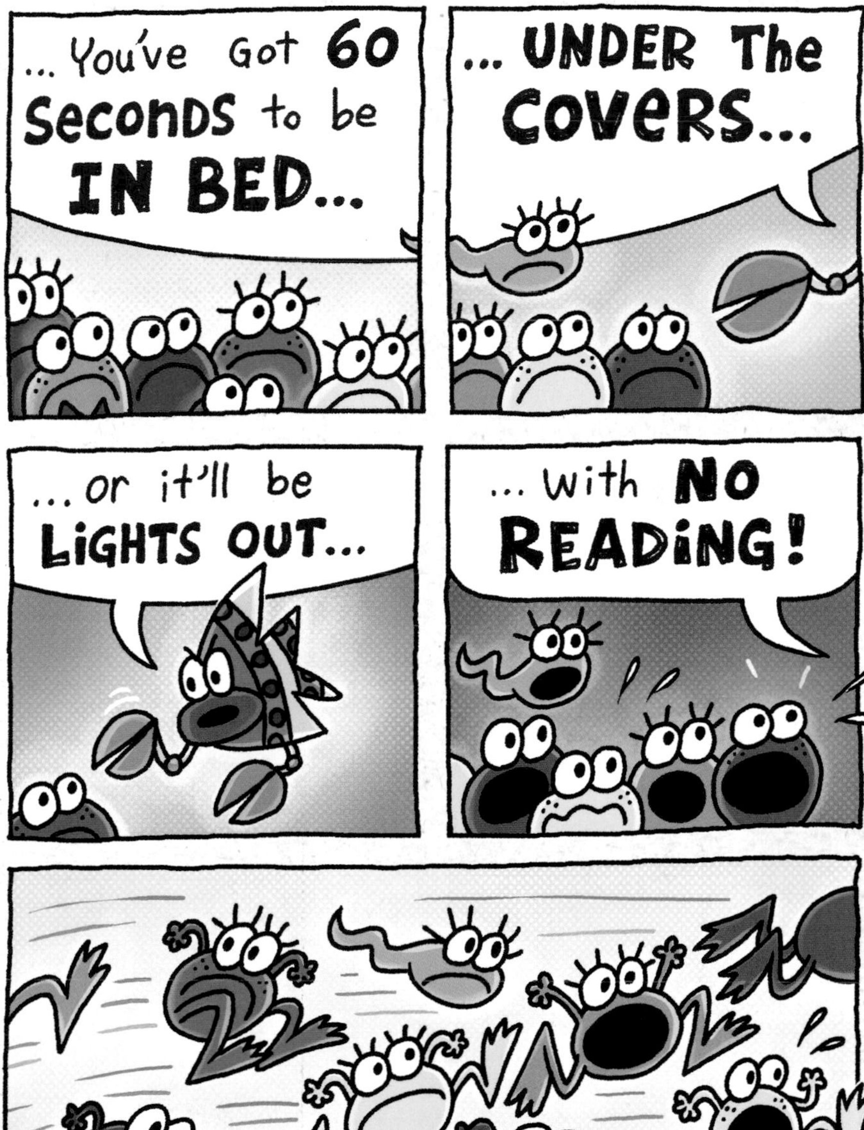
...You've Got 60 Seconds to be IN BED...
...UNDER The COVERS...
...or it'll be LIGHTS OUT...
...with NO READING!

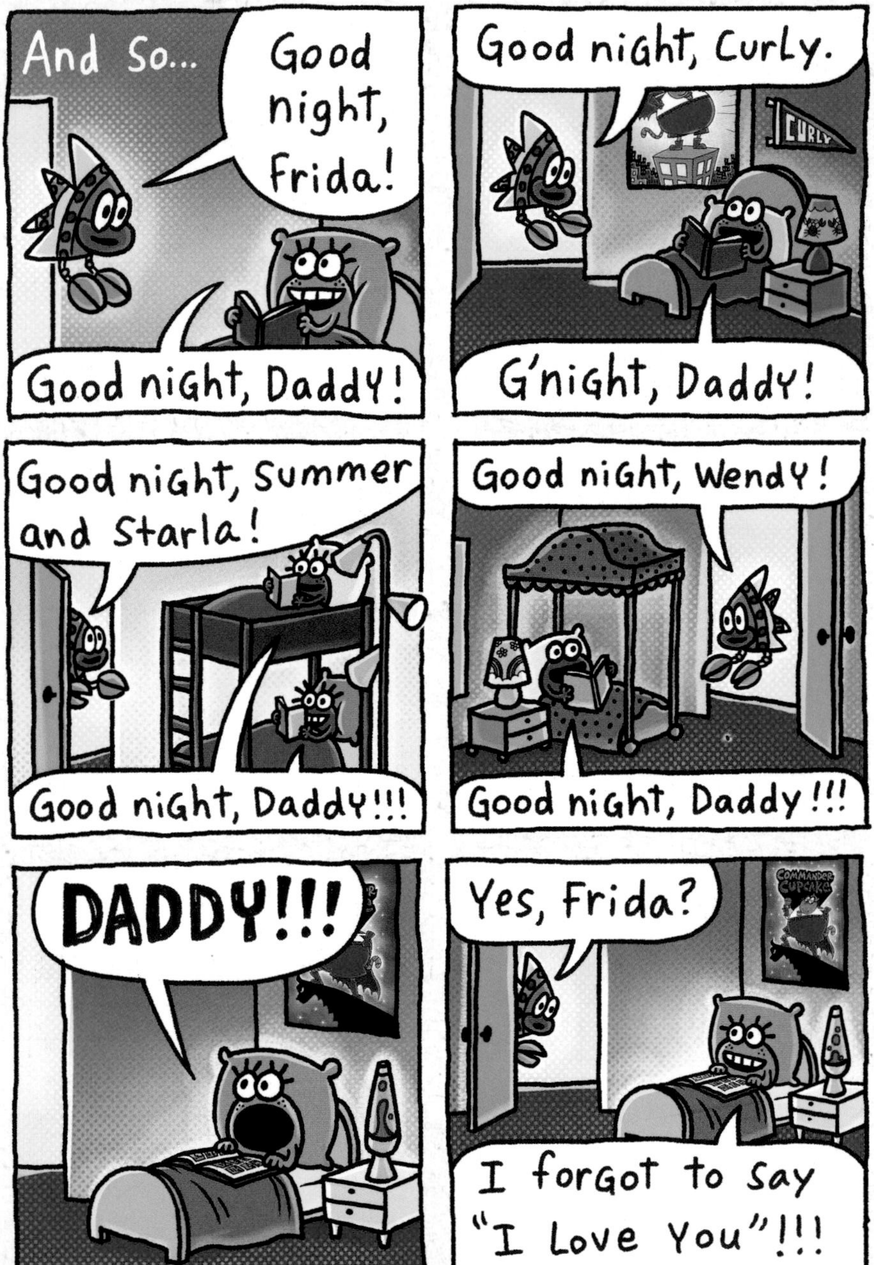
And So...
Good night, Frida!
Good night, Daddy!
Good night, Curly.
CURLY
G'night, Daddy!
Good night, Summer and Starla!
Good night, Daddy!!!
Good night, Wendy!
Good night, Daddy!!!
DADDY!!!
Yes, Frida?
COMMANDER CUPCAKE
I forgot to say "I Love You"!!!

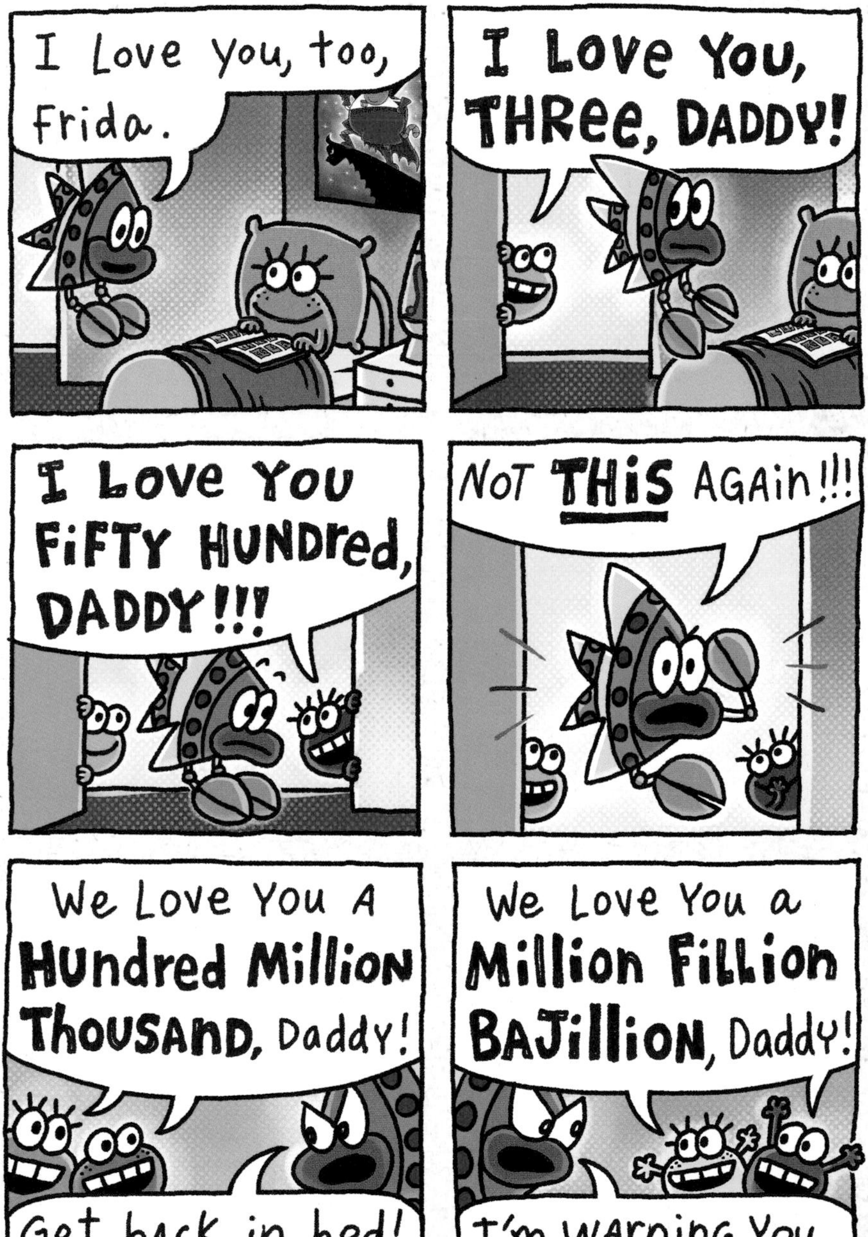
I Love you, too, Frida.
I Love You, THRee, DADDY!
I Love You FiFTY HUNDred, DADDY!!!
NOT THIS AGAin!!!
We Love You A Hundred Million THOUSAND, Daddy!
Get back in bed!
We Love You a Million Fillion BAJillion, Daddy!
I'm WARning You...

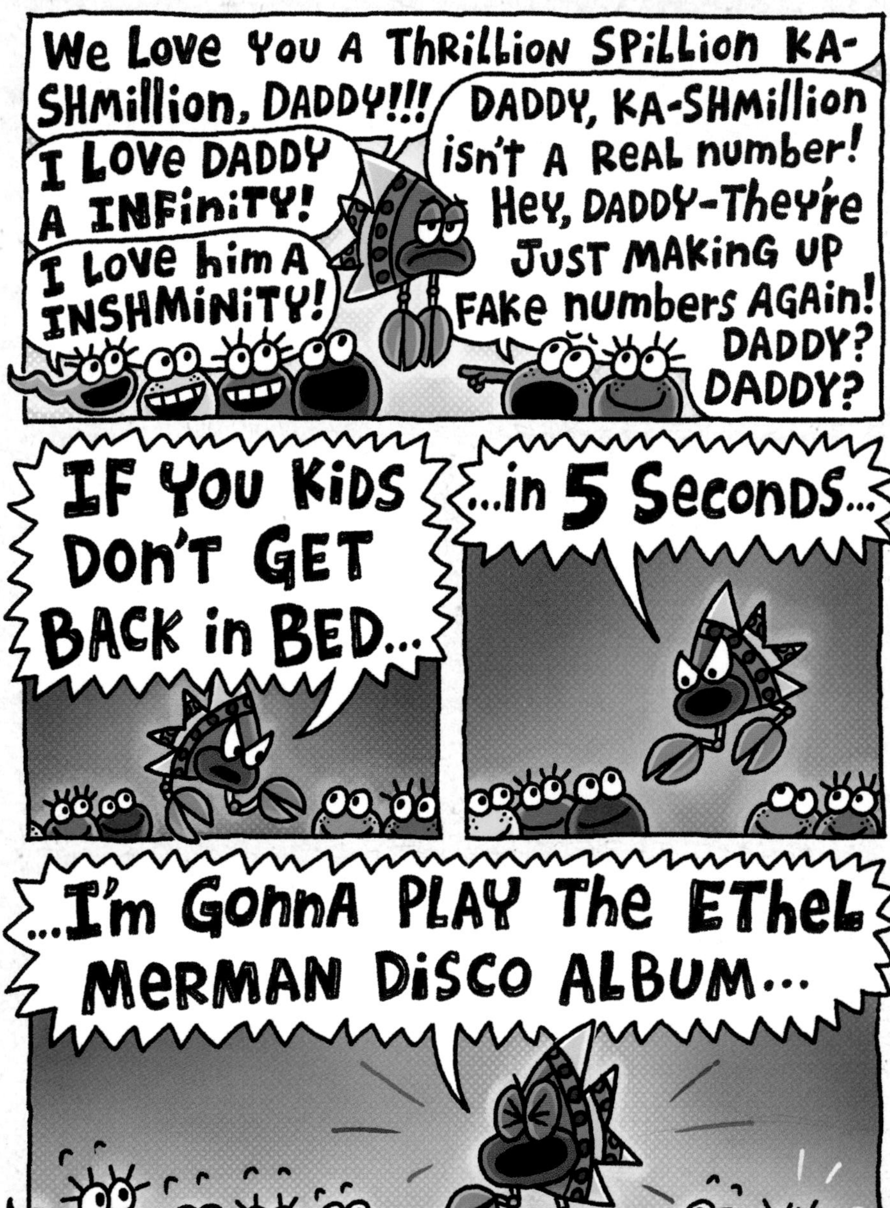
We Love You A Thrillion Spillion KA-SHmillion, DADDY!!!
I Love DADDY A INFinity!
I Love him A INSHMiNiTY!
DADDY, KA-SHmillion isn't A REAL number! Hey, DADDY-They're JUST MAKinG UP FAKE numbers AGAin! DADDY? DADDY?
IF YOU KiDS DON'T GET BACK in BED...
...in 5 SecONDS...
...I'm GonnA PLAY The EThel MeRMAN DiSCO ALBUM...

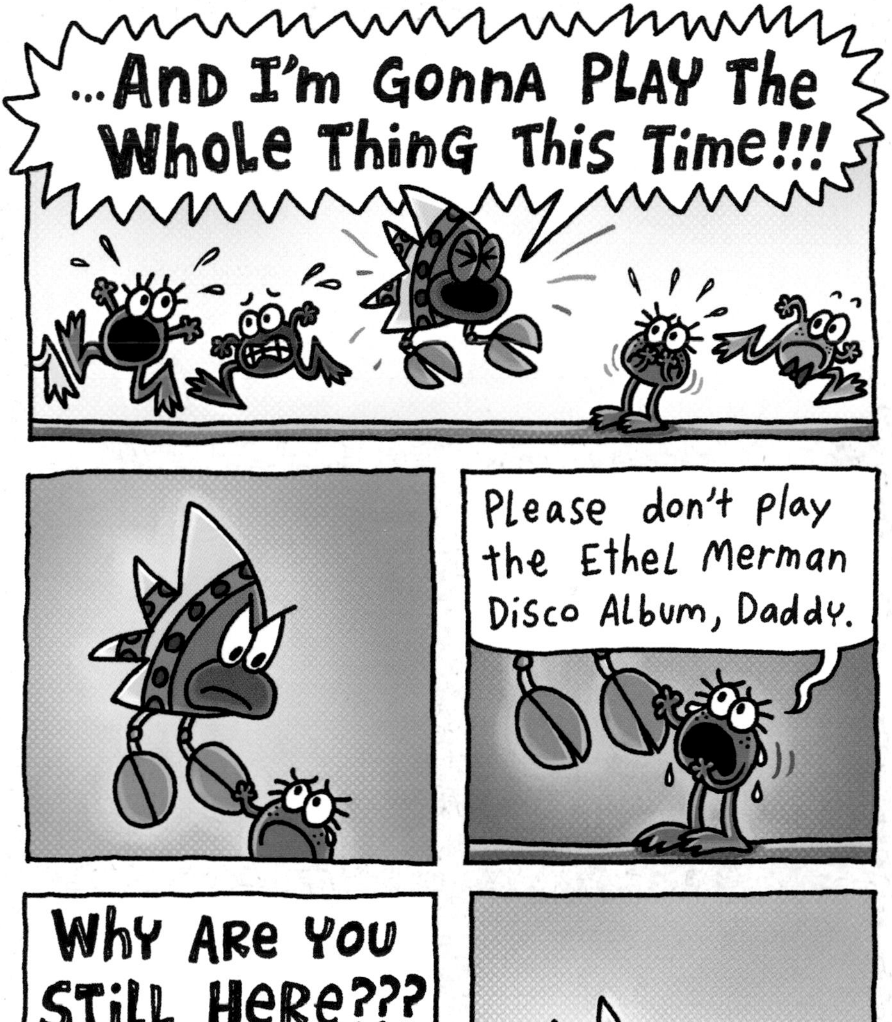
...AND I'M GONNA PLAY THE WHOLE THING THIS TIME!!!
Please don't play the Ethel Merman Disco Album, Daddy.
WHY ARE YOU STILL HERE???

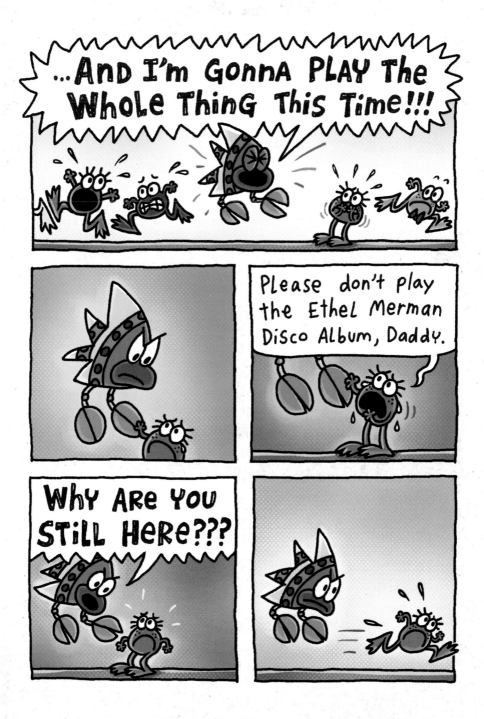

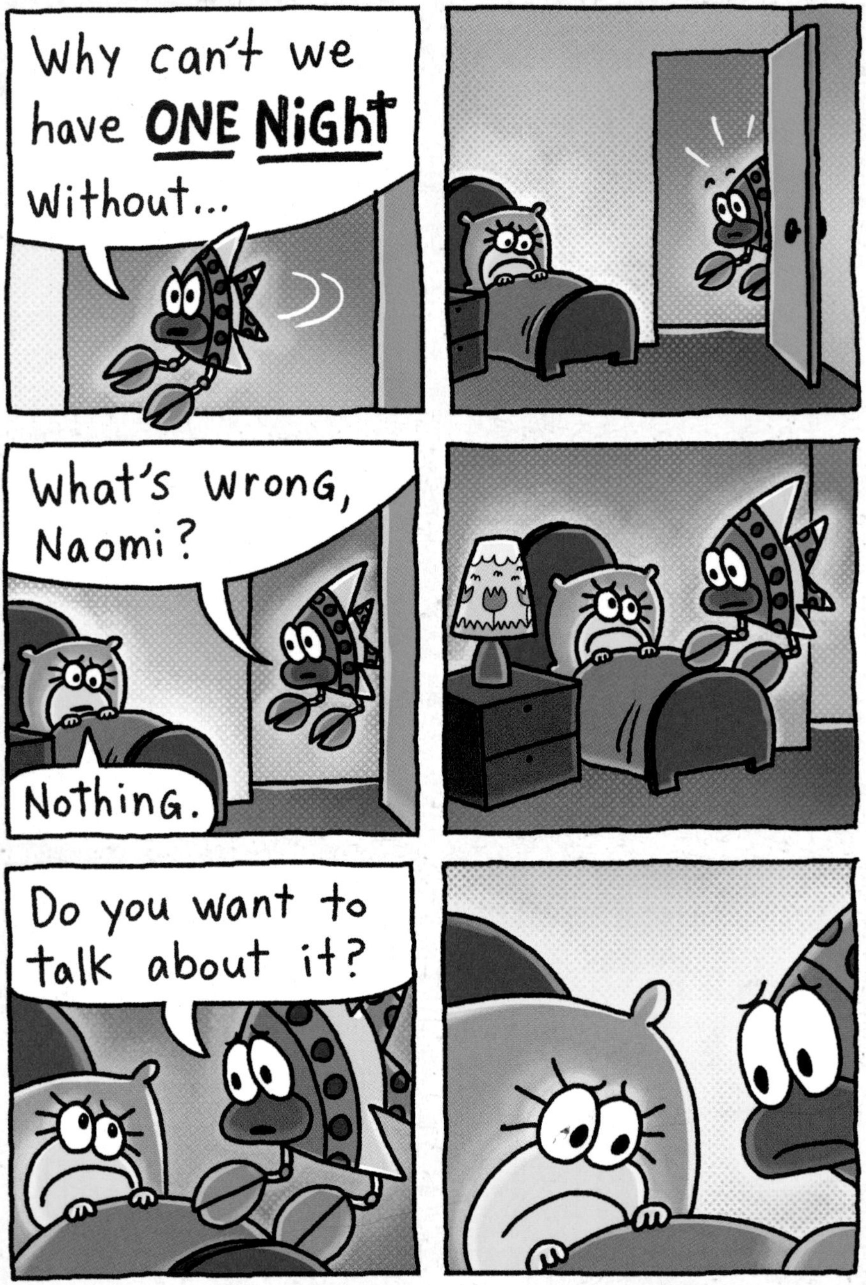
Why can't we have ONE NiGhT without...
What's WRONG, Naomi?
NothinG.
Do you want to talk about it?

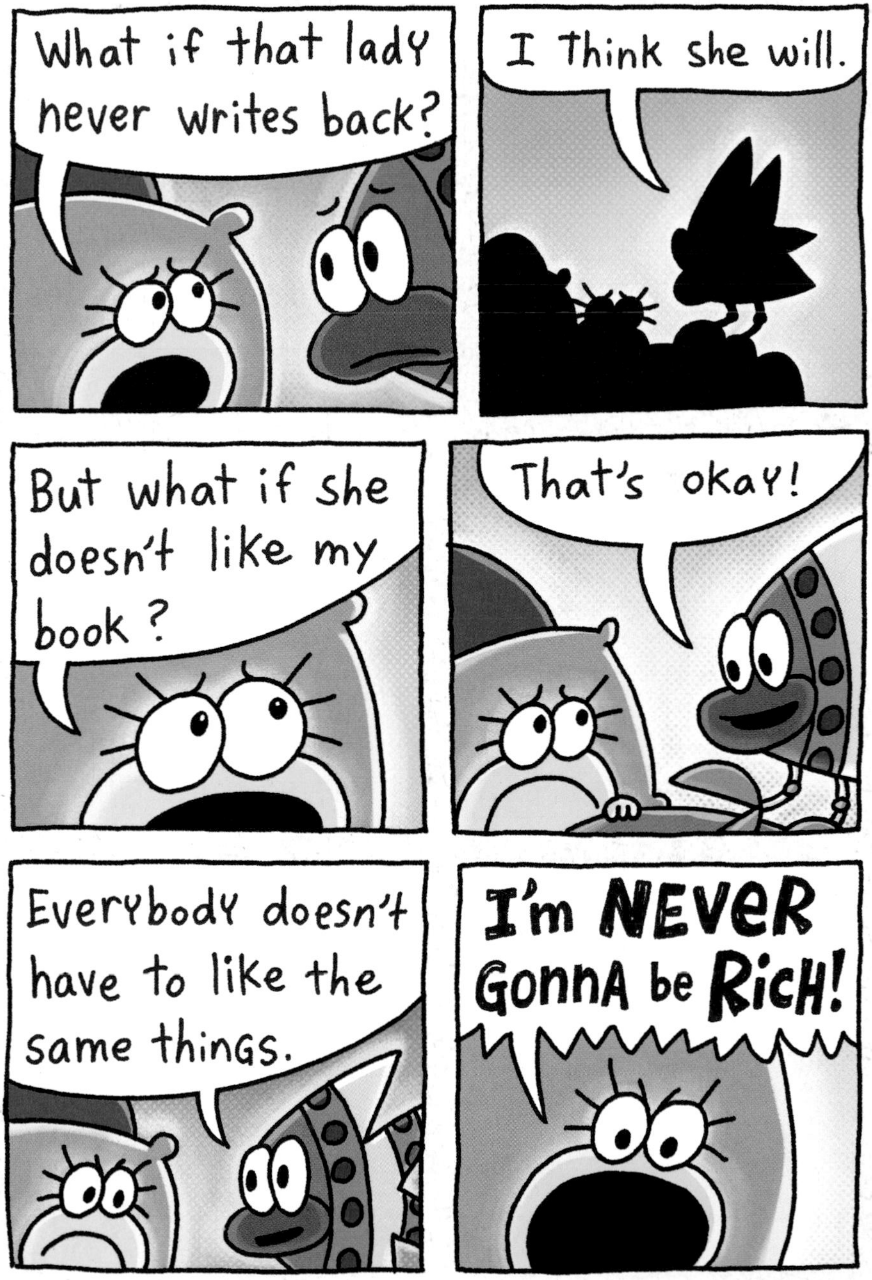
What if that lady never writes back?
I Think she will.
But what if she doesn't like my book?
That's okay!
Everybody doesn't have to like the same things.
I'm NEVER GONNA be RICH!

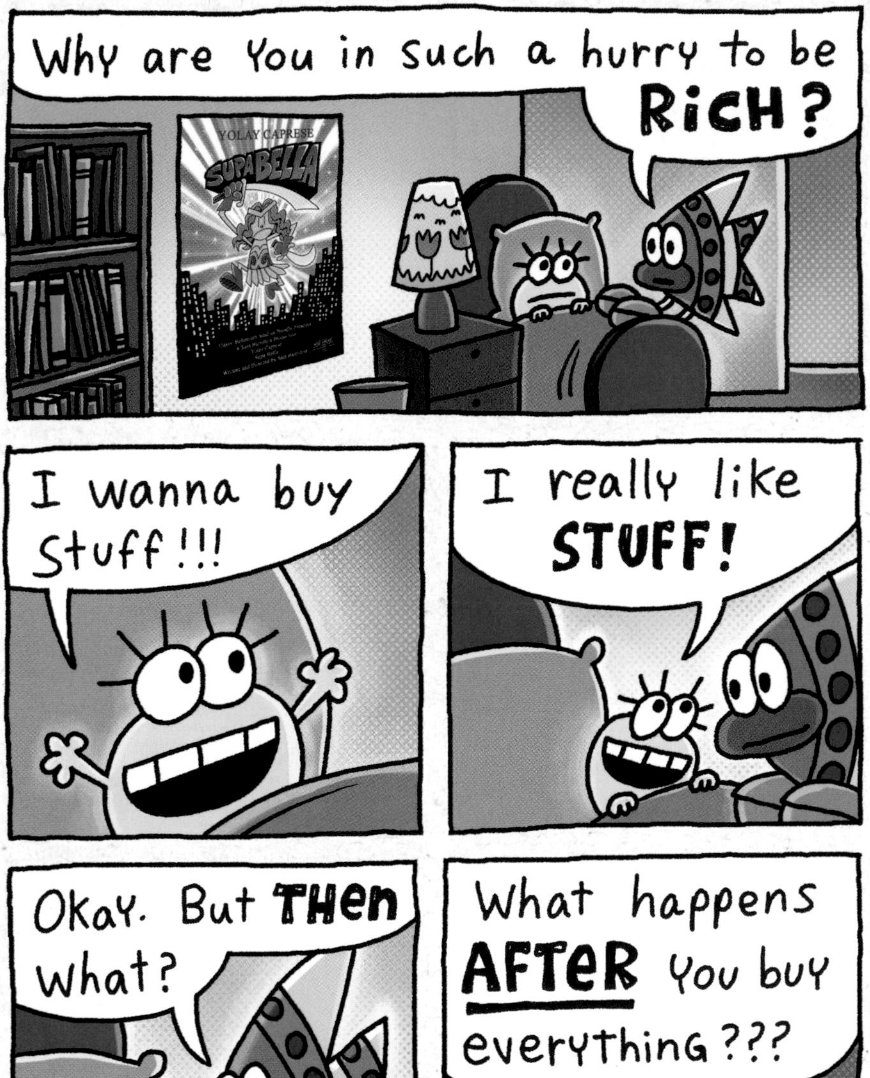
Why are You in such a hurry to be RICH?
YOLAY CAPRESE
SUPABELLA
I wanna buy Stuff!!!
I really like STUFF!
Okay. But THEN what?
What happens AFTER you buy everything???

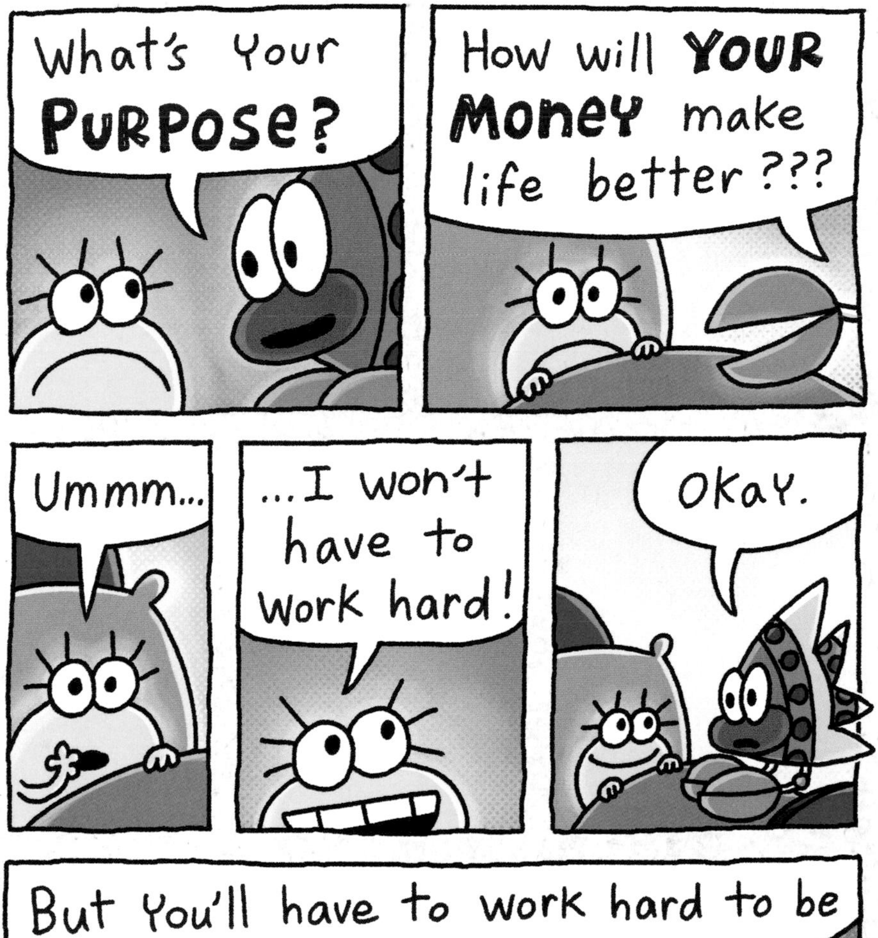
What's Your PURPOSE?
How will YOUR MONEY make life better???
Ummm...
...I won't have to work hard!
OKAY.
But You'll have to work hard to be RICH, right?
Yeah, Probably.

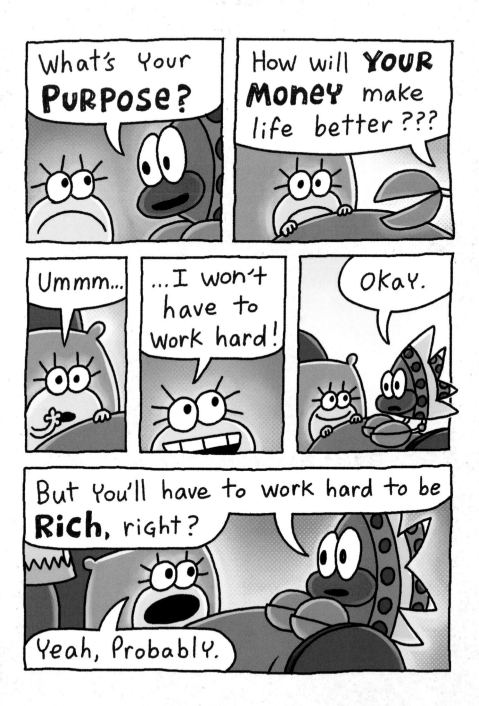

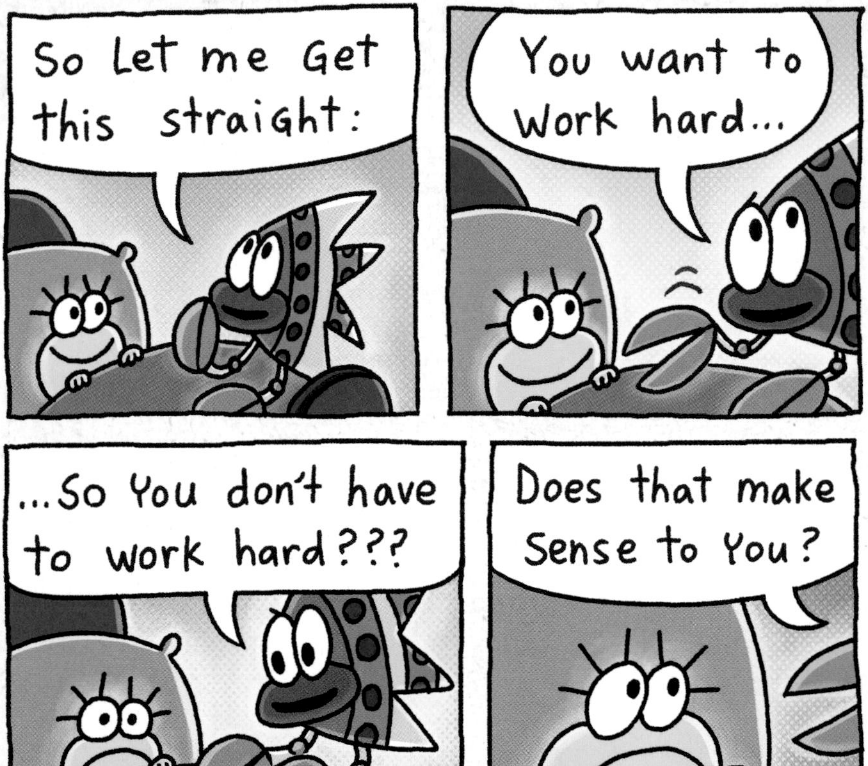
So Let me Get this straight:
You want to Work hard...
...So You don't have to work hard???
Does that make Sense to You?
NOT When YOU SAY it like THAT!
Gassy Behemoth Studios Proudly Presents
A Sam Hamilton Production
Yolay Caprese
Supa Bella
Written and Directed by Sam Hamilton

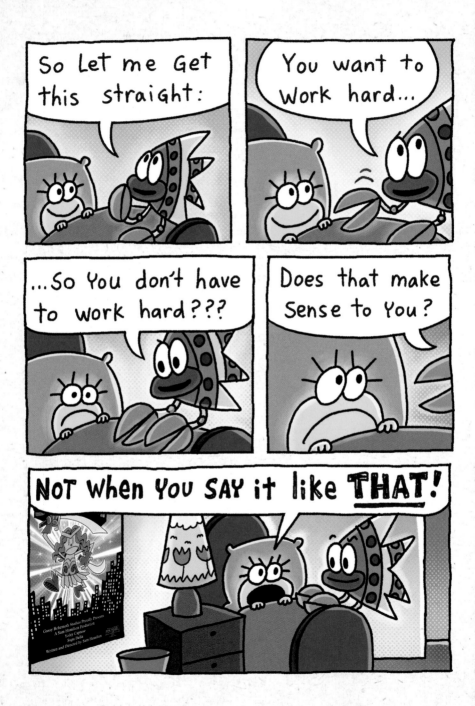

CHAPTER 3

The Big Surprise

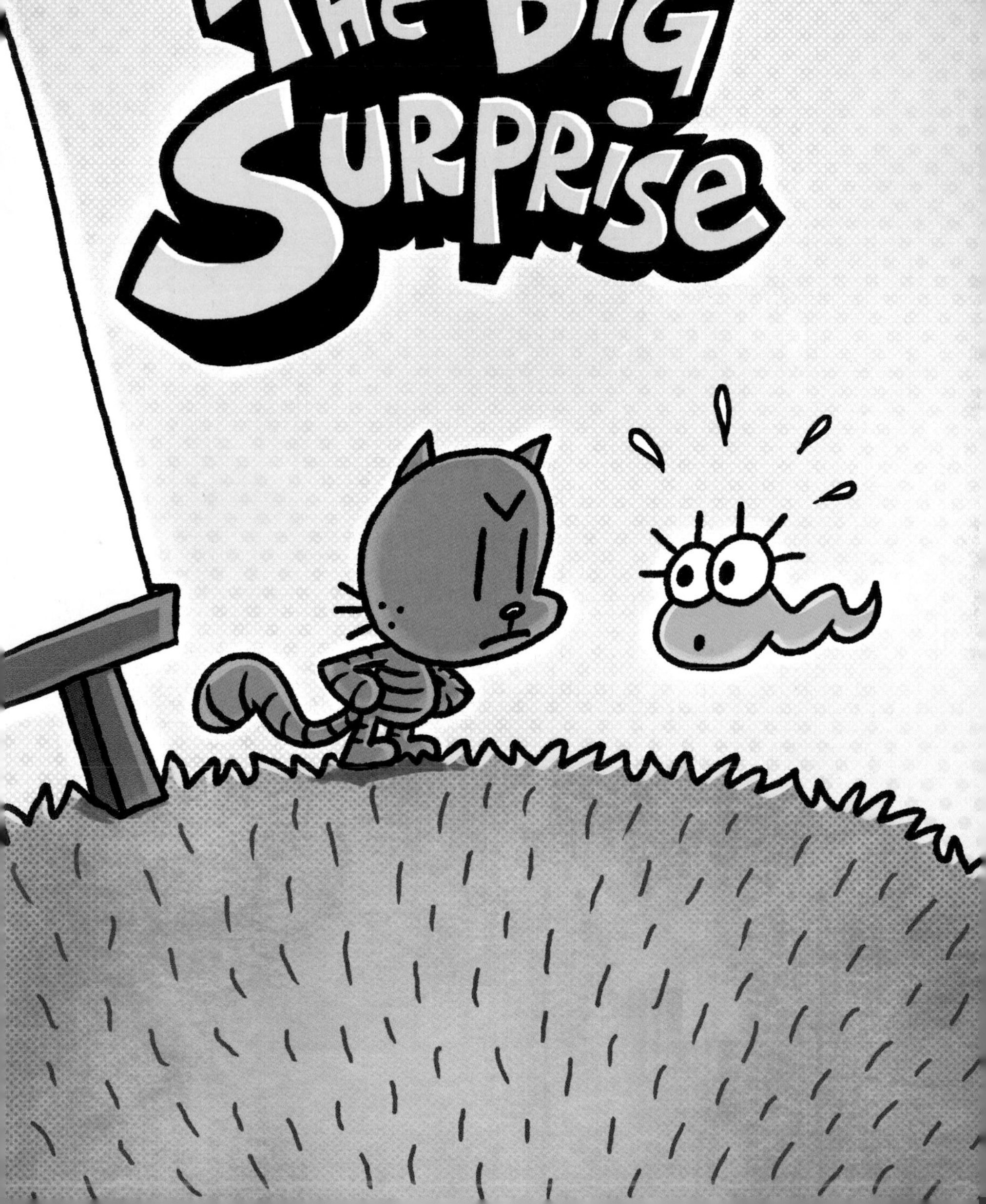

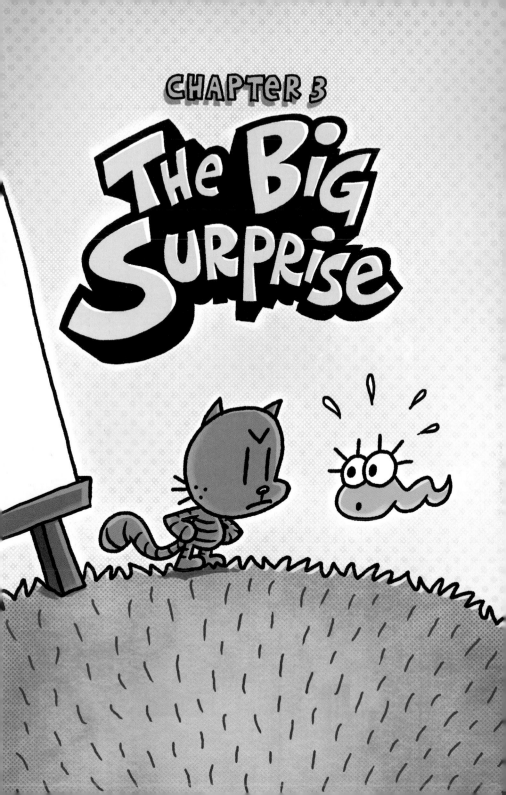

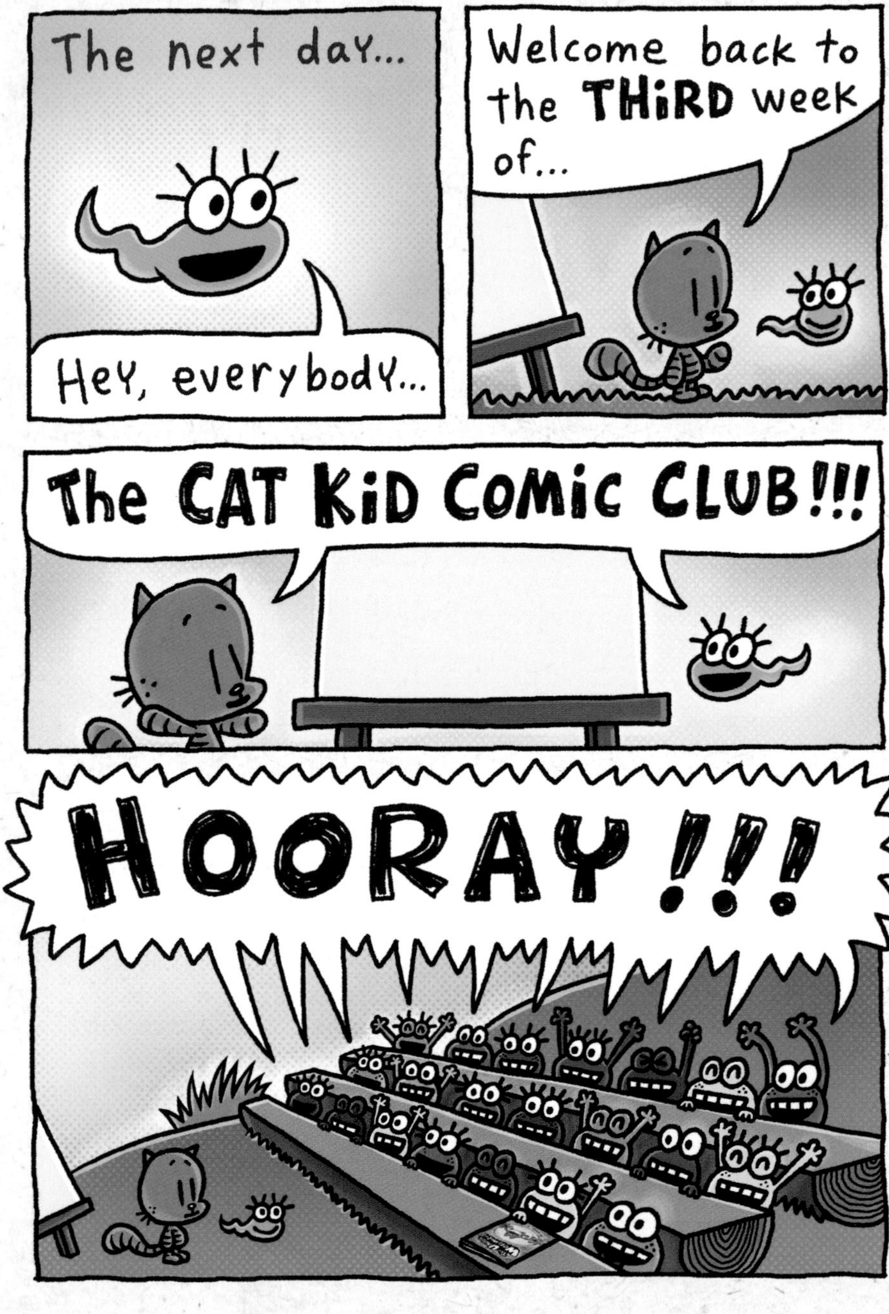
The next day...
Hey, everybody...
Welcome back to the THIRD week of...
The CAT KID COMIC CLUB!!!
HOORAY!!!

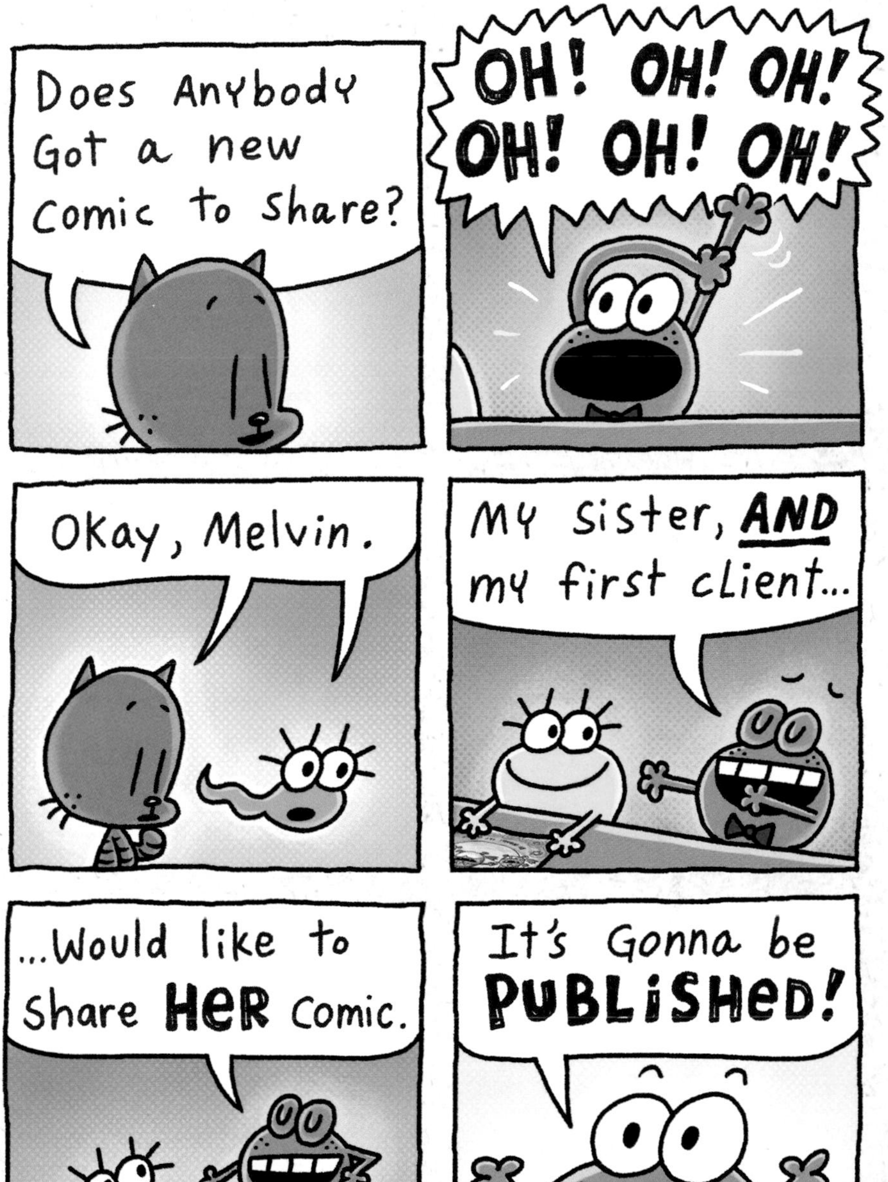
Does Anybody Got a new Comic to Share?
OH! OH! OH! OH! OH! OH!
Okay, Melvin.
My Sister, AND my first cLient...
...Would like to Share HER Comic.
It's Gonna be PUBLiSHeD!

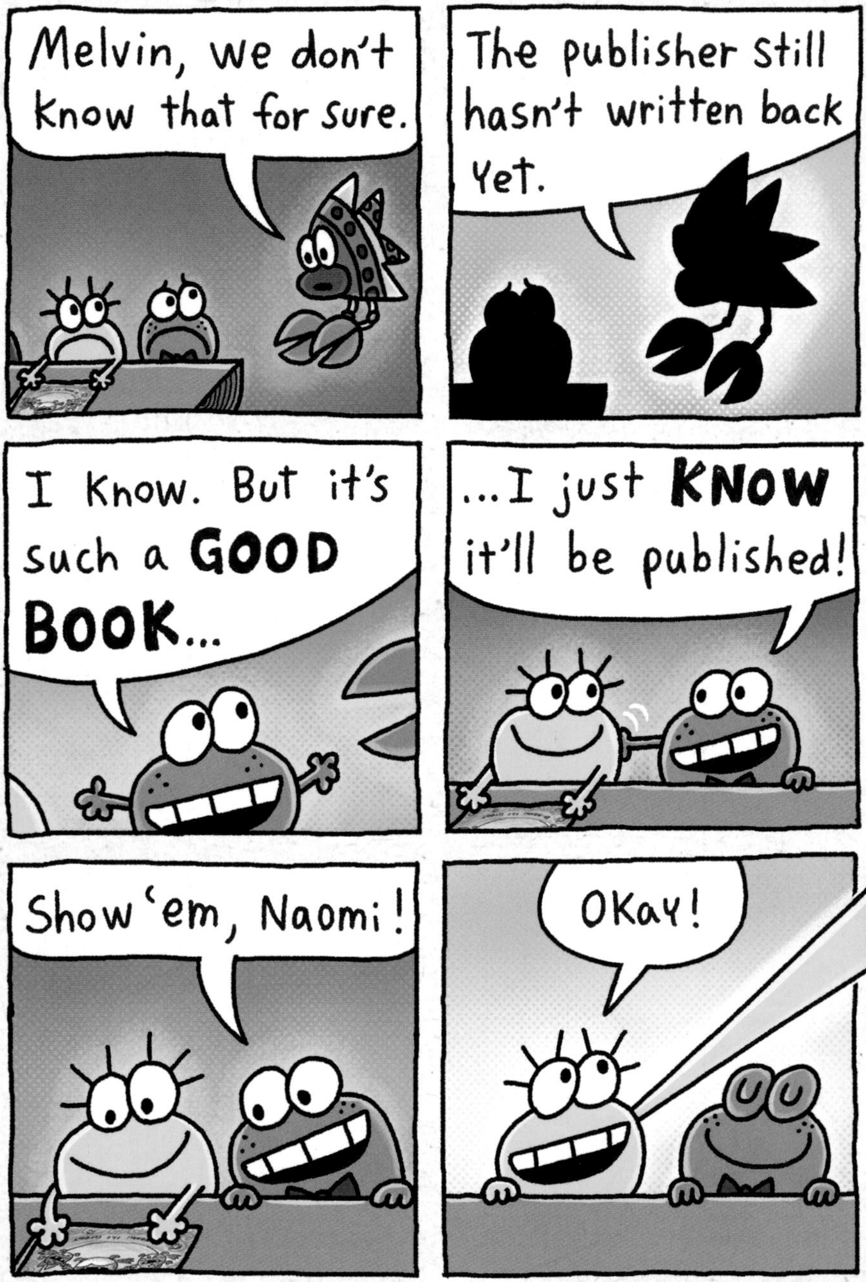
Melvin, we don't know that for sure.
The publisher still hasn't written back yet.
I know. But it's such a GOOD BOOK...
...I just KNOW it'll be published!
Show 'em, Naomi!
OKay!

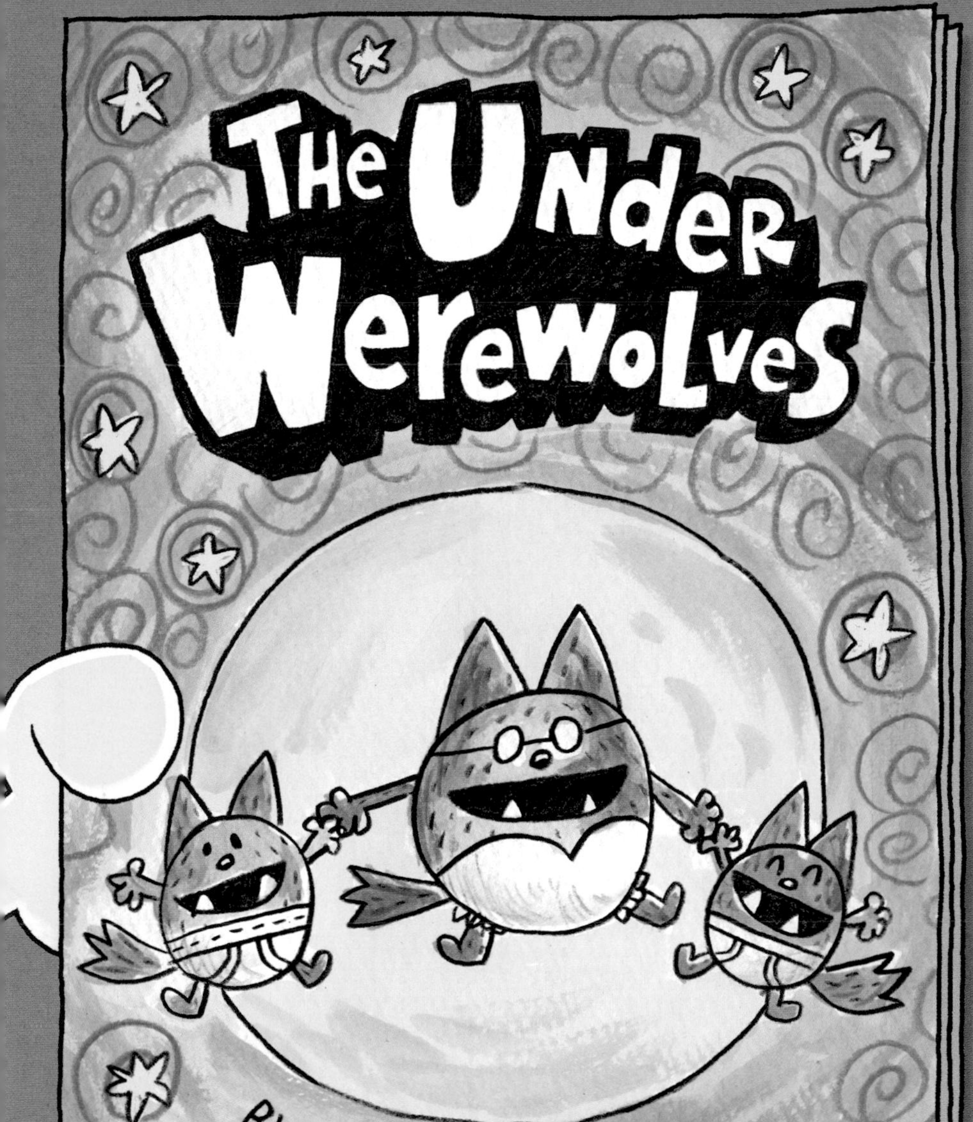
The Under Werewolves
By Naomi the Great

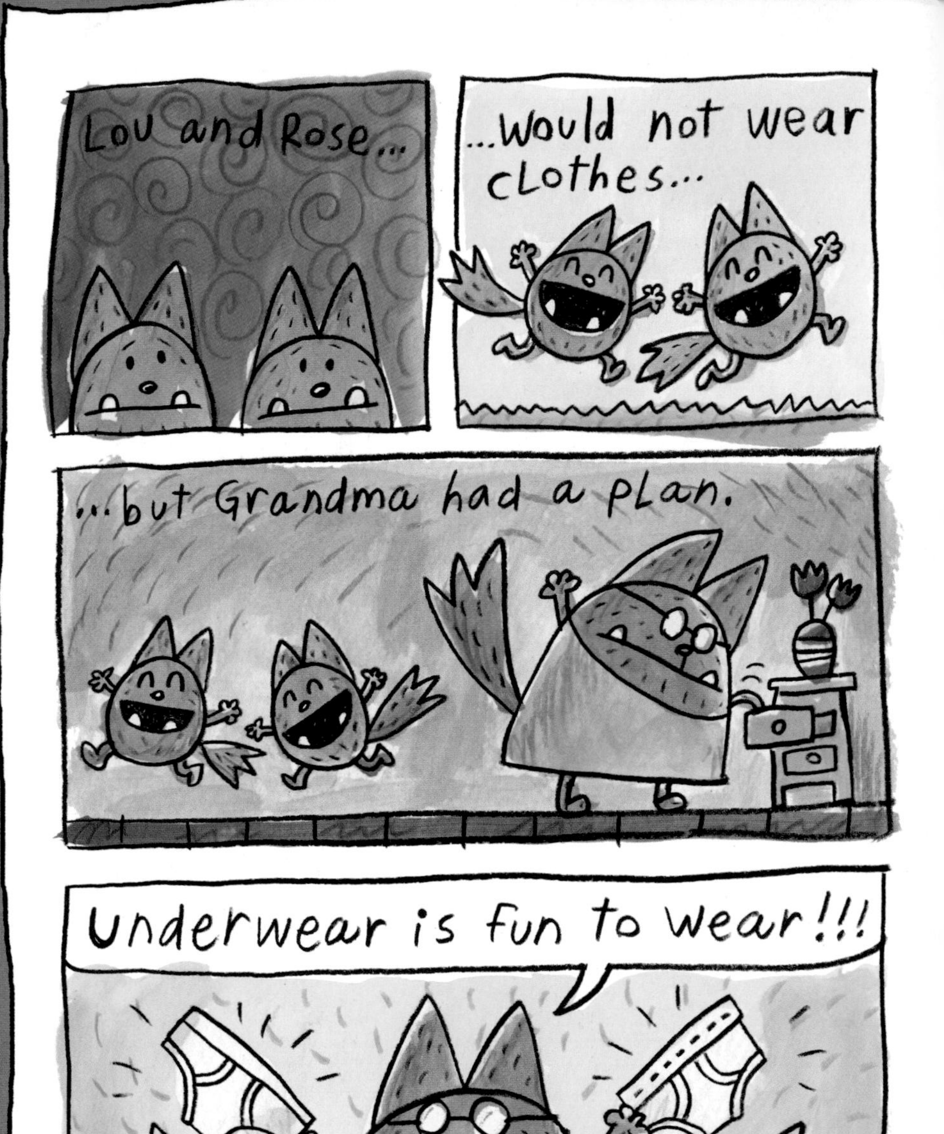
Lou and Rose...
...would not wear clothes...
...but Grandma had a plan.
Underwear is fun to wear!!!

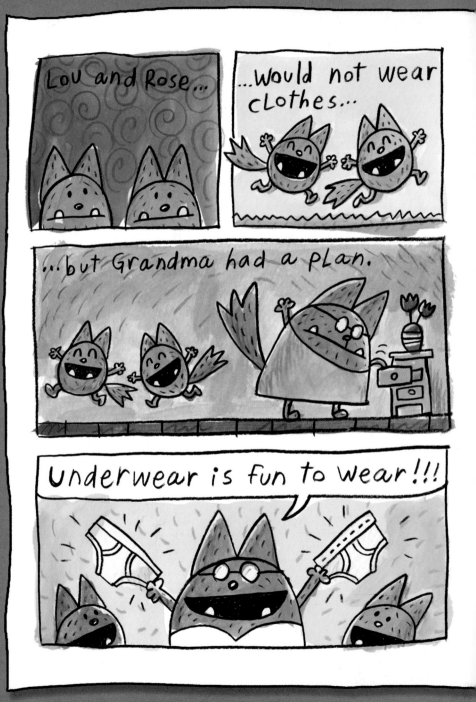

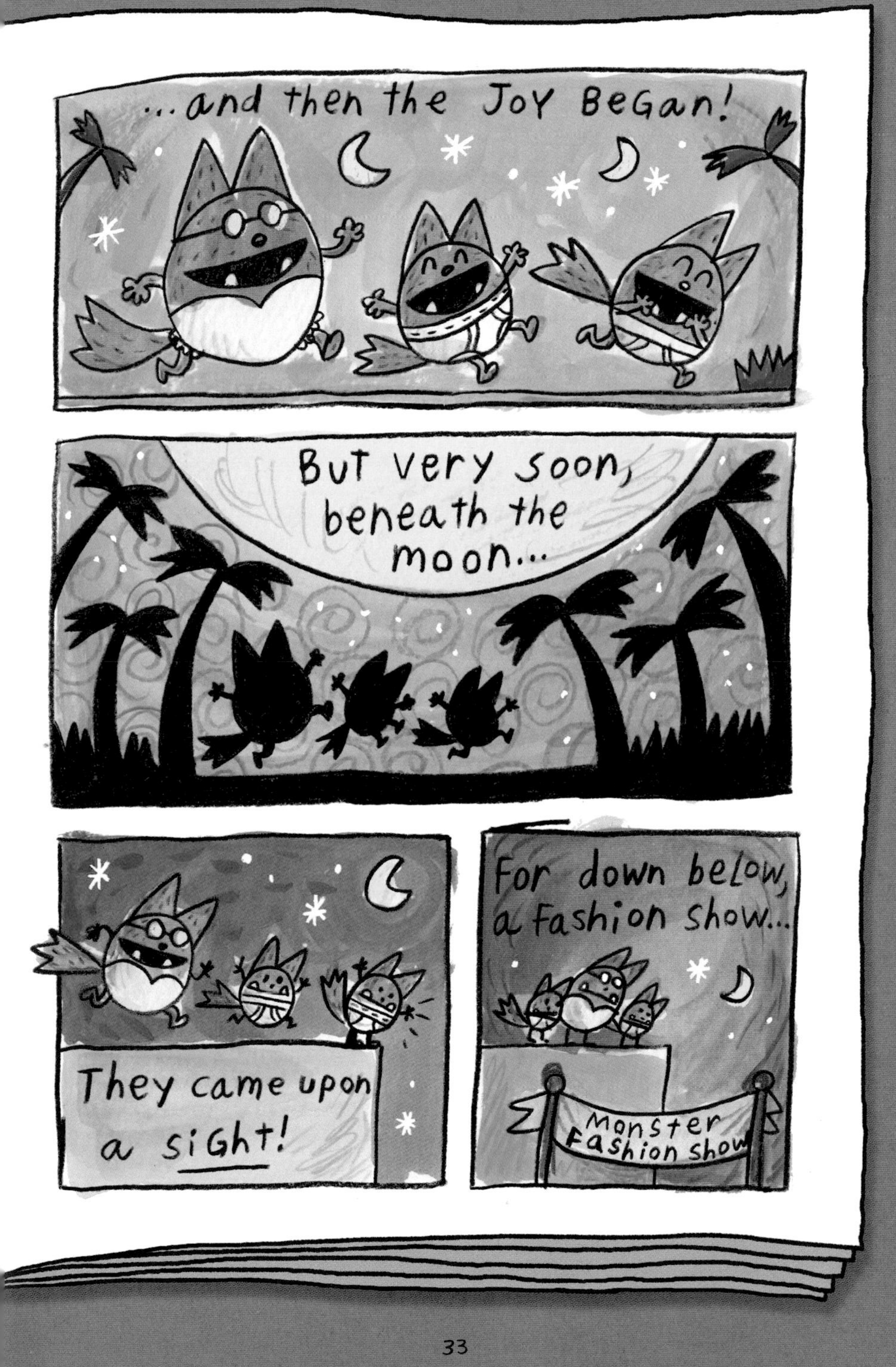
...and then the JOY BeGan!
But very soon, beneath the moon...
They came upon a SiGht!
For down below, a Fashion show...
Monster Fashion Show

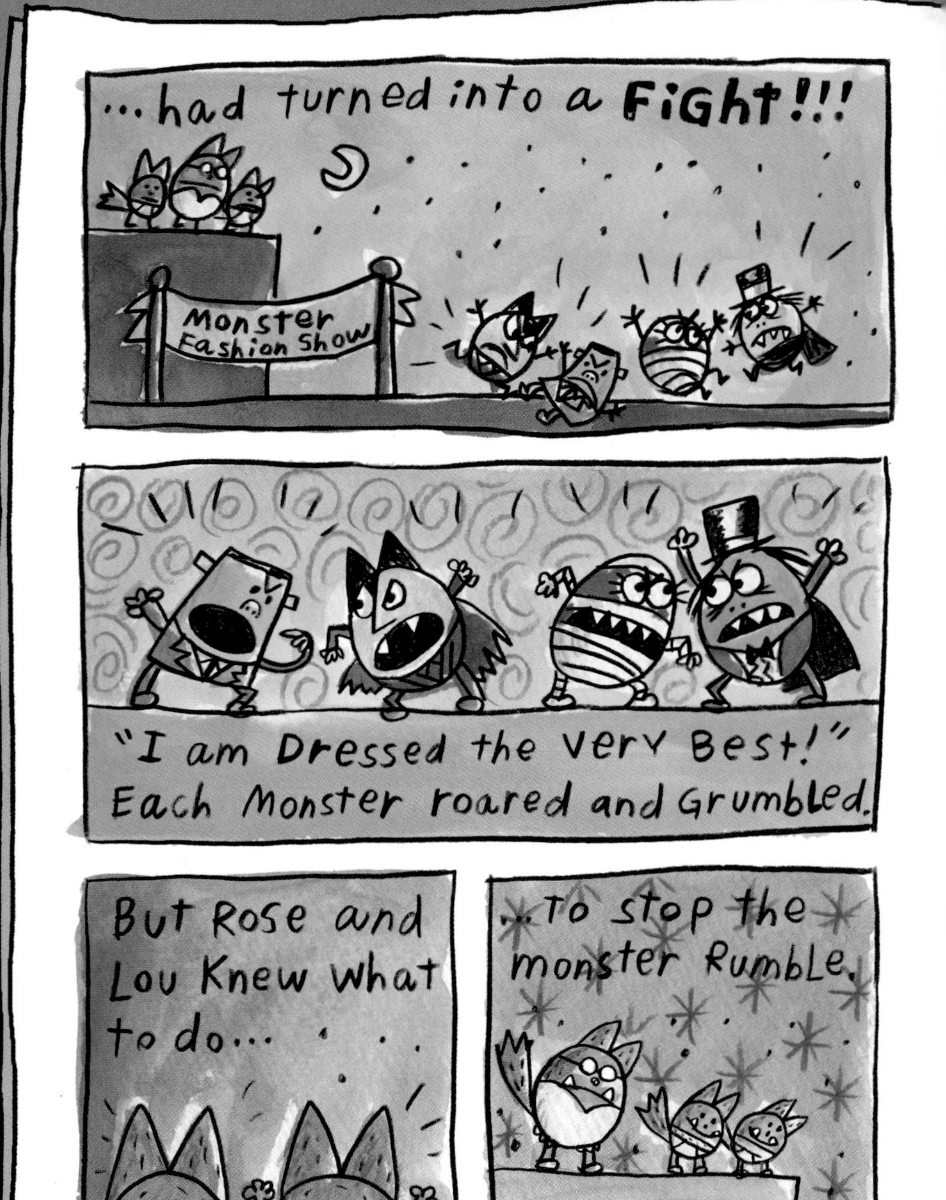
...had turned into a FiGHT!!!
Monster Fashion Show
"I am Dressed the Very Best!"
Each Monster roared and Grumbled.
But Rose and Lou Knew what to do...
...To stop the monster Rumble.

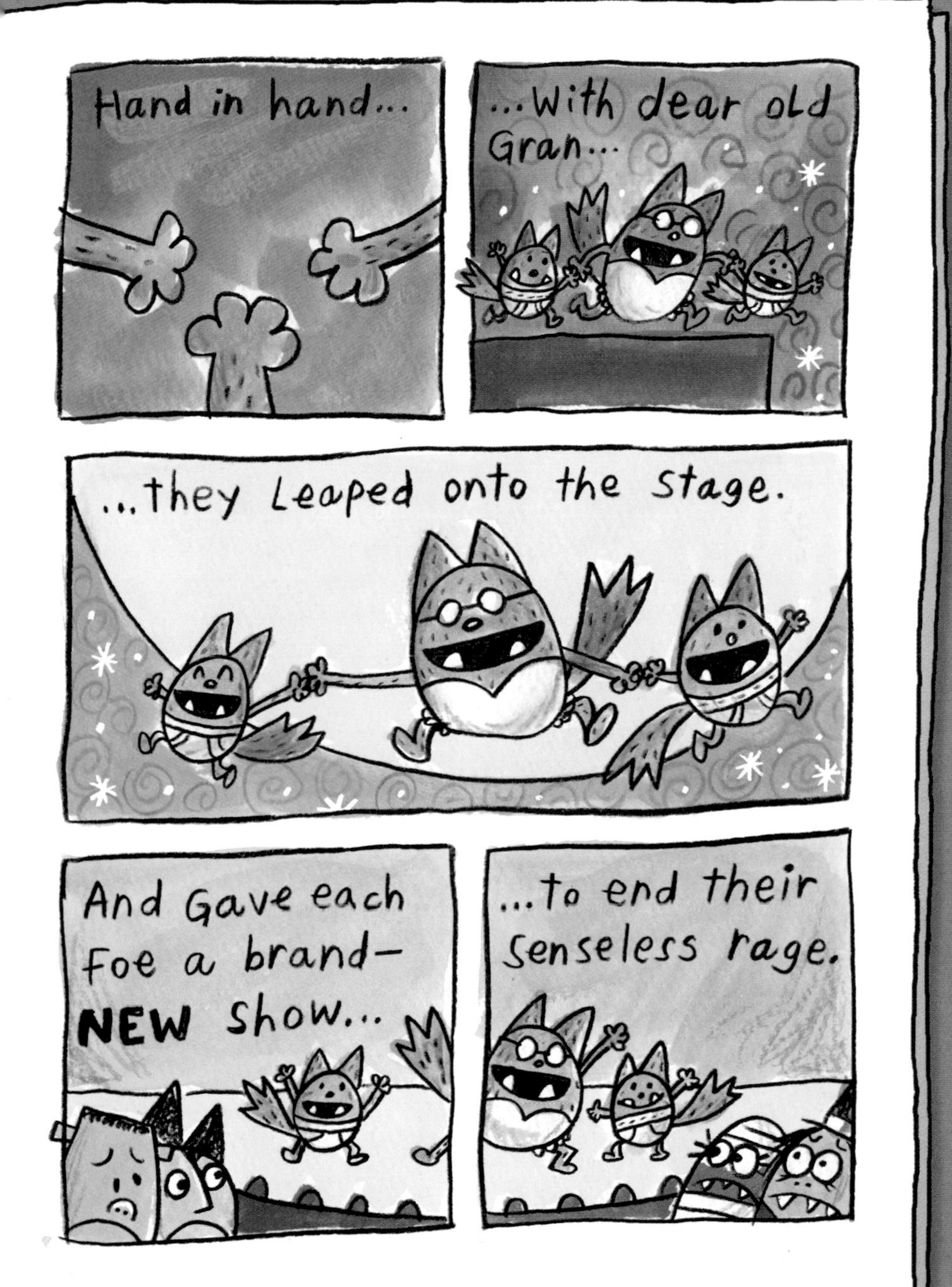
Hand in hand...
...With dear old Gran...
...they Leaped onto the stage.
And Gave each Foe a brand-NEW show...
...to end their senseless rage.

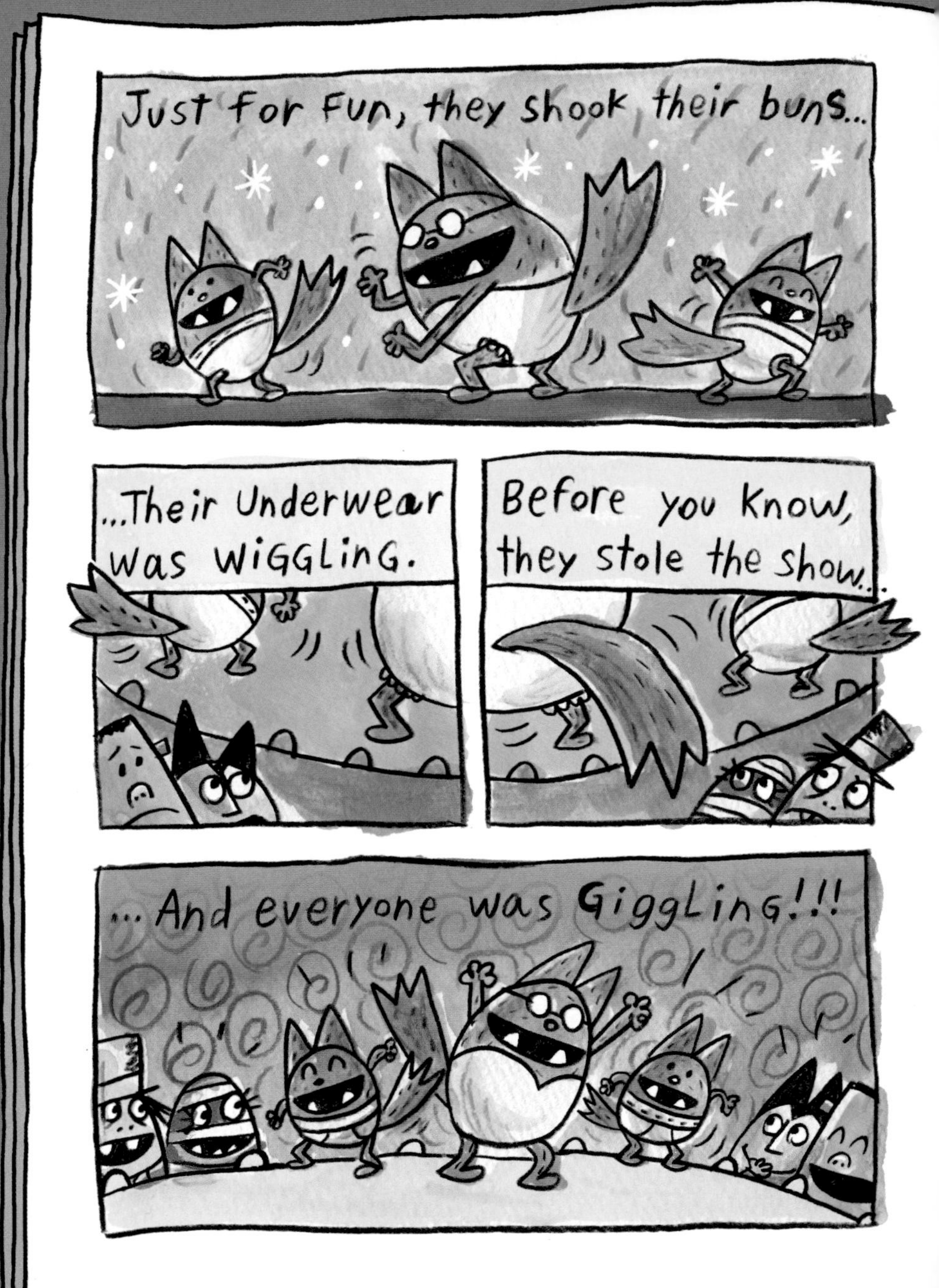
Just for Fun, they shook their buns...
...Their Underwear was WiGGLinG.
Before you know, they stole the show...
...And everyone was GiggLinG!!!

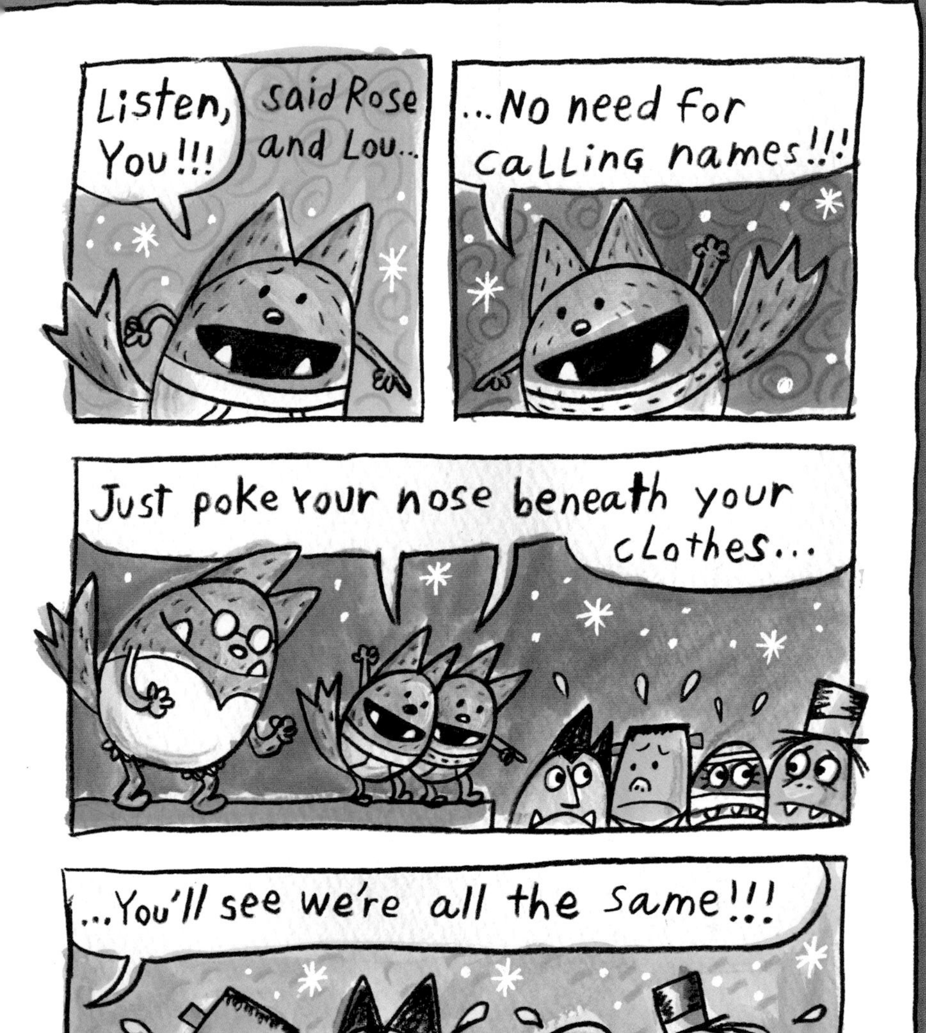
Listen, You!!!
said Rose and Lou...
...No need for calling names!!!
Just poke your nose beneath your clothes...
...You'll see we're all the same!!!

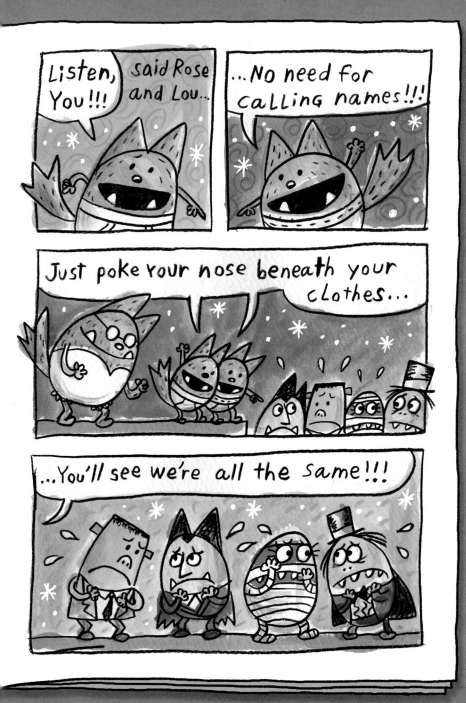

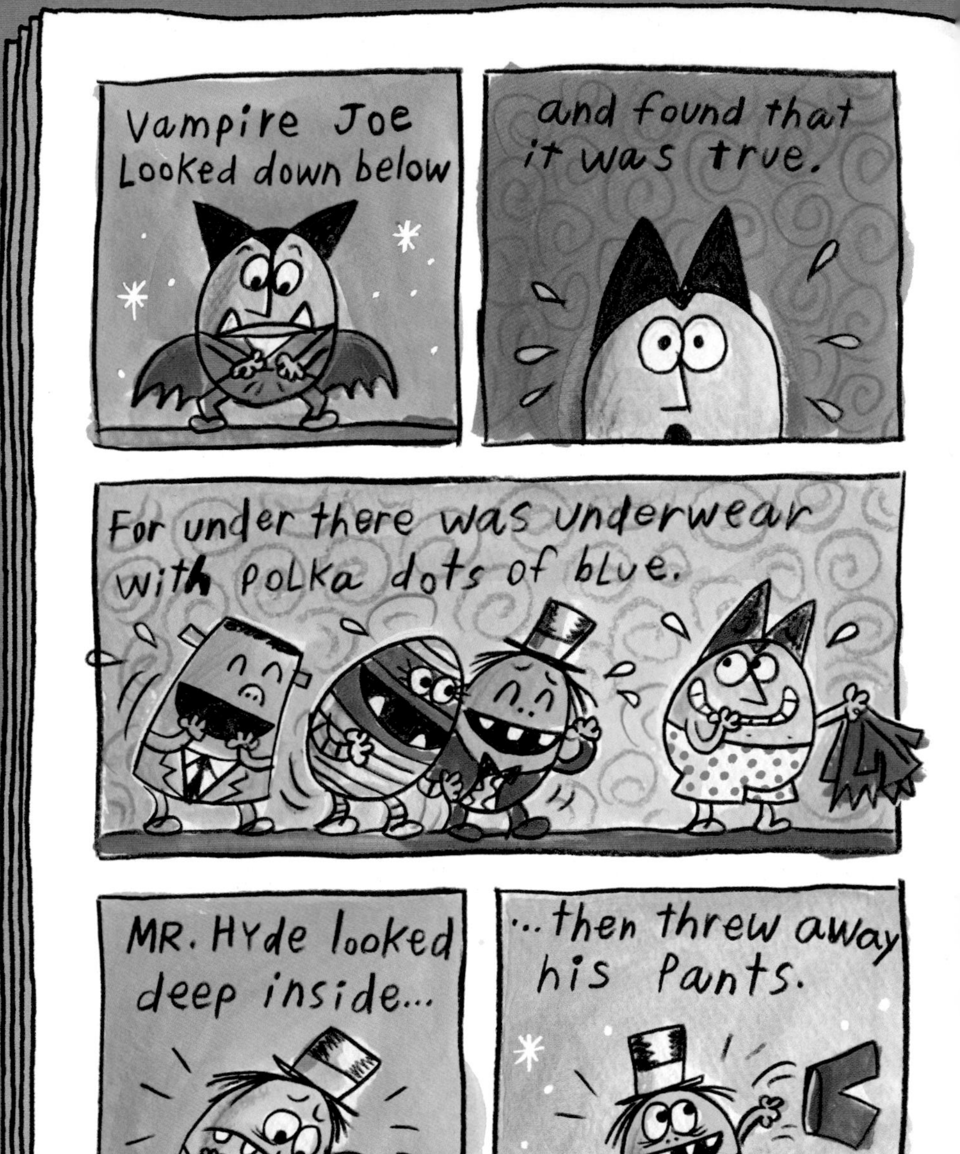
Vampire Joe
Looked down below
and found that
it was true.
For under there was underwear
with polka dots of blue.
MR. Hyde looked
deep inside...
...then threw away
his Pants.

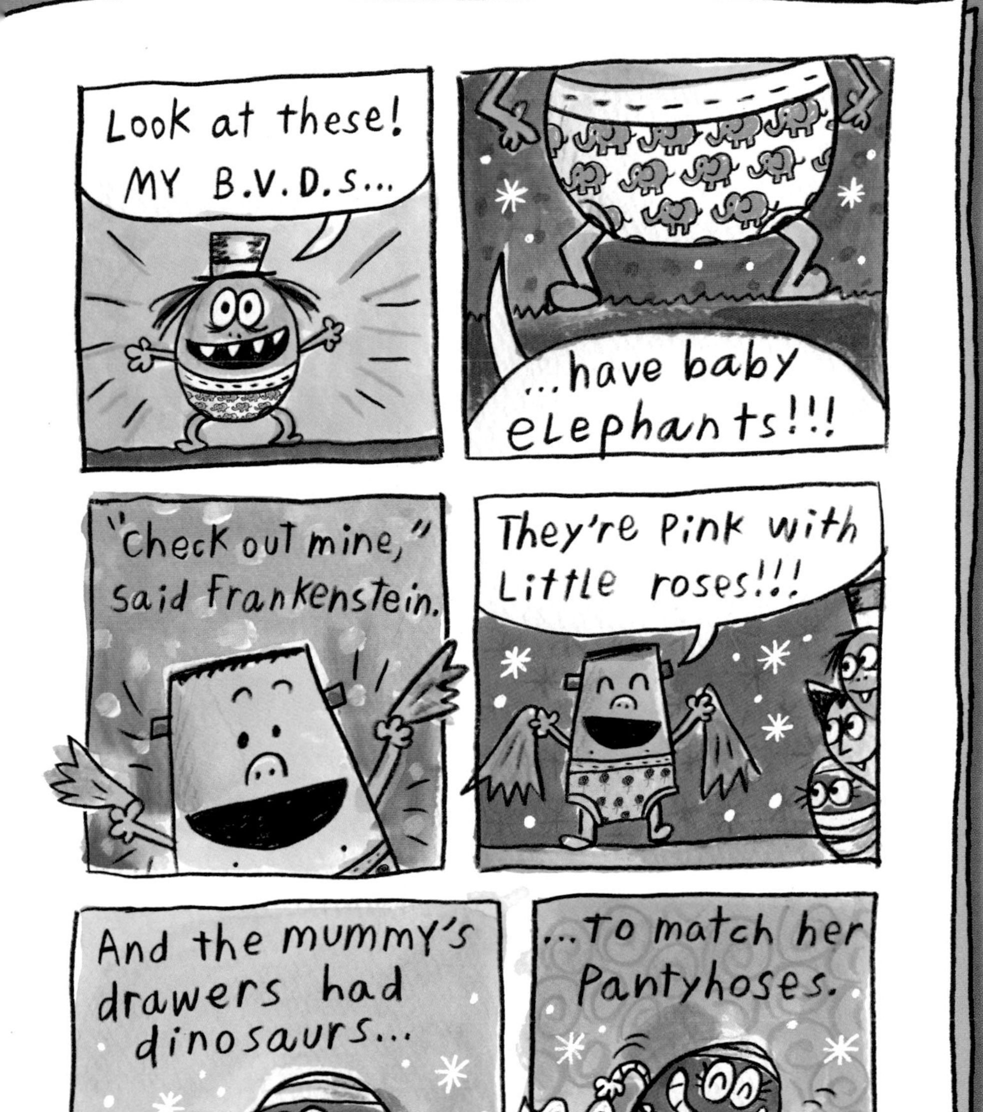
Look at these! MY B.V.D.s...
...have baby elephants!!!
"Check out mine," said Frankenstein.
They're Pink with Little roses!!!
And the mummy's drawers had dinosaurs...
...to match her Pantyhoses.

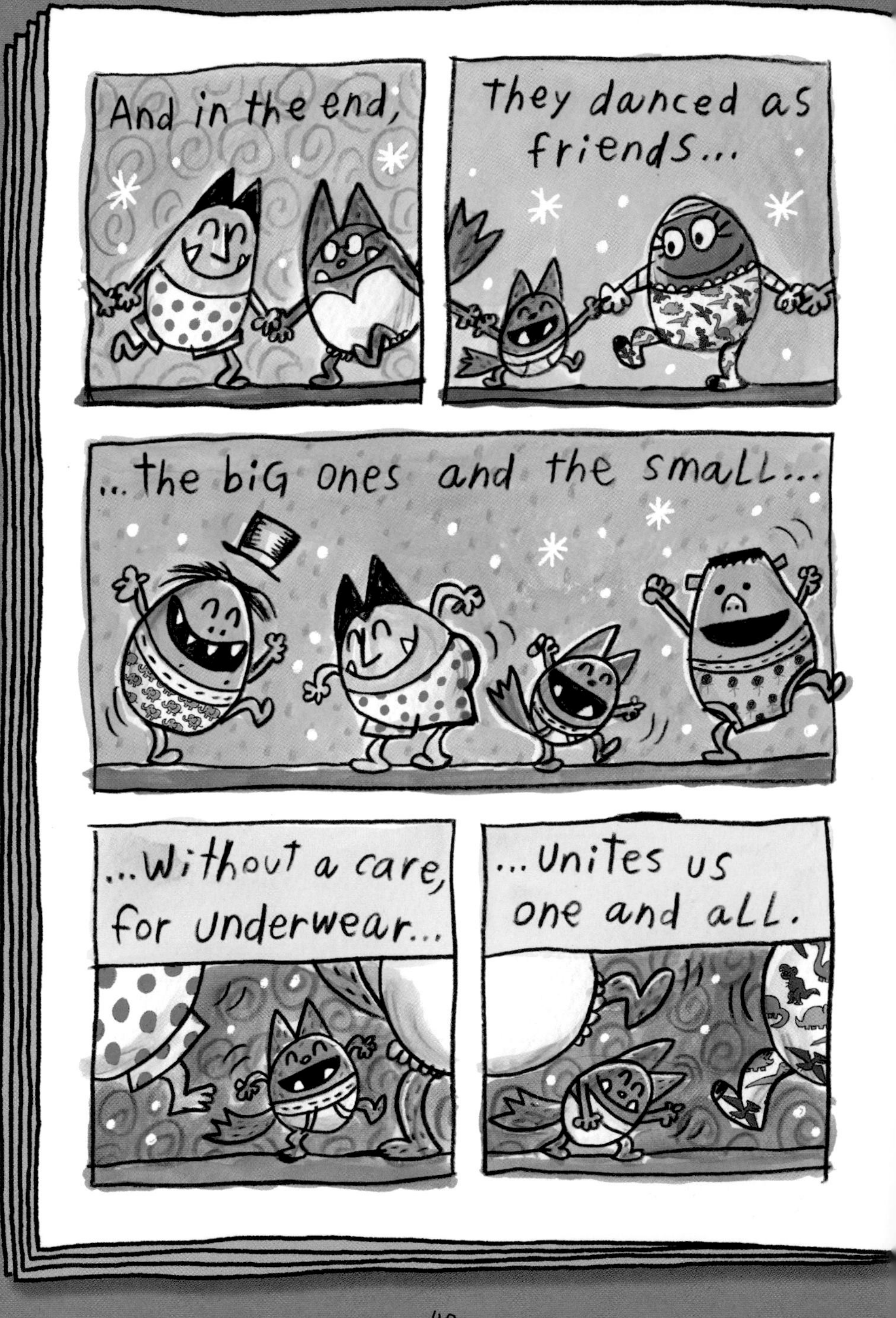
And in the end,
they danced as friends...
...the biG ones and the smaLL...
...Without a care, for underwear...
...Unites us one and aLL.

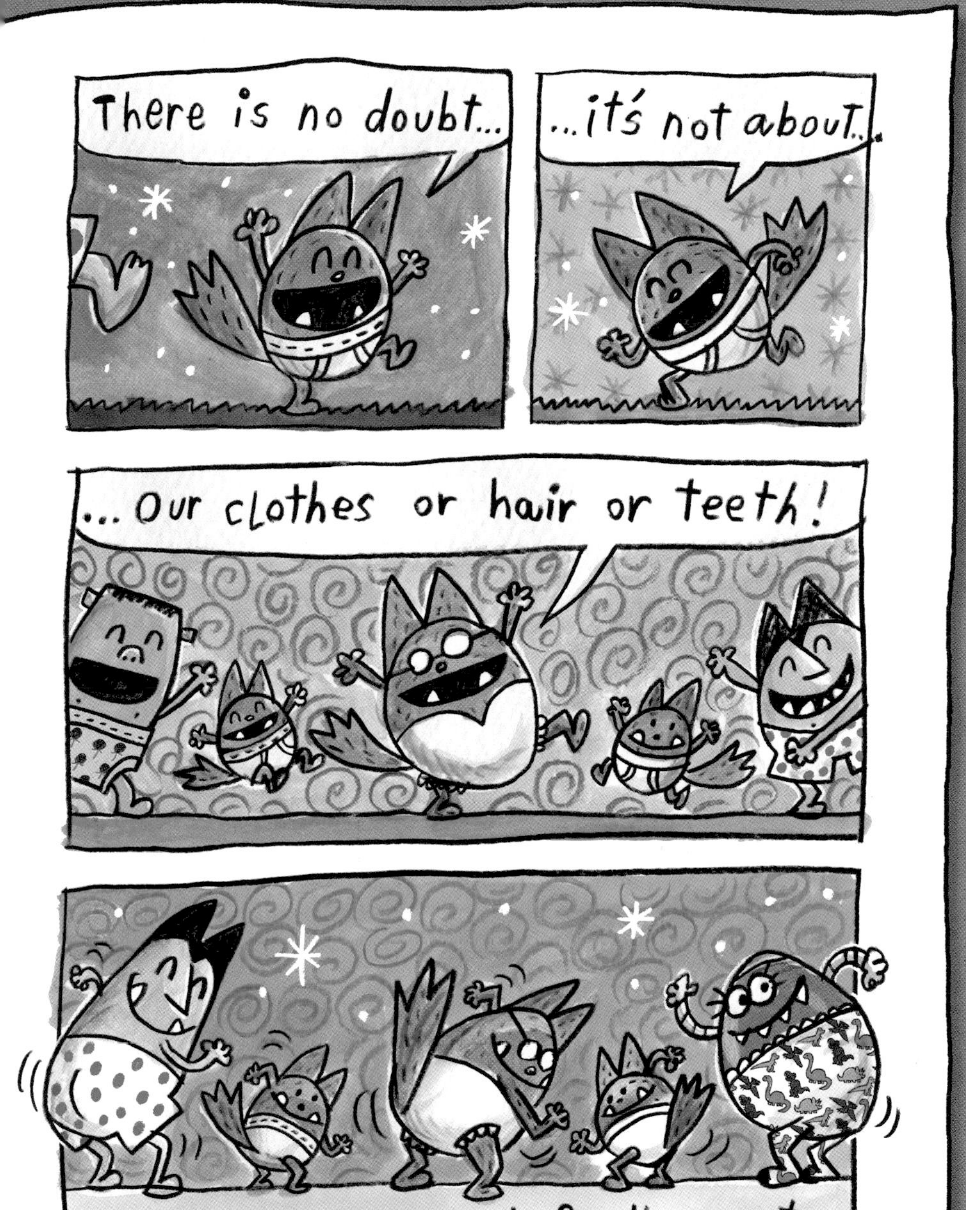
There is no doubt...
...it's not about...
...our clothes or hair or teeth!
The only ounce that Really counts...

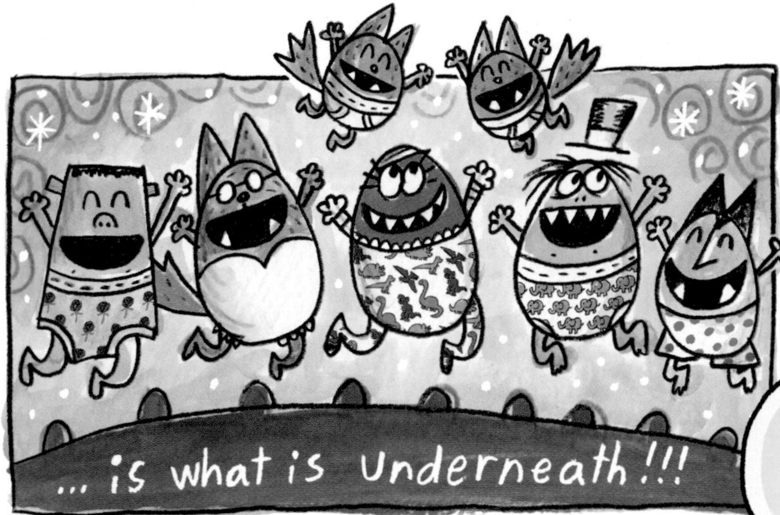
... is what is underneath!!!

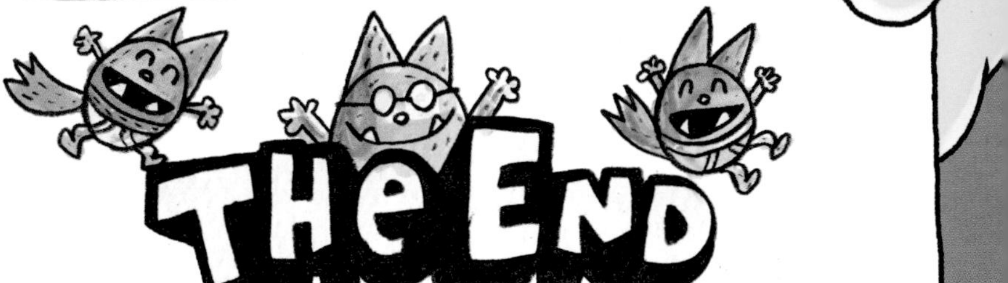
THE END

About the Author / Illustrator

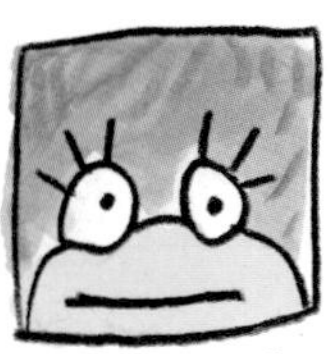
Naomi the Great

Naomi the Great is the world-Renowned creator of Monster Cheese Sandwich.

When she is not making books, Naomi the Great enjoys reading, watching videos, and playing the drums.

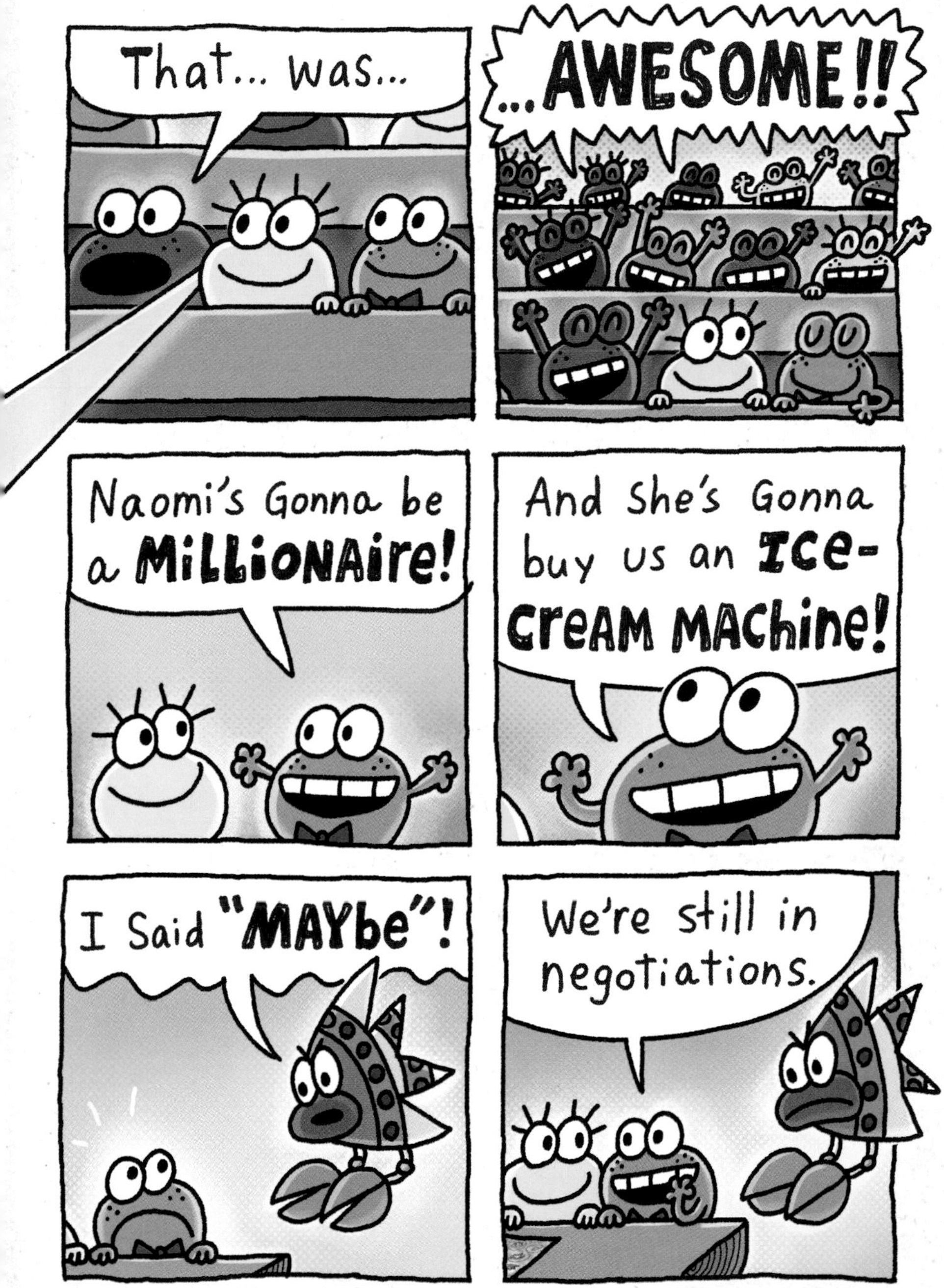
That... was...
...AWESOME!!
Naomi's Gonna be a MILLIONAIRE!
And She's Gonna buy us an ICE-CREAM MACHINE!
I Said "MAYbe"!
We're still in negotiations.

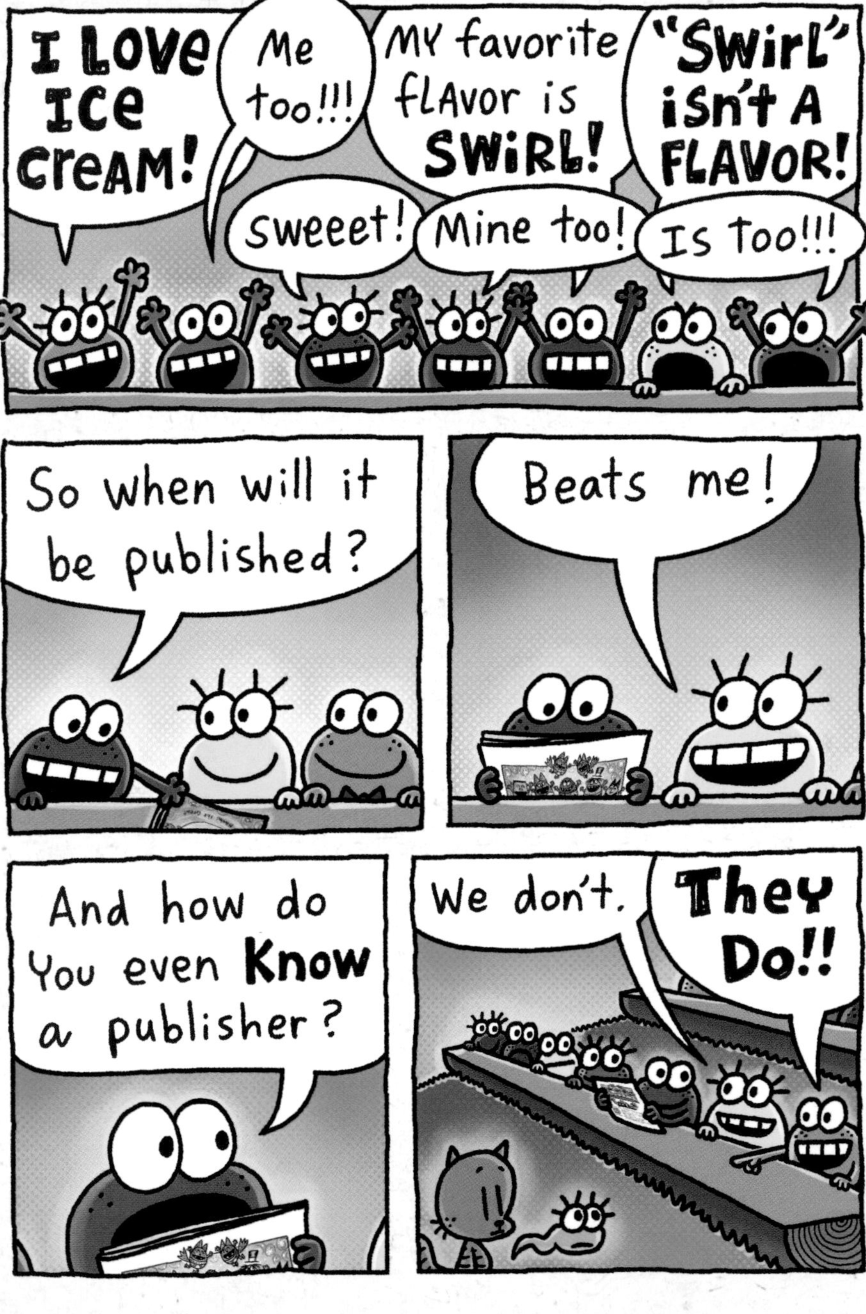
I LOVE ICE CREAM!
Me too!!!
MY favorite fLAvor is SWIRL!
"SWirL" isn't A FLAVOR!
Sweeet!
Mine too!
Is Too!!!
So when will it be published?
Beats me!
And how do You even Know a publisher?
We don't.
They Do!!

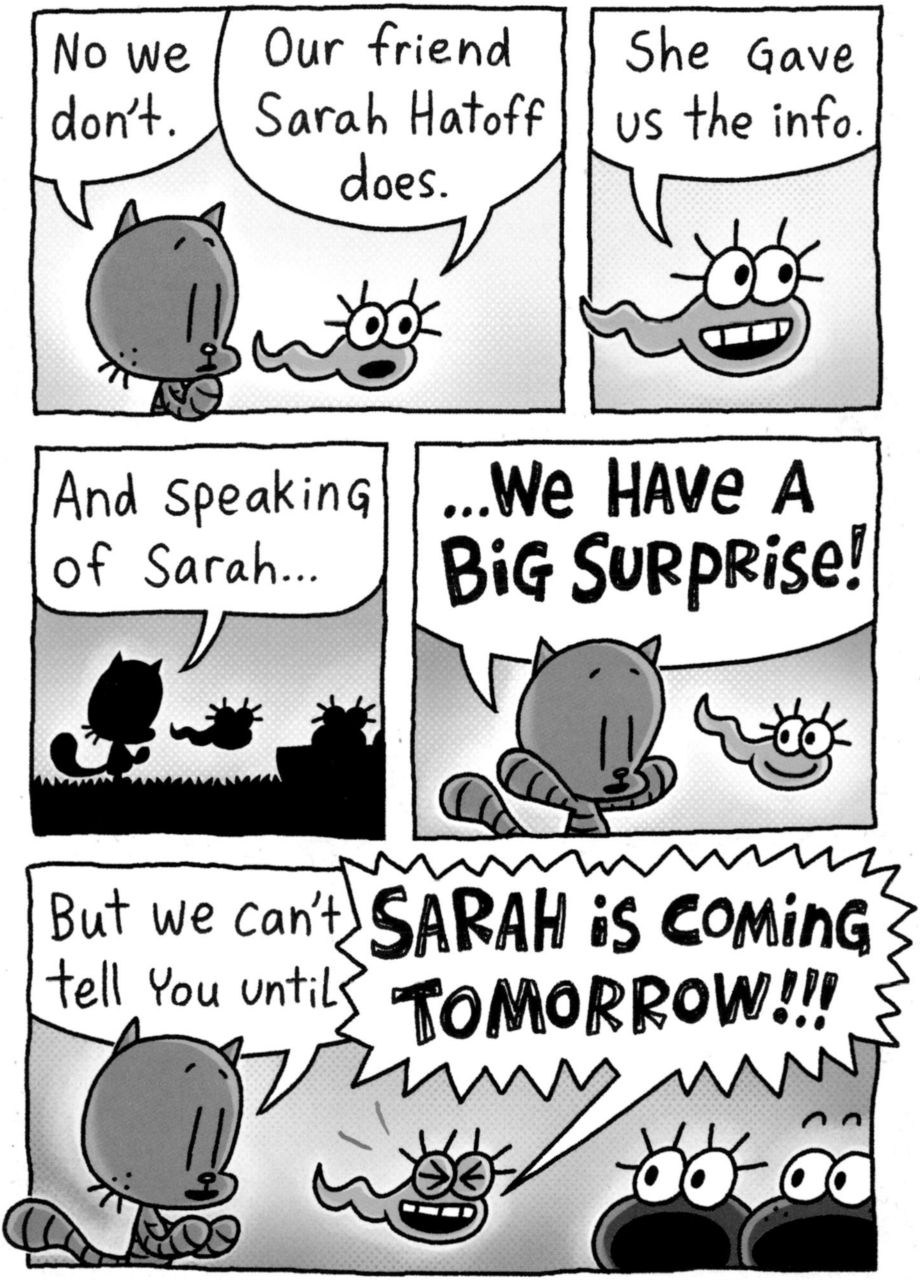
No we don't.
Our friend Sarah Hatoff does.
She Gave us the info.
And speaking of Sarah...
...WE HAVE A BIG SURPRISE!
But we can't tell You until
SARAH IS COMING TOMORROW!!!

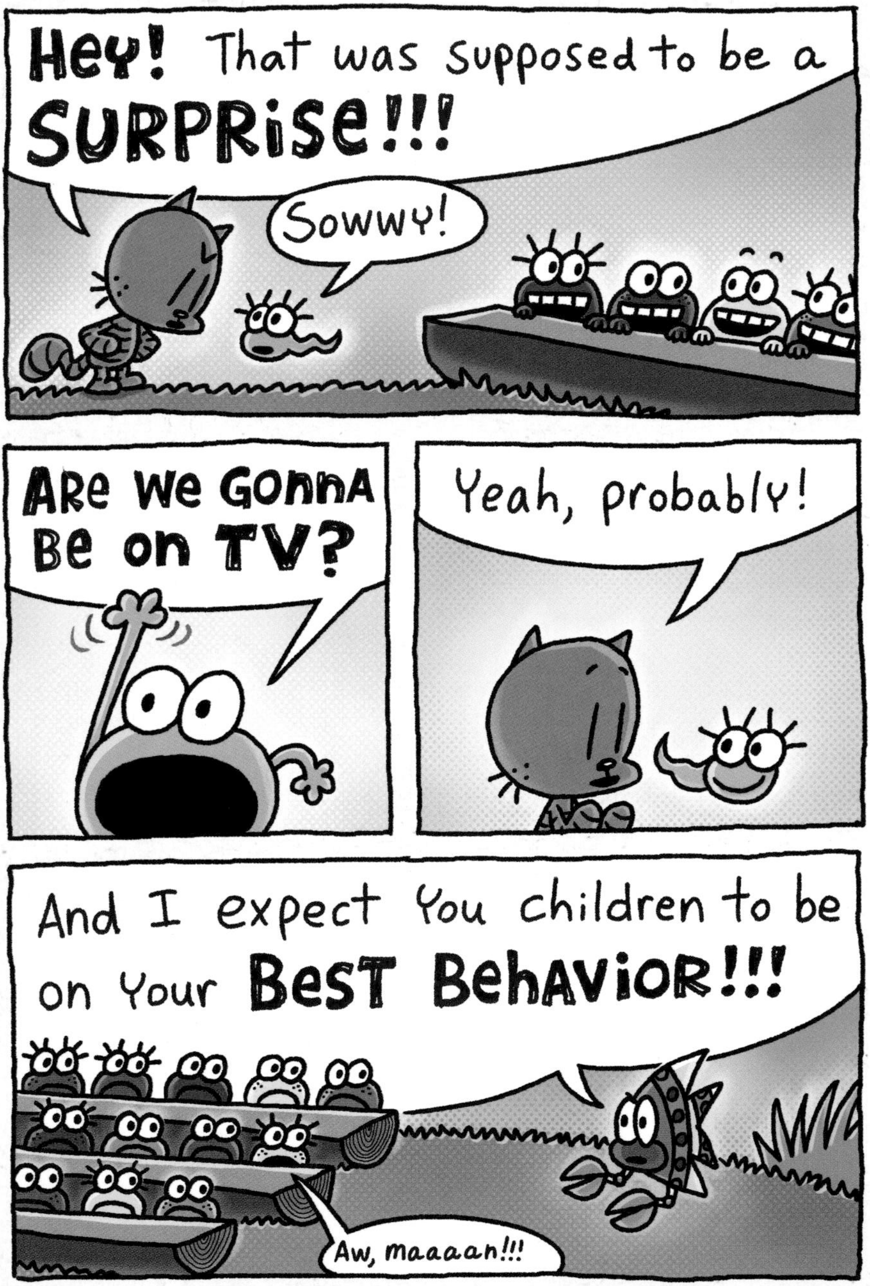
HEY! That was supposed to be a SURPRISE!!!
Sowwy!
ARE WE GONNA BE ON TV?
Yeah, probably!
And I expect You children to be on Your BEST BEHAVIOR!!!
Aw, maaaan!!!

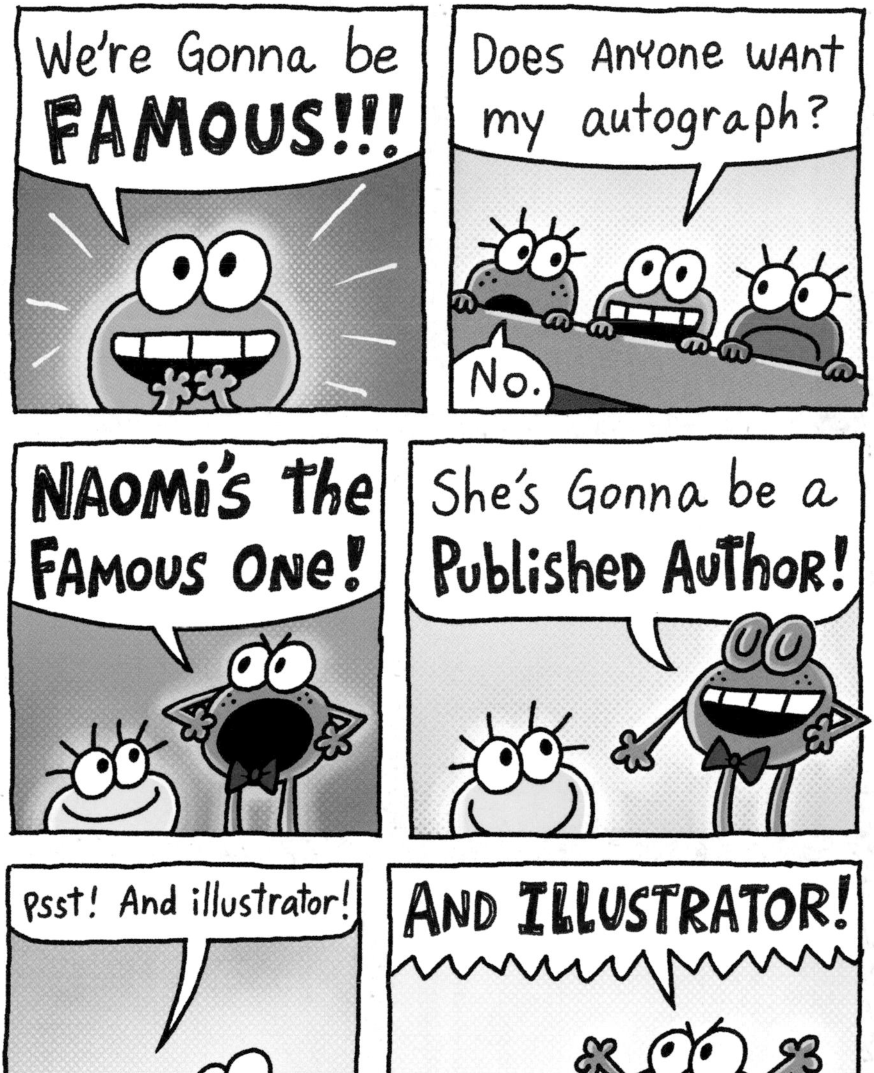
We're Gonna be FAMOUS!!!
Does AnYone WAnt my autograph?
No.
NAOMi's the FAMOUS ONe!
She's Gonna be a Published Author!
Psst! And illustrator!
AND ILLUSTRATOR!

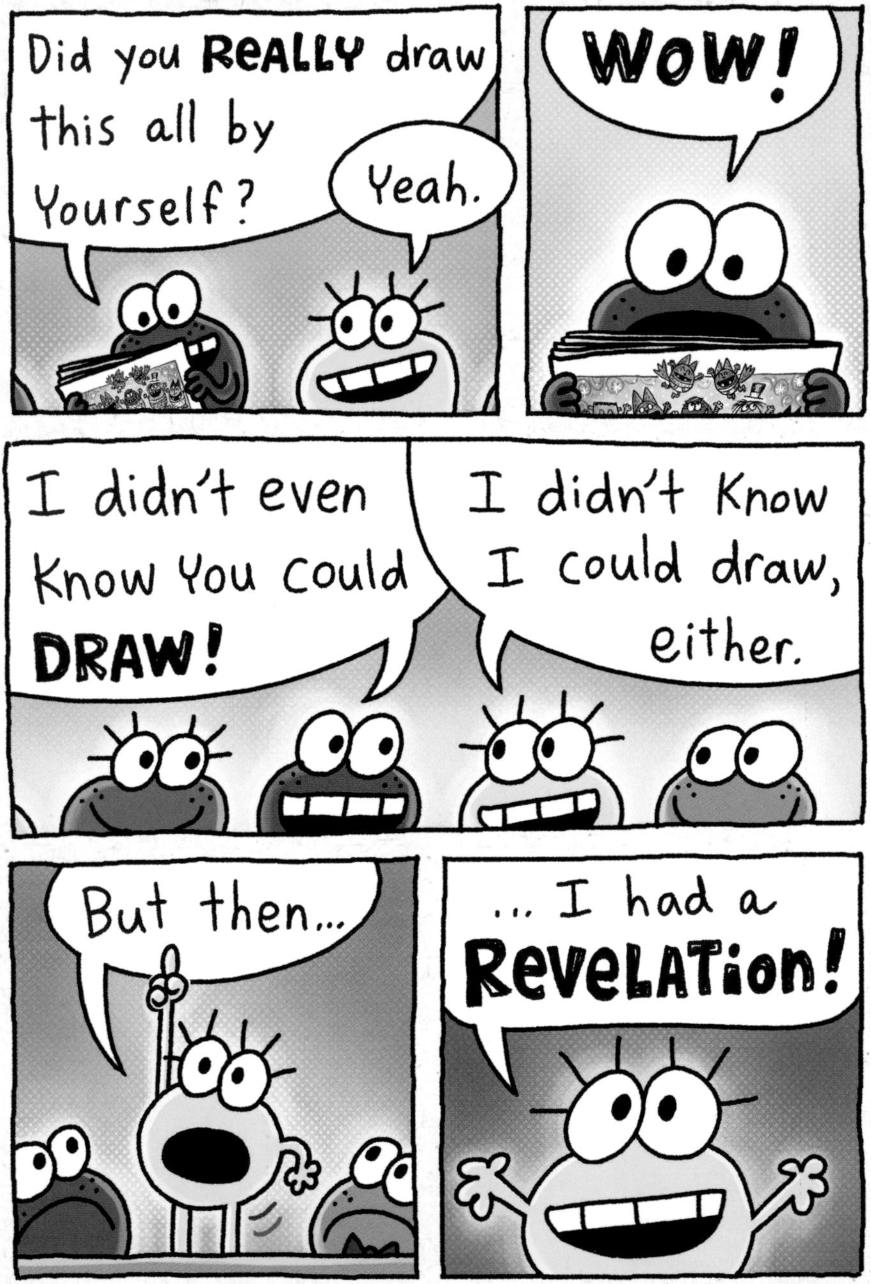
Did you REALLY draw this all by Yourself?
Yeah.
WOW!
I didn't even Know You could DRAW!
I didn't Know I could draw, either.
But then...
... I had a REVELATION!

CHAPTER 4

NAOMI'S REVELATION

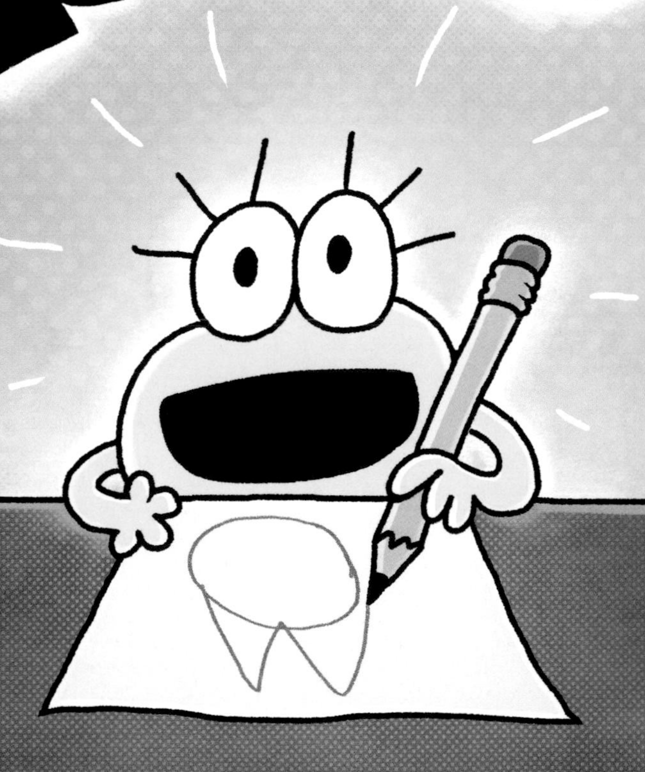

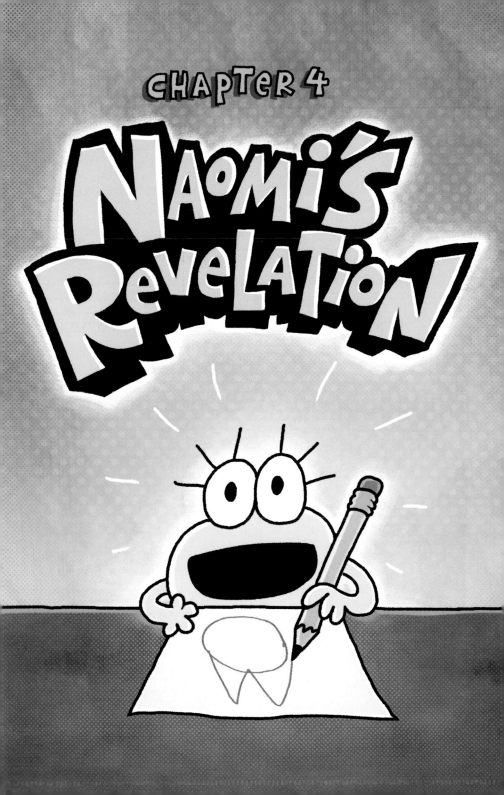

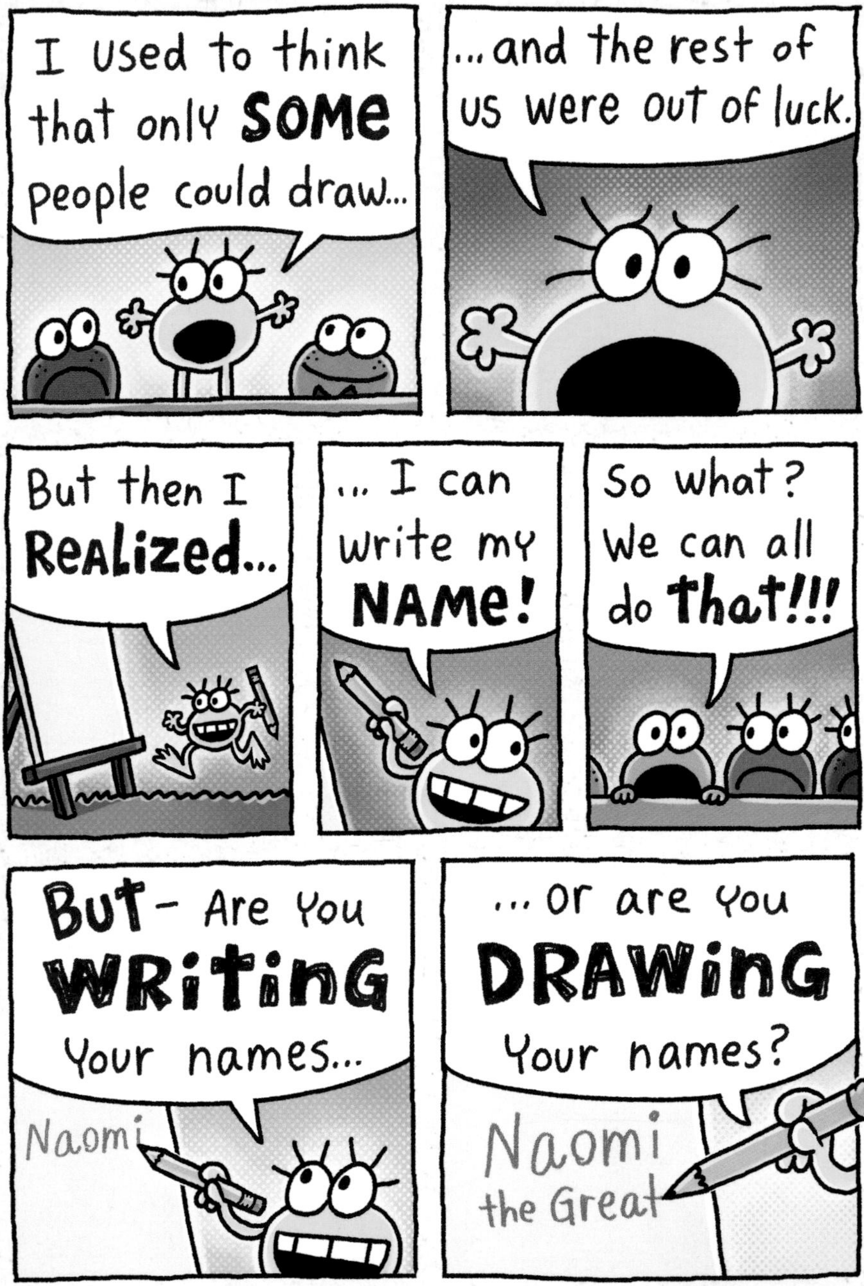
I used to think that only SOME people could draw...
...and the rest of us were out of luck.
But then I REALIZED...
... I can write my NAME!
So what? We can all do THAT!!!
BUT- Are you WRITING your names...
Naomi
... Or are you DRAWING your names?
Naomi the Great

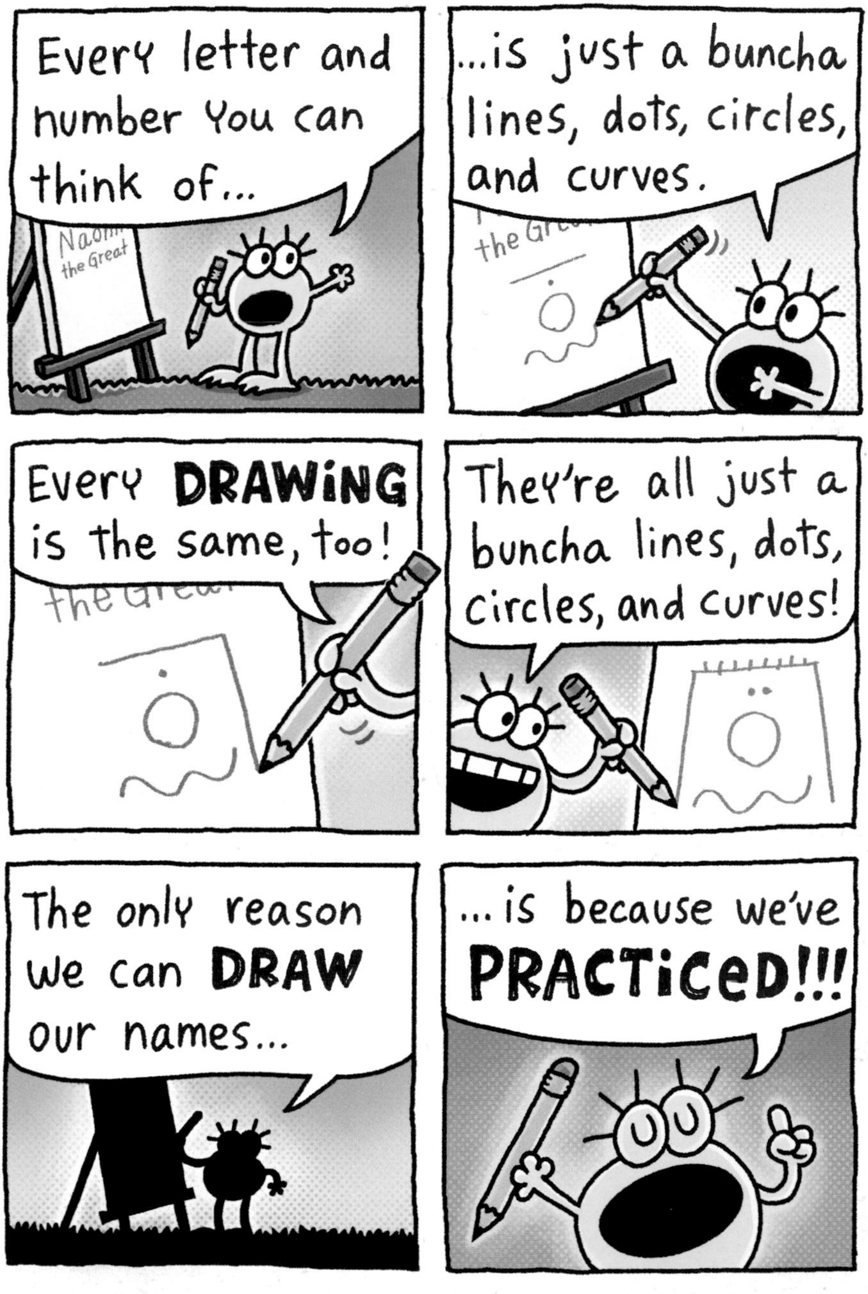

Every letter and number You can think of...
Naomi the Great
...is just a buncha lines, dots, circles, and curves.
Every DRAWiNG is the same, too!
They're all just a buncha lines, dots, circles, and curves!
The only reason we can DRAW our names...
...is because we've PRACTiCeD!!!

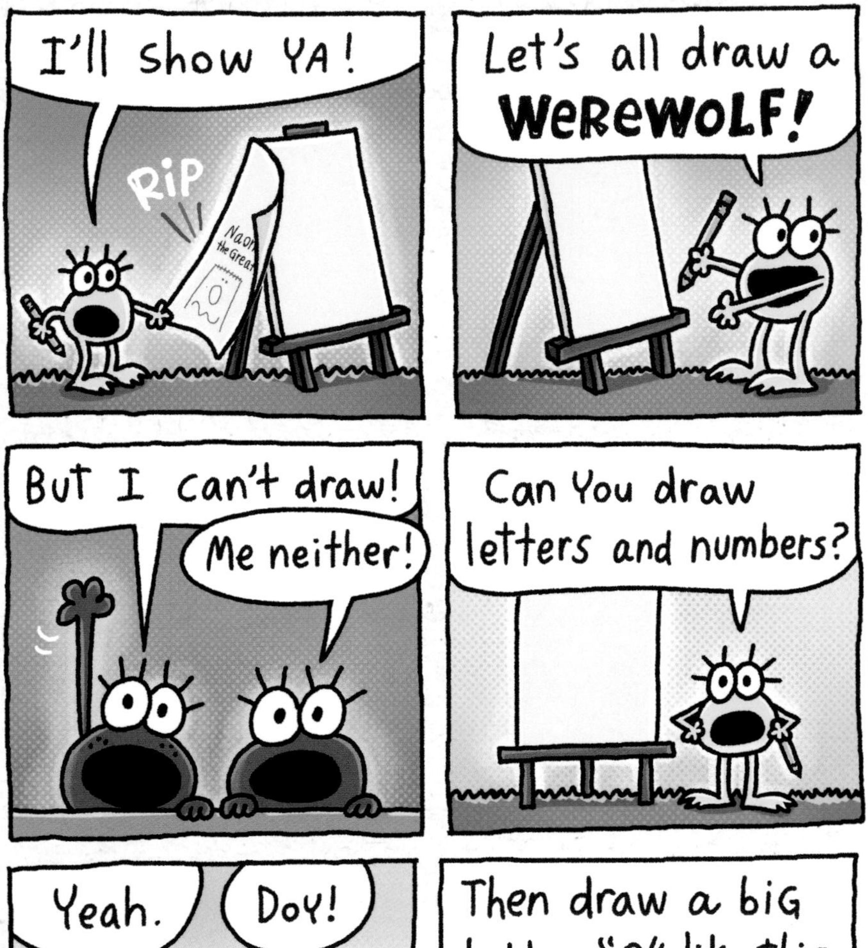

I'll show YA!
RIP
Let's all draw a
WEREWOLF!
But I can't draw!
Me neither!
Can You draw
letters and numbers?
Yeah.
DOY!
Then draw a biG
letter "O" like this.

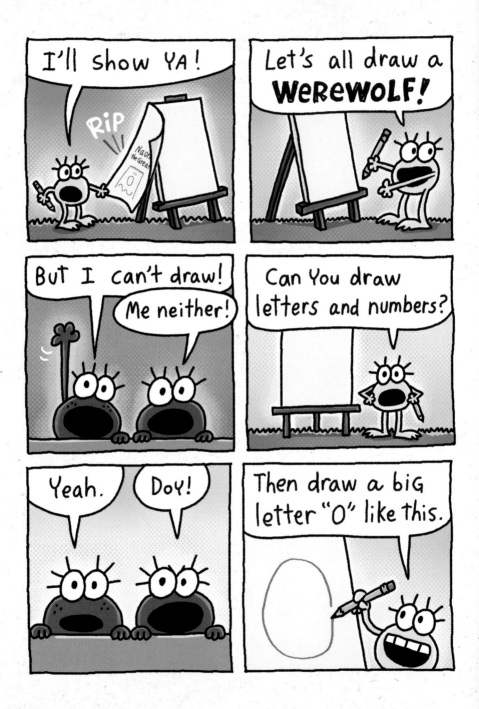

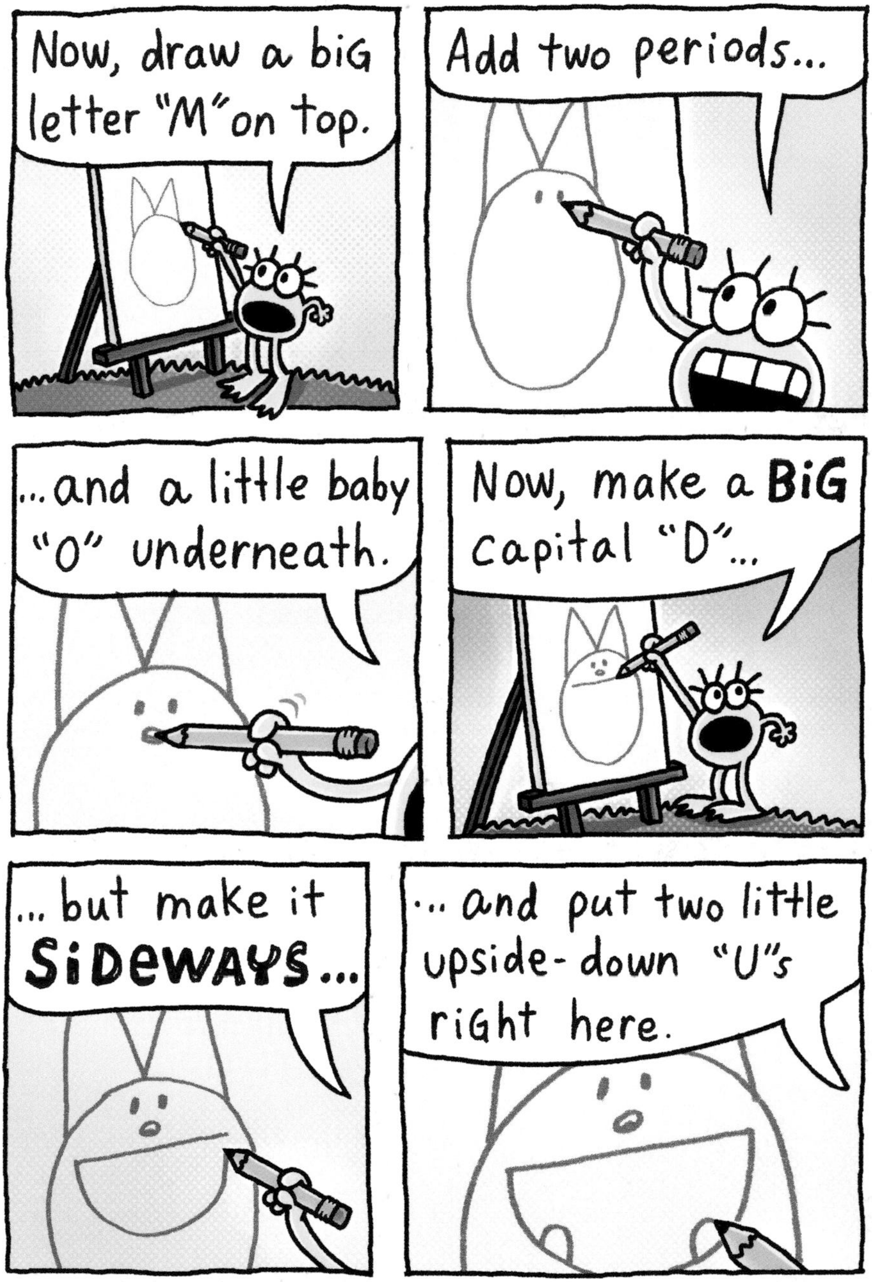
Now, draw a biG letter "M" on top.
Add two periods...
...and a little baby "O" underneath.
Now, make a BiG capital "D"...
...but make it SiDEWAYS...
...and put two little upside-down "U"s riGht here.

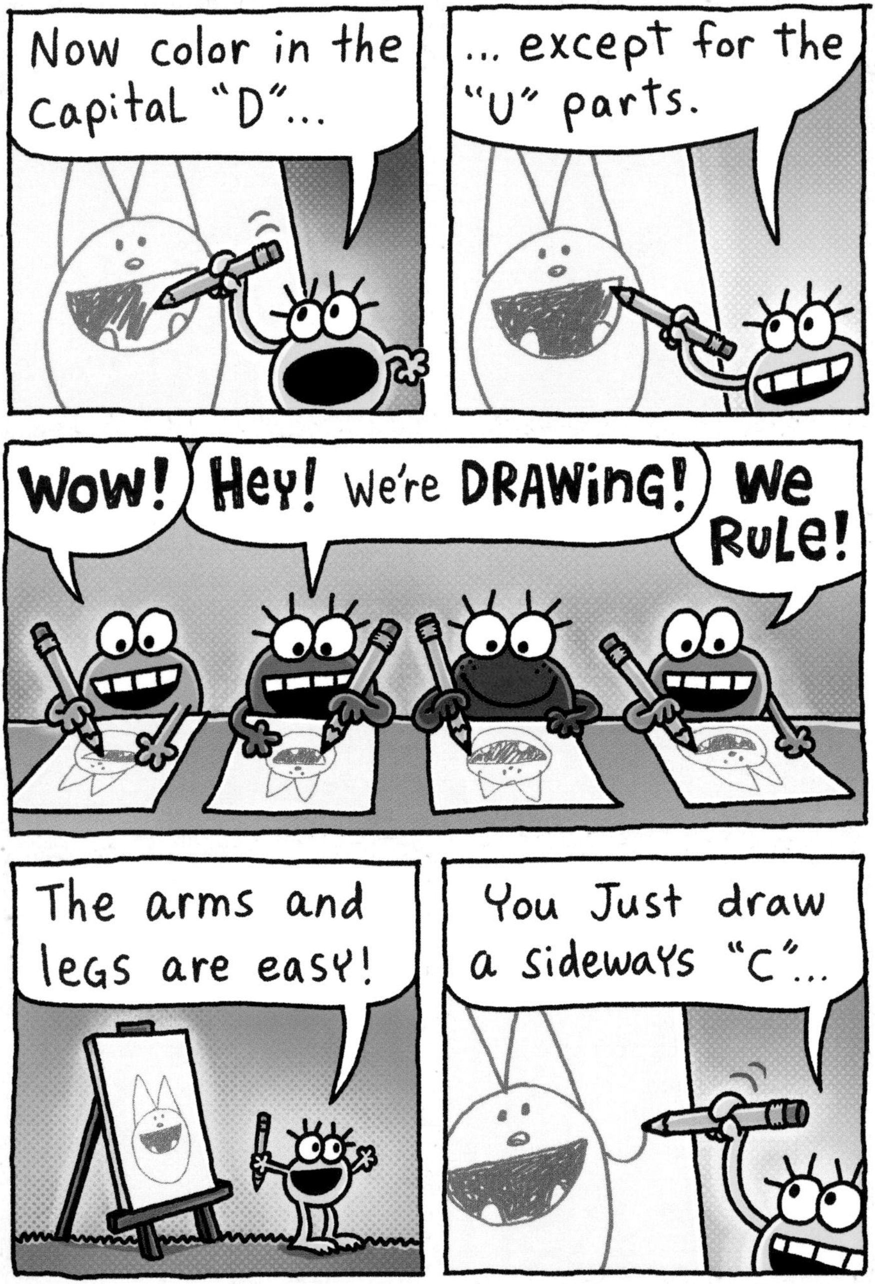
Now color in the capital "D"...
... except for the "U" parts.
WOW!
HEY! We're DRAWING!
WE RULE!
The arms and legs are easy!
You just draw a sideways "C"...

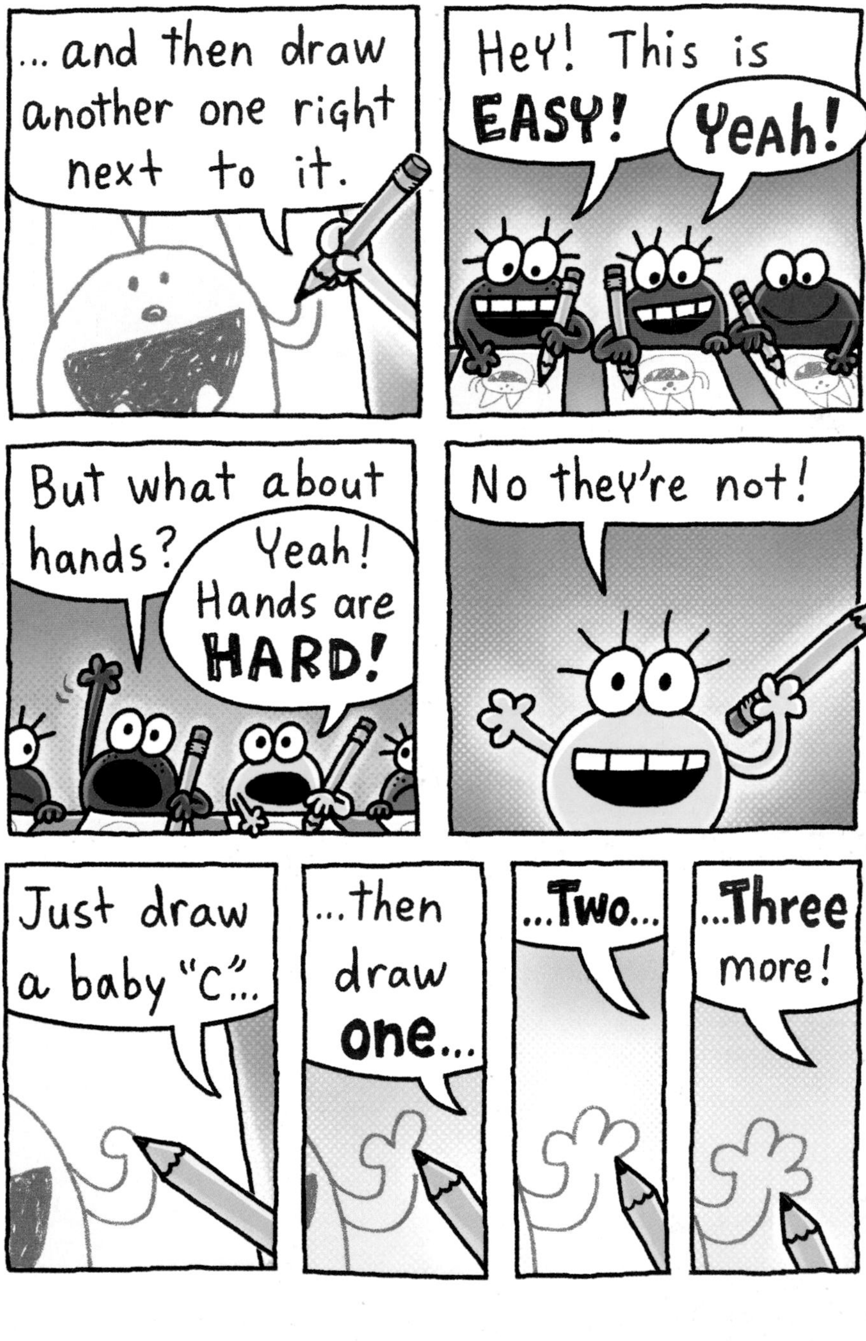
...and then draw another one right next to it.
Hey! This is EASY!
Yeah!
But what about hands?
Yeah! Hands are HARD!
No they're not!
Just draw a baby "C"...
...then draw one...
...Two...
...Three more!

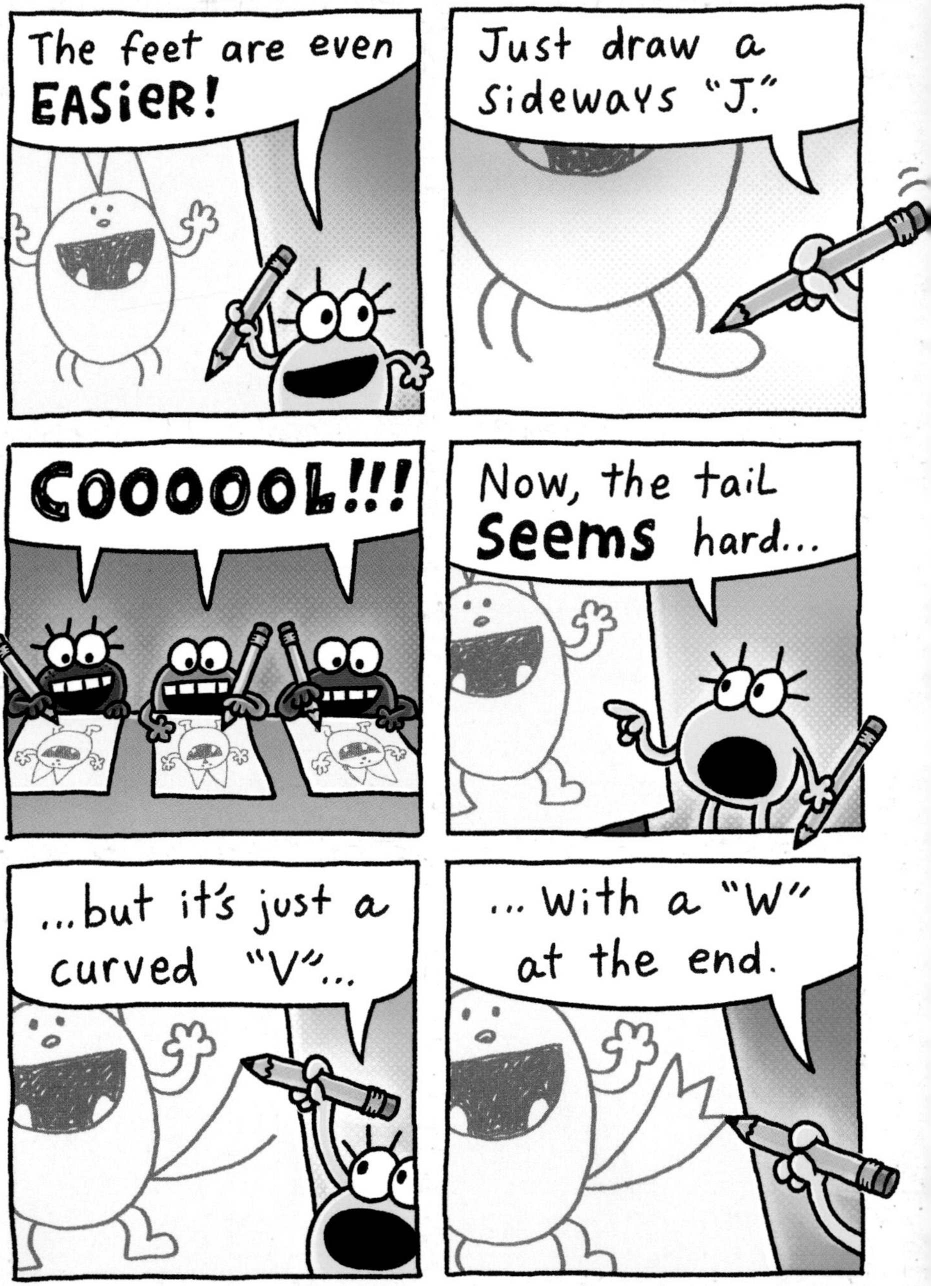
The feet are even EASIER!
Just draw a sideways "J."
COOOOOL!!!
Now, the tail Seems hard...
...but it's just a curved "V"...
... with a "W" at the end.

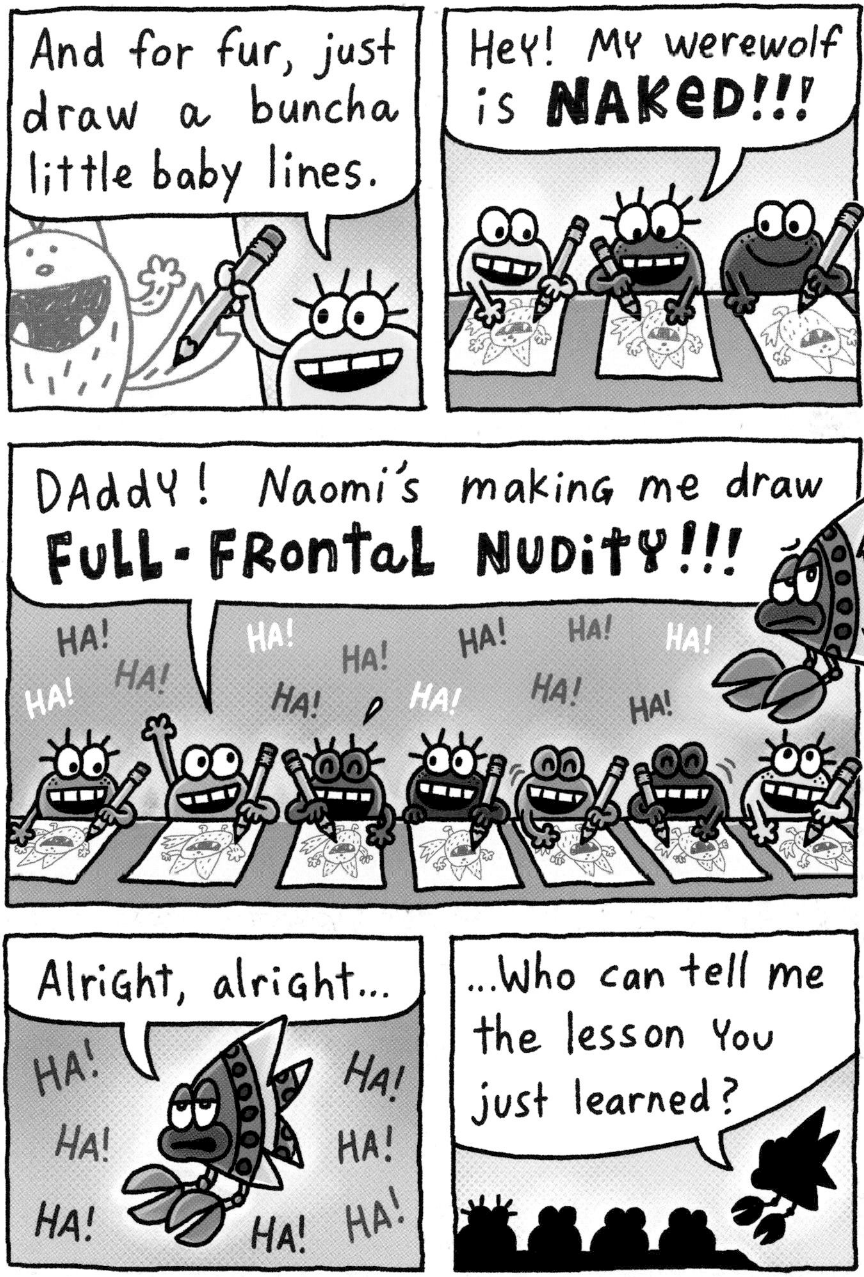
And for fur, just draw a buncha little baby lines.
Hey! My werewolf is NAKED!!!
DAddy! Naomi's making me draw FULL-FRontaL NUDity!!!
HA! HA! HA! HA! HA! HA! HA! HA! HA! HA! HA! HA!
Alright, alright...
HA! HA! HA! HA! HA! HA! HA!
...Who can tell me the lesson You just learned?

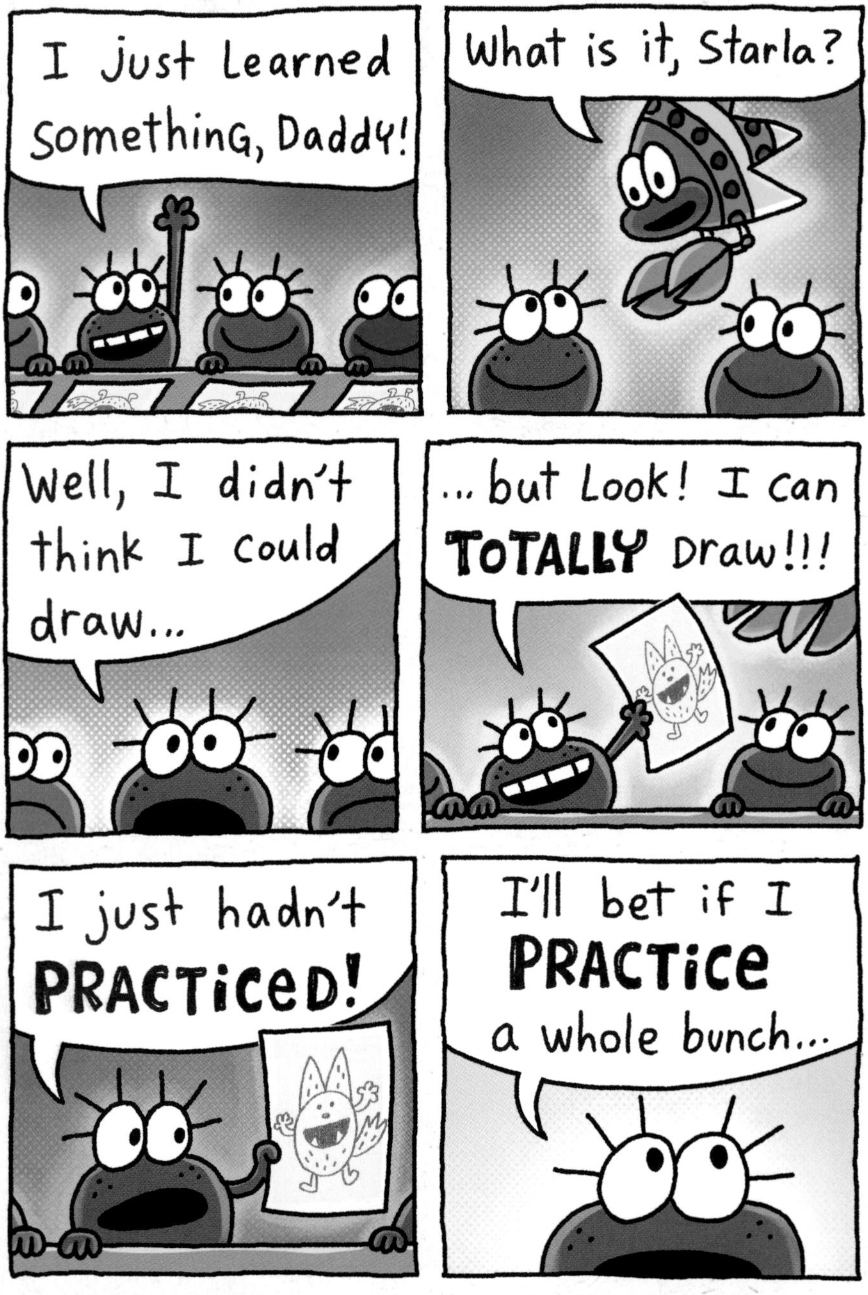

I just Learned Something, Daddy!
What is it, Starla?
Well, I didn't think I could draw...
...but Look! I can TOTALLY Draw!!!
I just hadn't PRACTICED!
I'll bet if I PRACTICE a whole bunch...

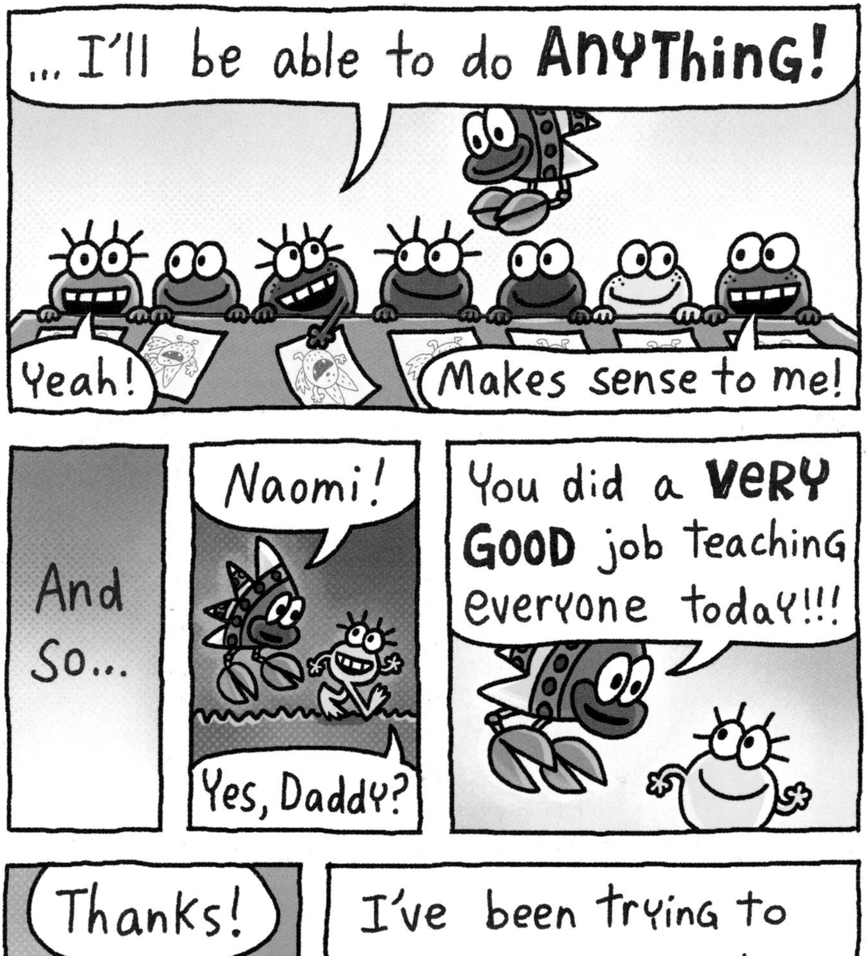

... I'll be able to do ANYTHING!
Yeah!
Makes sense to me!
And So...
Naomi!
Yes, Daddy?
You did a VERY GOOD job teaching everyone today!!!
Thanks!
I've been trying to teach you kids that lesson ALL YEAR...

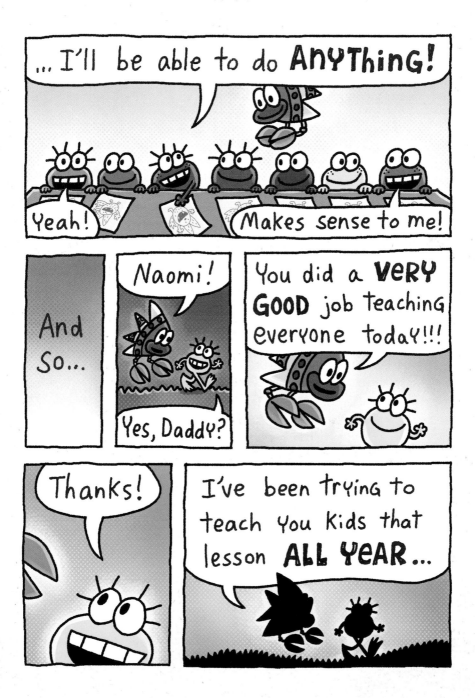

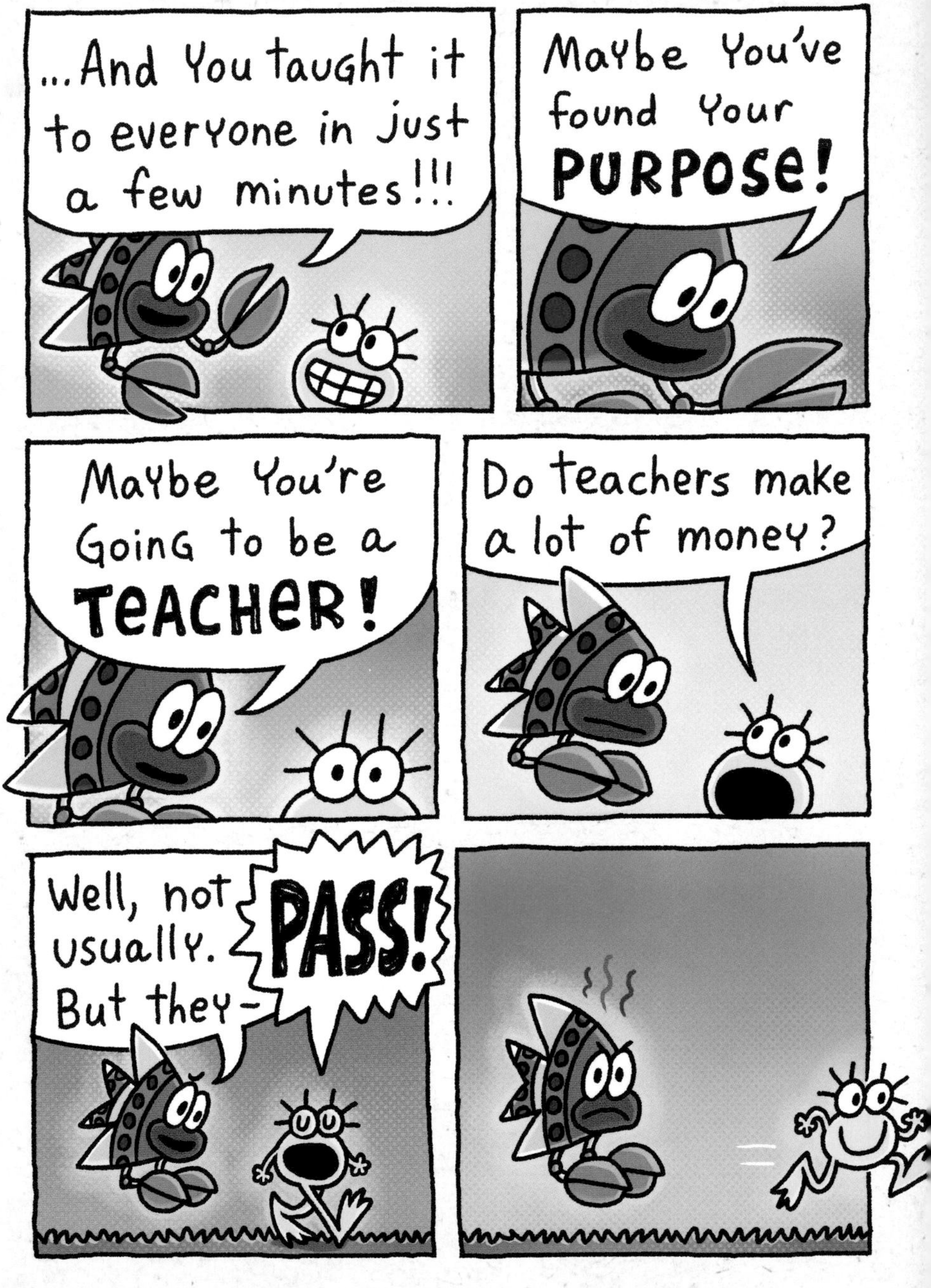
...And You taught it to everyone in just a few minutes!!!
Maybe You've found Your PURPOSE!
Maybe You're Going to be a TEACHER!
Do teachers make a lot of money?
Well, not usually. But they-
PASS!

CHAPTER 5

SHE WRITES BACK

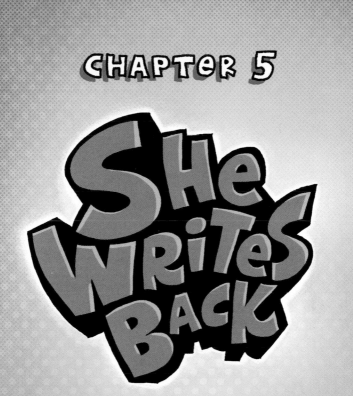

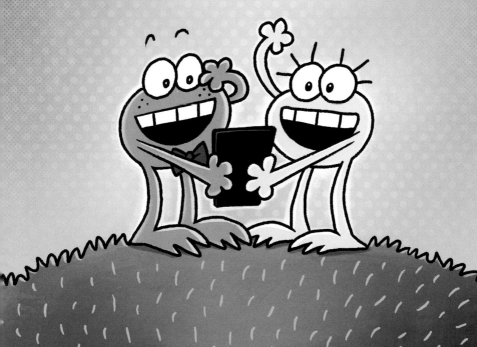

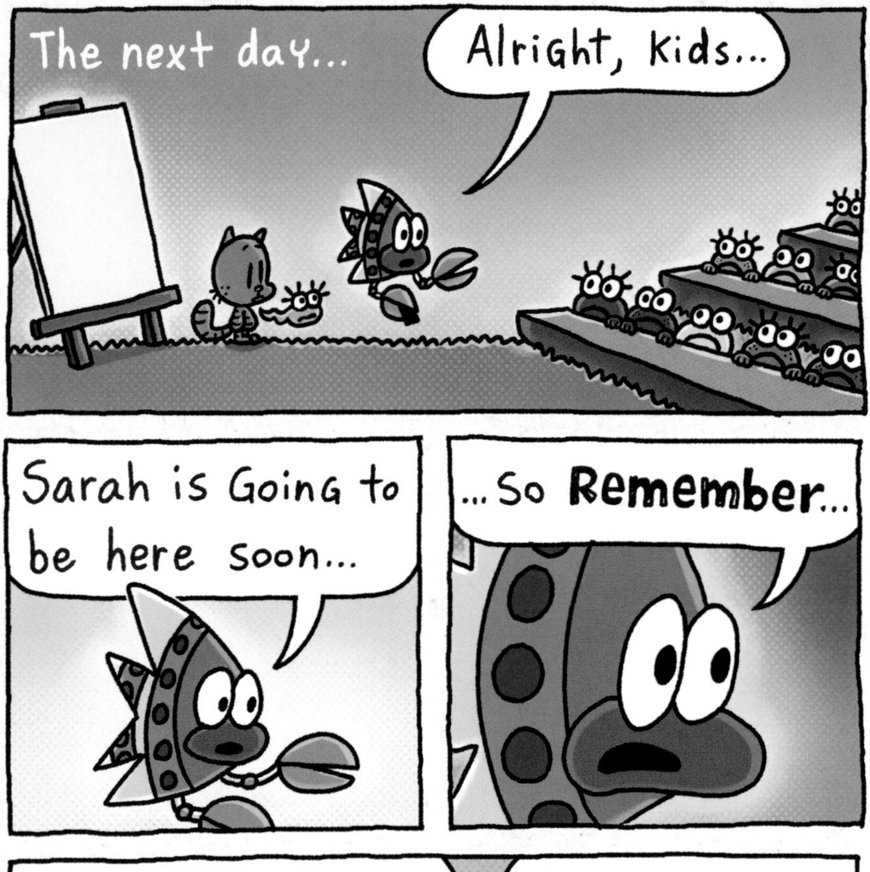
The next day...
Alright, kids...
Sarah is Going to be here soon...
...So Remember...
...I Want You kids to be on Your BEST BEHAVIOR!
Yeah, we know!

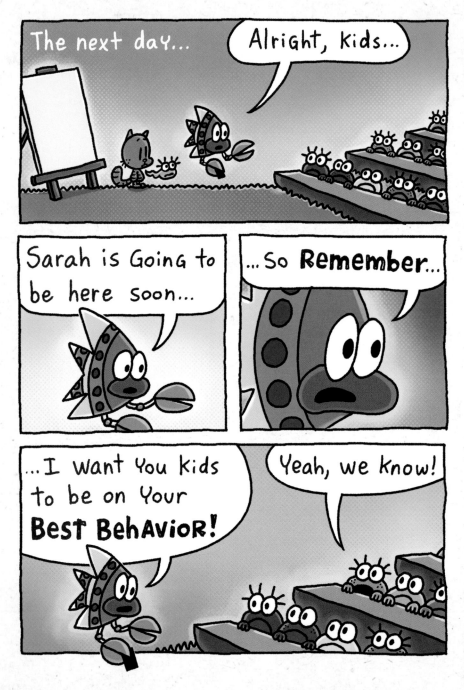

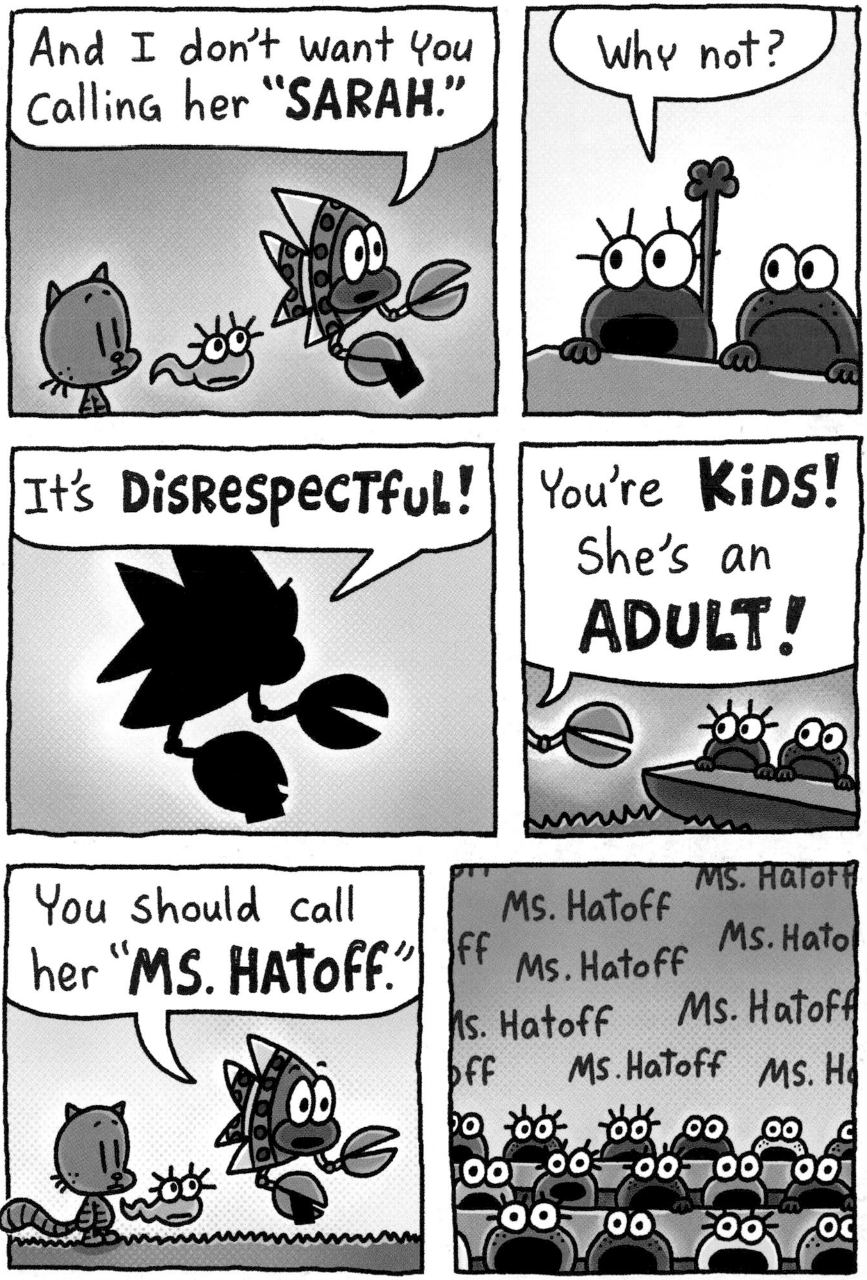
And I don't want you calling her "SARAH."
Why not?
It's DISRESPECTFUL!
You're KIDS! She's an ADULT!
You should call her "MS. HATOFF."
Ms. Hatoff
Ms. Hatoff
Ms. Hatoff
Ms. Hatoff
Ms. Hatoff

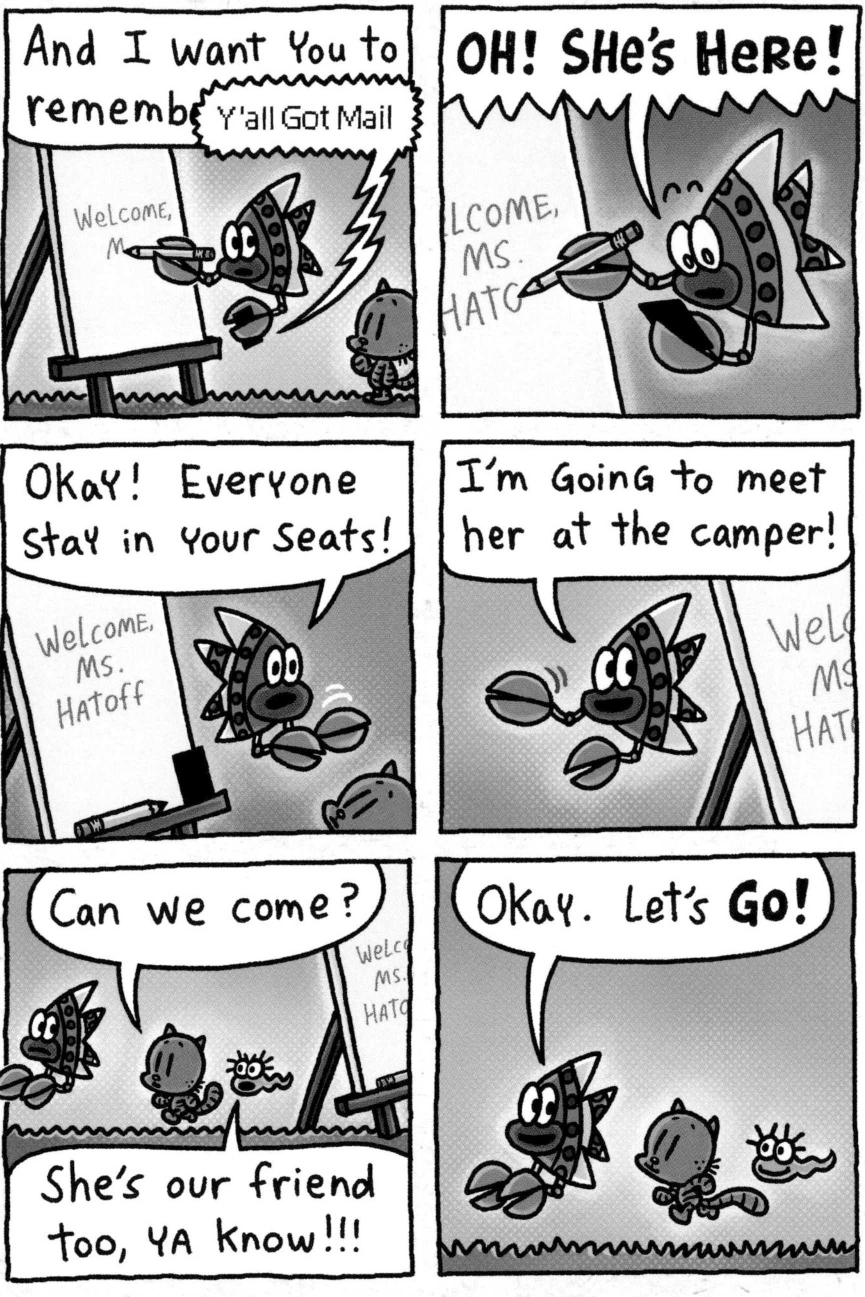
And I want you to rememb
Y'all Got Mail
OH! SHe's Here!
WelcoME,
M
LCOME,
MS.
HATO
OKaY! EverYone stay in Your Seats!
WelcoME,
MS.
HATOff
I'm Going to meet her at the camper!
Can we come?
She's our friend too, YA know!!!
OKaY. Let's GO!

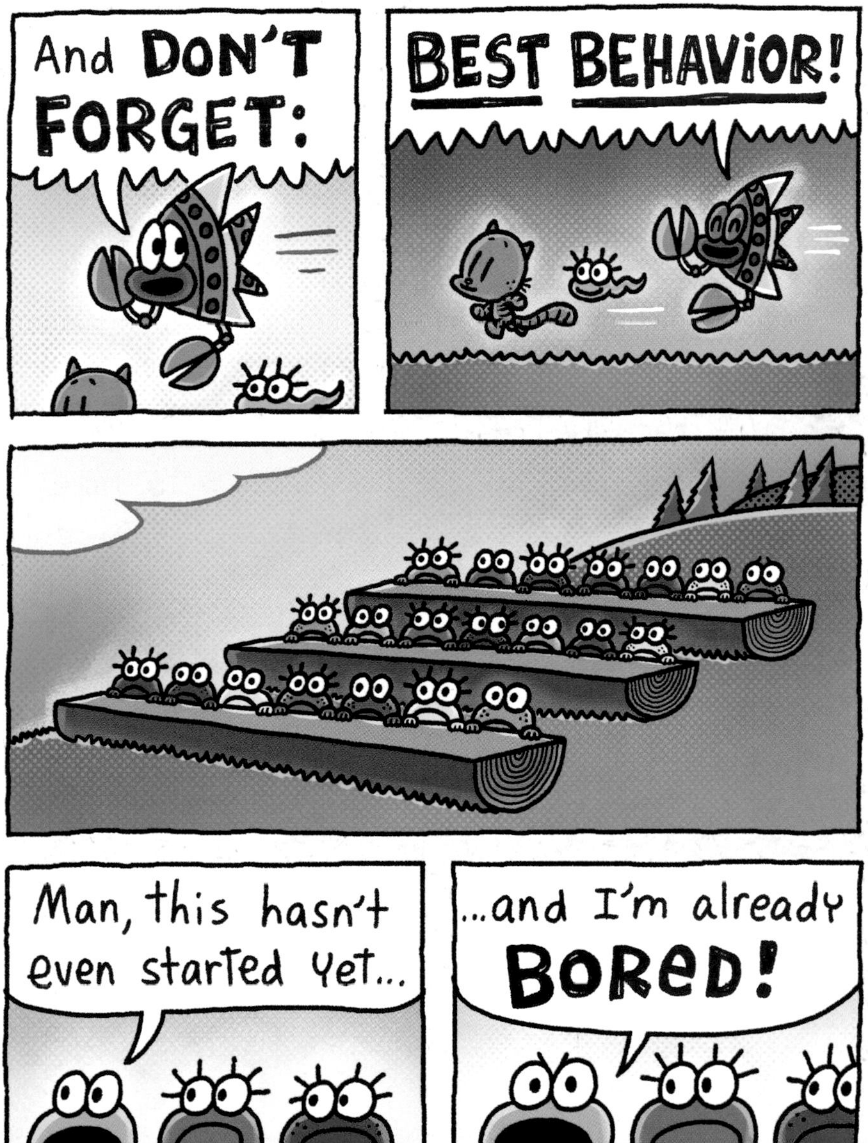
And DON'T FORGET:
BEST BEHAVIOR!
Man, this hasn't even started yet...
...and I'm already BORED!

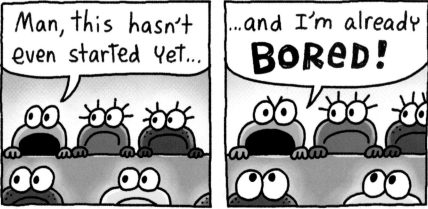

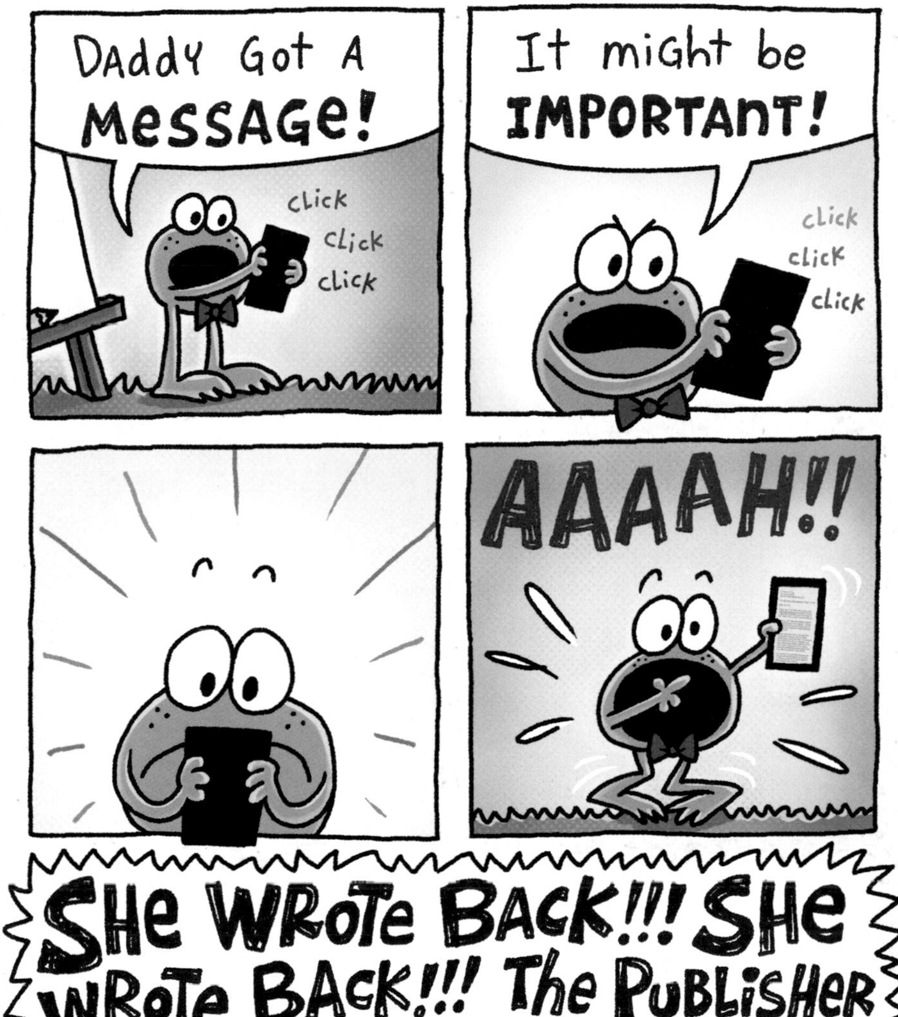
Daddy Got A MESSAGE!
click click click
It might be IMPORTANT!
click click click
AAAAH!!
SHE WROTE BACK!!! SHE WROTE BACK!!! The PUBLISHER LADY FINALLY WROTE BACK!

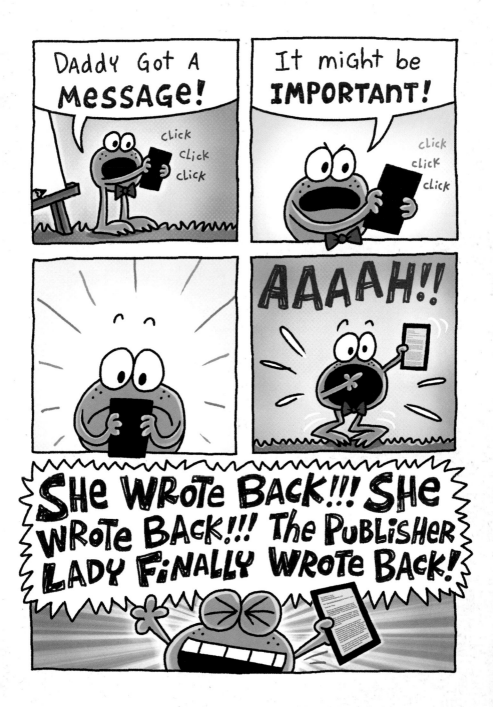

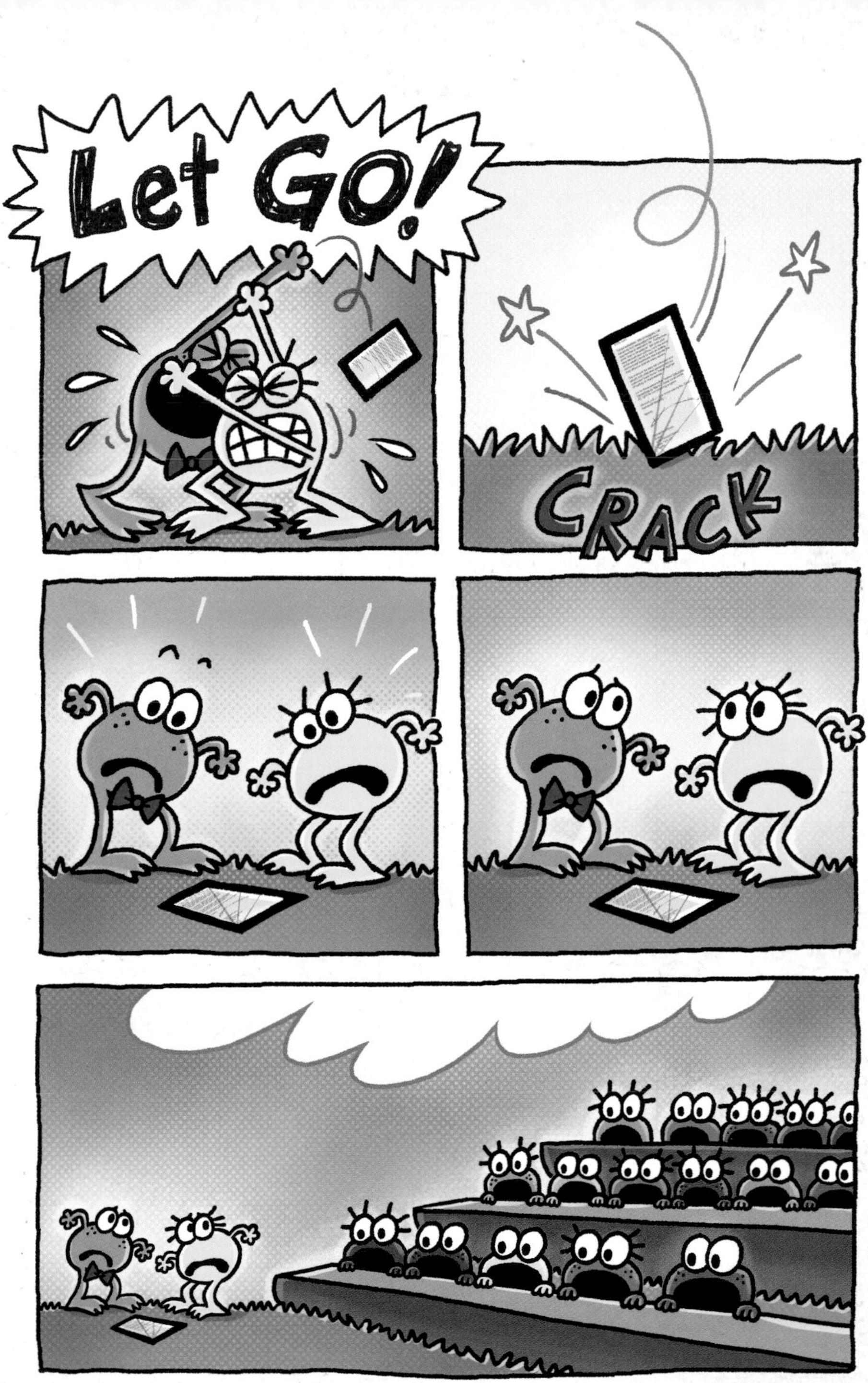
Let GO!
CRACK

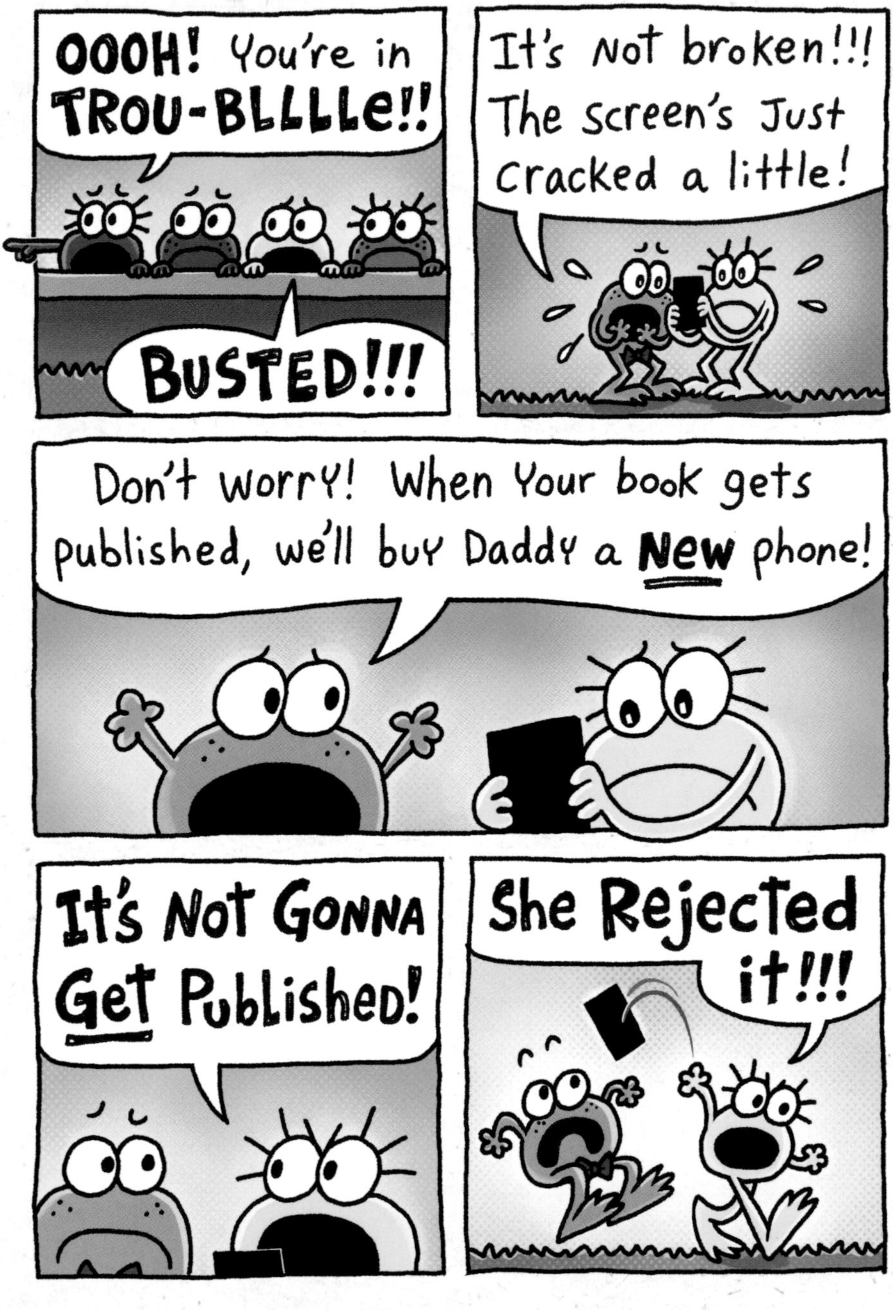
OOOH! You're in TROU-BLLLLe!!
BUSTED!!!
It's Not broken!!! The screen's Just cracked a little!
Don't worry! When Your book gets published, we'll buy Daddy a New phone!
It's Not GONNA Get Published!
She Rejected it!!!

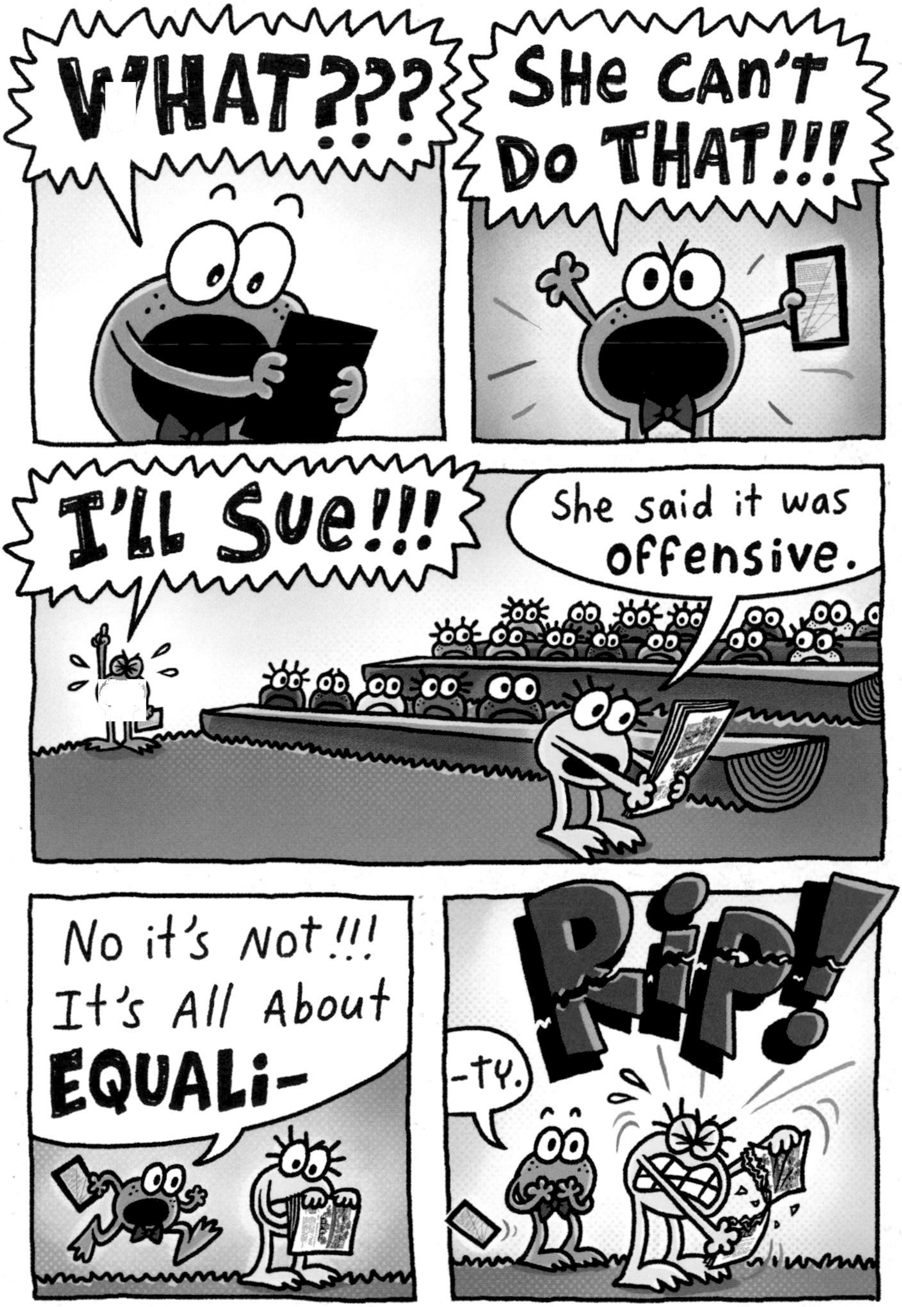
WHAT???
She Can't Do THAT!!!
I'll Sue!!!
She said it was offensive.
No it's Not!!! It's All About EQUALi-
RiP!
-TY.

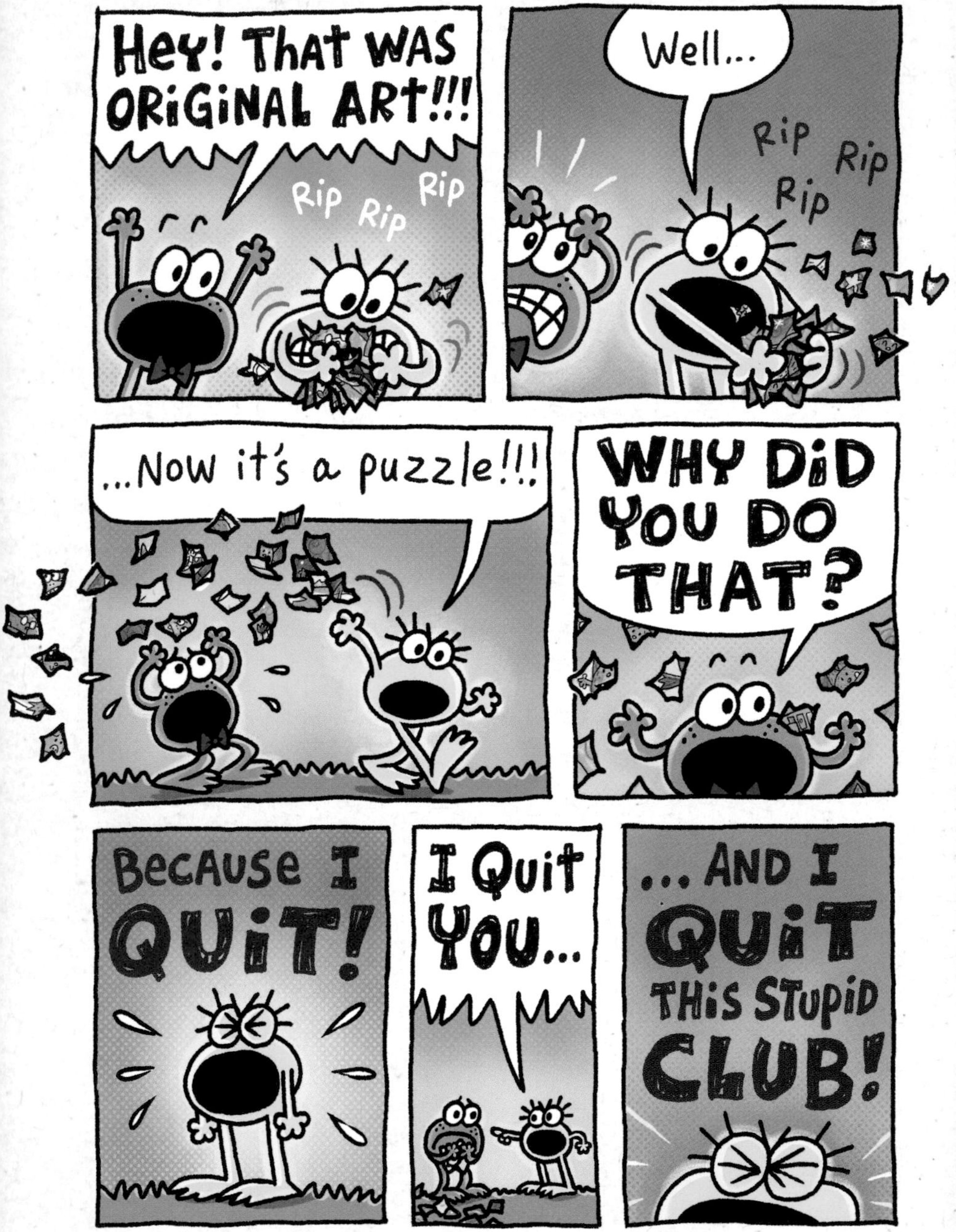
Hey! That WAS ORIGINAL ART!!!
Rip Rip Rip
Well...
Rip Rip Rip
...Now it's a puzzle!!!
WHY DID YOU DO THAT?
BECAUSE I QUIT!
I Quit YOU...
... AND I QUIT THIS STUPID CLUB!

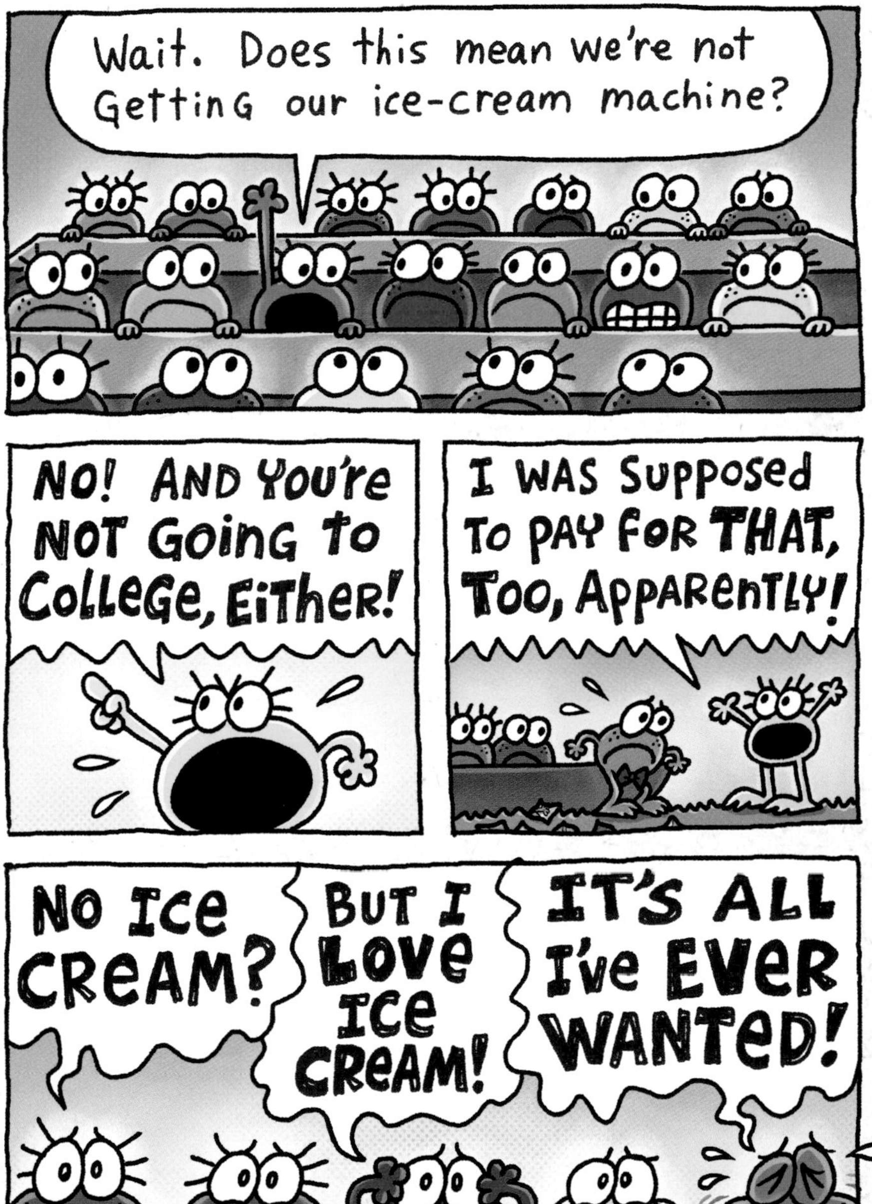
Wait. Does this mean we're not Getting our ice-cream machine?
NO! AND YOU'RE NOT GOING TO COLLEGE, EITHER!
I WAS SUPPOSED TO PAY FOR THAT, TOO, APPARENTLY!
NO ICE CREAM?
BUT I LOVE ICE CREAM!
IT'S ALL I'VE EVER WANTED!

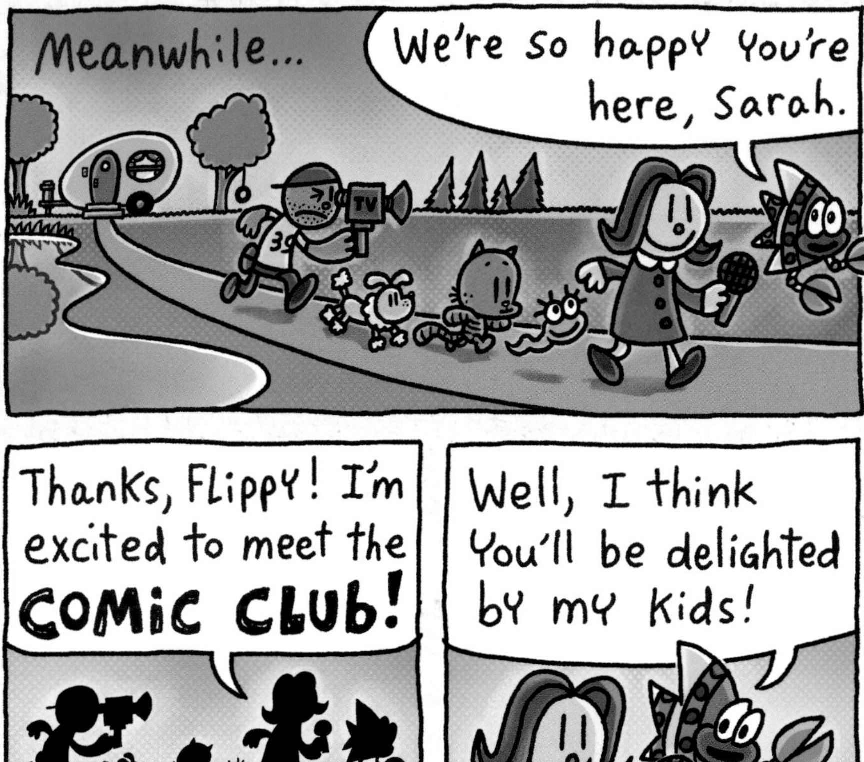
Meanwhile...
We're so happy you're here, Sarah.
Thanks, Flippy! I'm excited to meet the COMIC CLUB!
Well, I think you'll be delighted by my kids!
They're so CREATIVE...
... so MATURE...
... and always on their BEST BEHAVIOR!!!

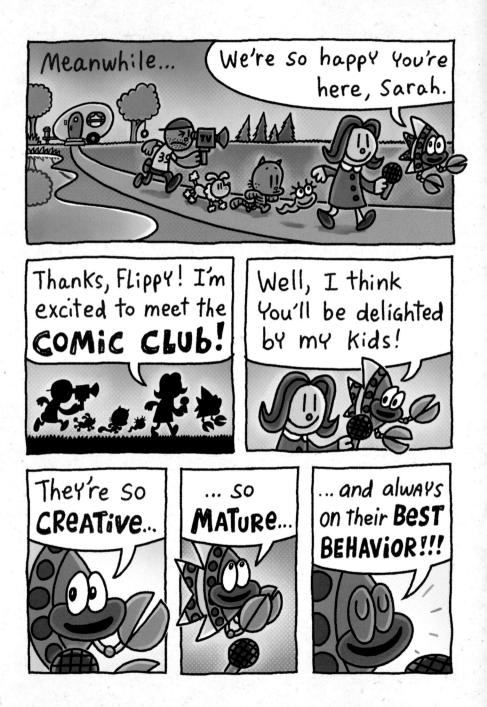

CHAPTER 6

Our Worst Behavior

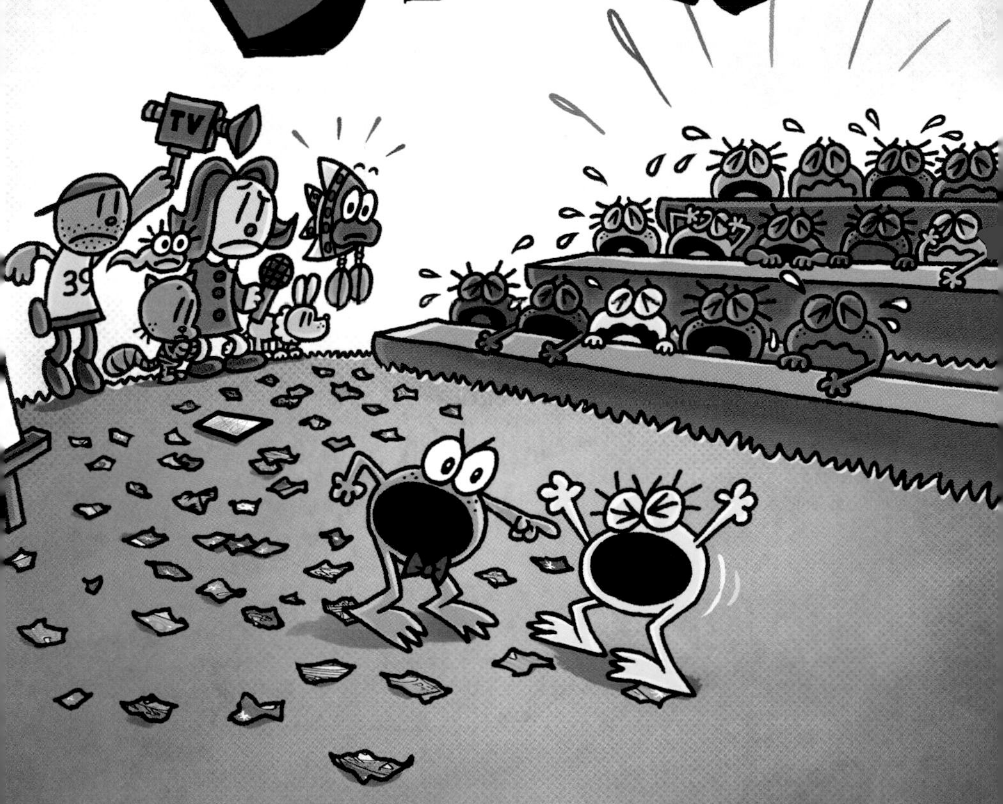
TV
39

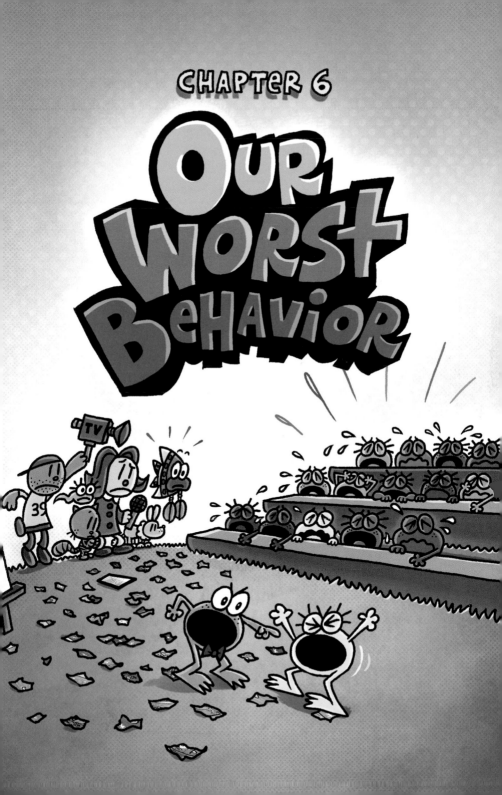

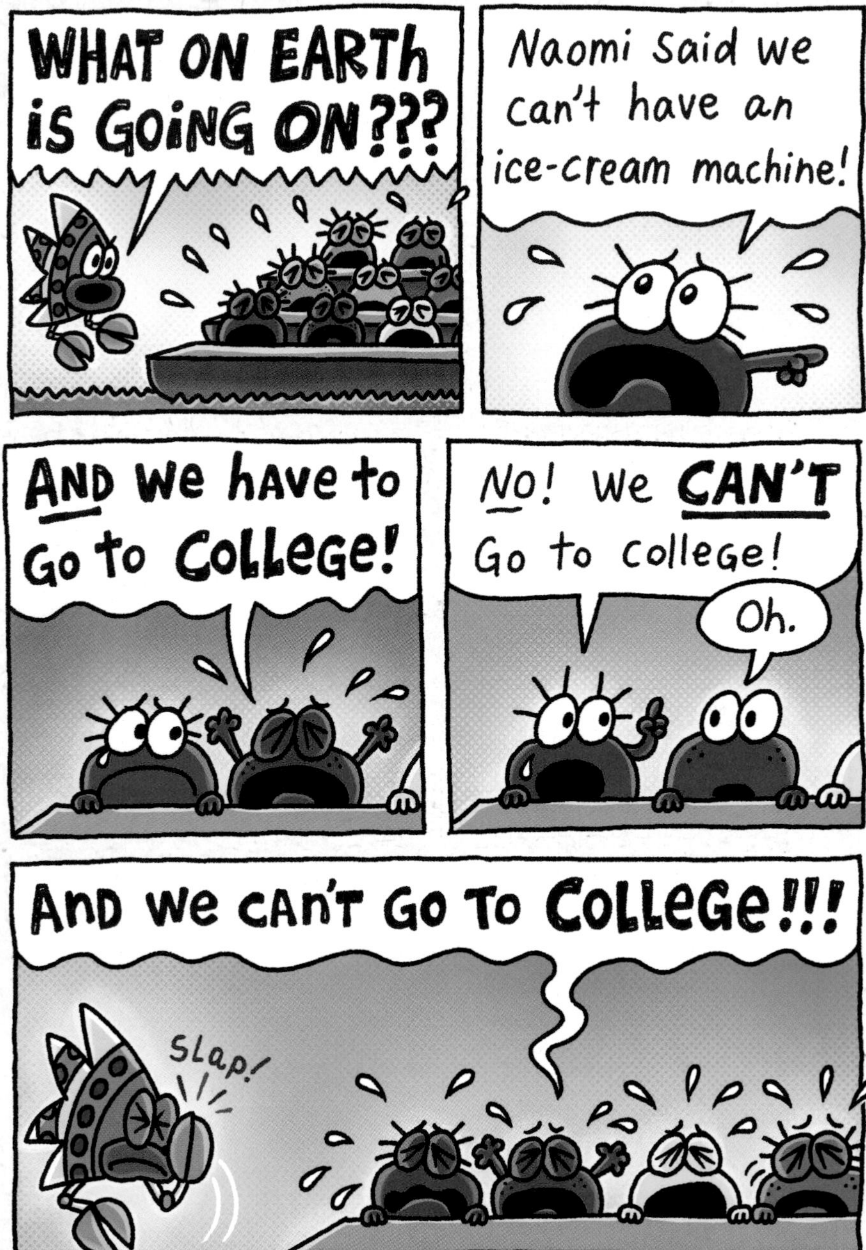
WHAT ON EARTH is GOING ON???
Naomi Said we can't have an ice-cream machine!
AND we have to Go to COLLeGe!
NO! We CAN'T Go to college!
Oh.
AND we CAN'T GO TO COLLeGe!!!
SLap!

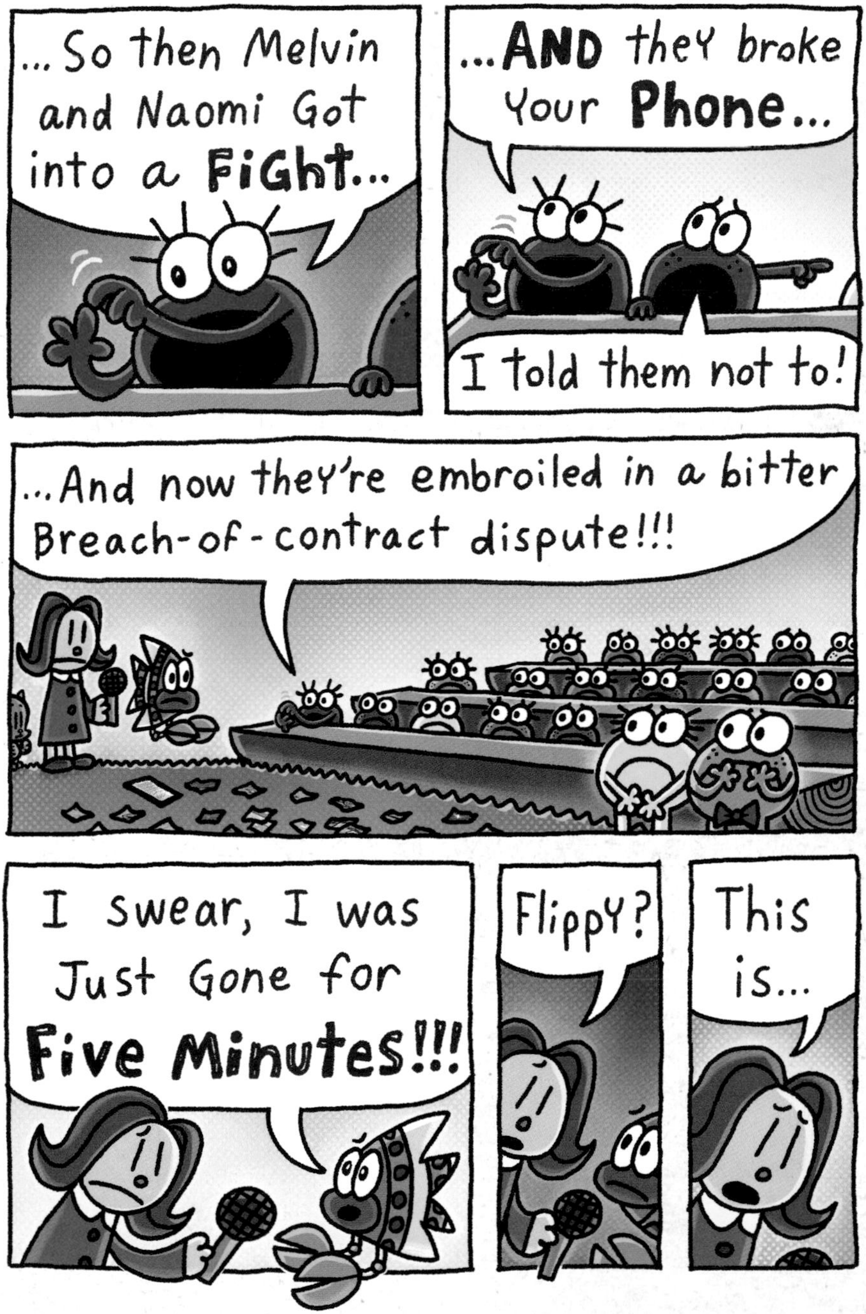
...So then Melvin and Naomi Got into a FiGHT...
...AND they broke Your Phone...
I told them not to!
...And now they're embroiled in a bitter Breach-of-contract dispute!!!
I swear, I was Just Gone for Five Minutes!!!
Flippy?
This is...

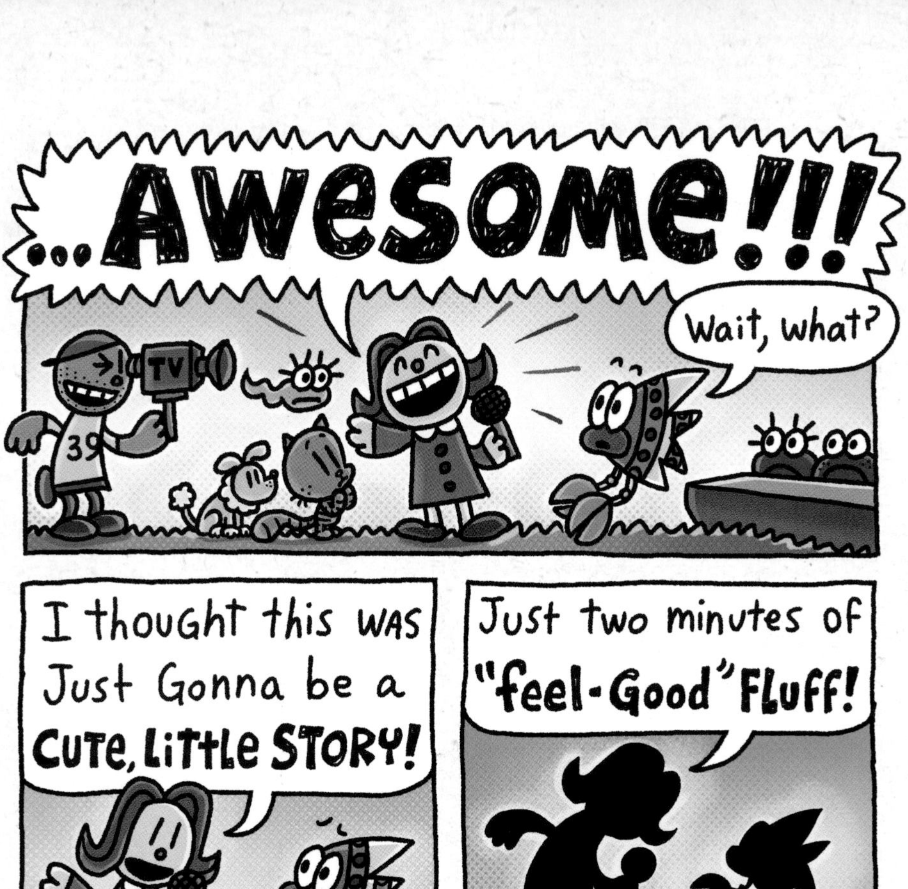
...AWESOME!!!
Wait, what?
TV
39
I thought this WAS Just Gonna be a CUTE, LITTLE STORY!
Just two minutes of "feel-Good" FLUFF!
But this story has PASSION...
...DRAMA...

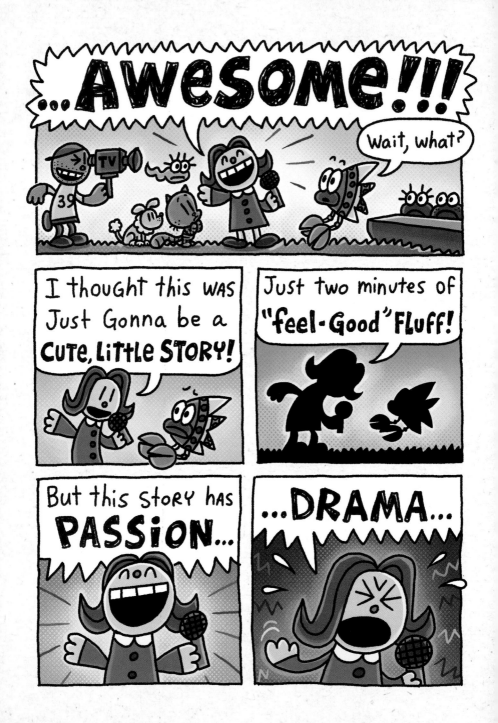

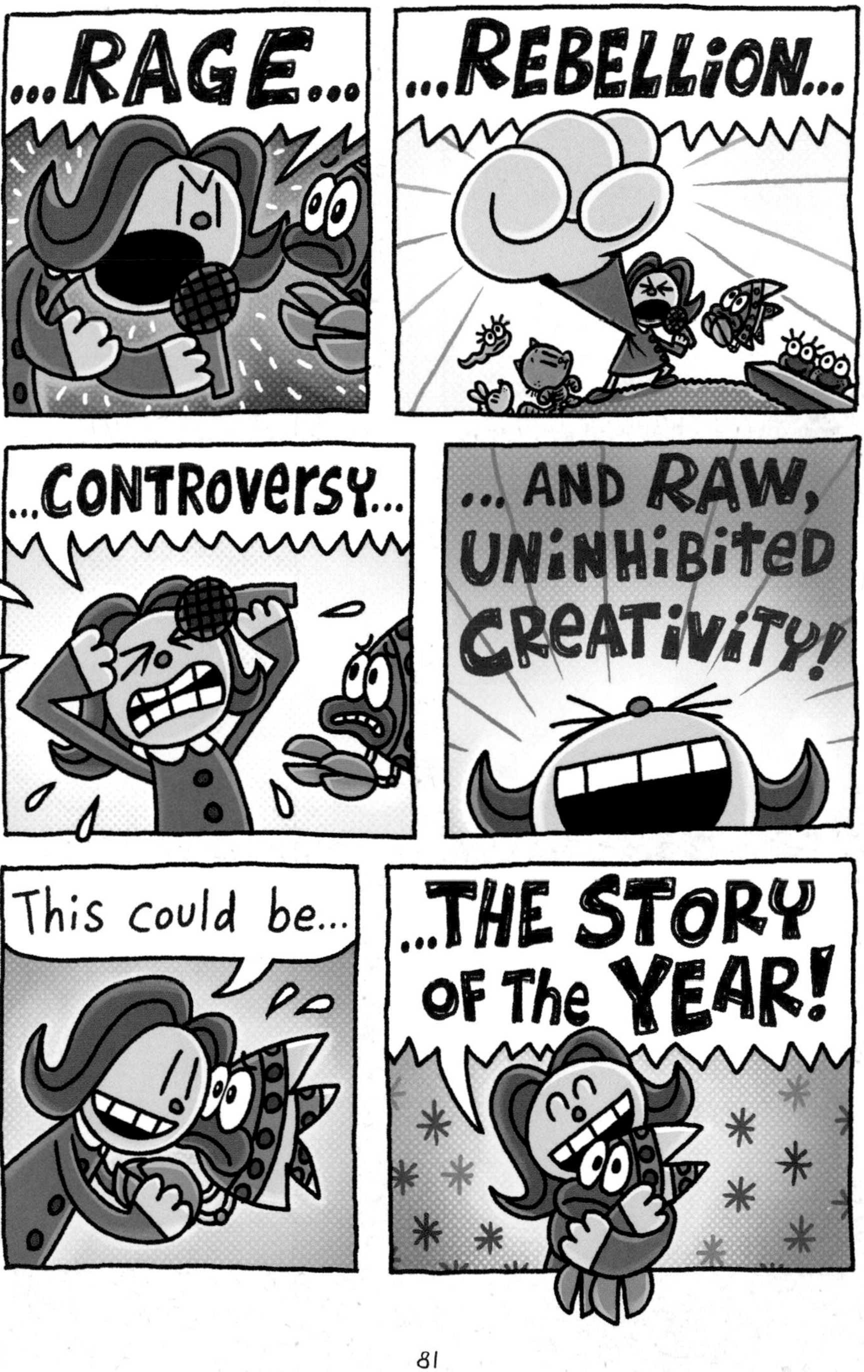
...RAGE...
...REBELLION...
...CONTROVERSY...
... AND RAW, UNINHIBITED CREATIVITY!
This could be...
...THE STORY OF THE YEAR!

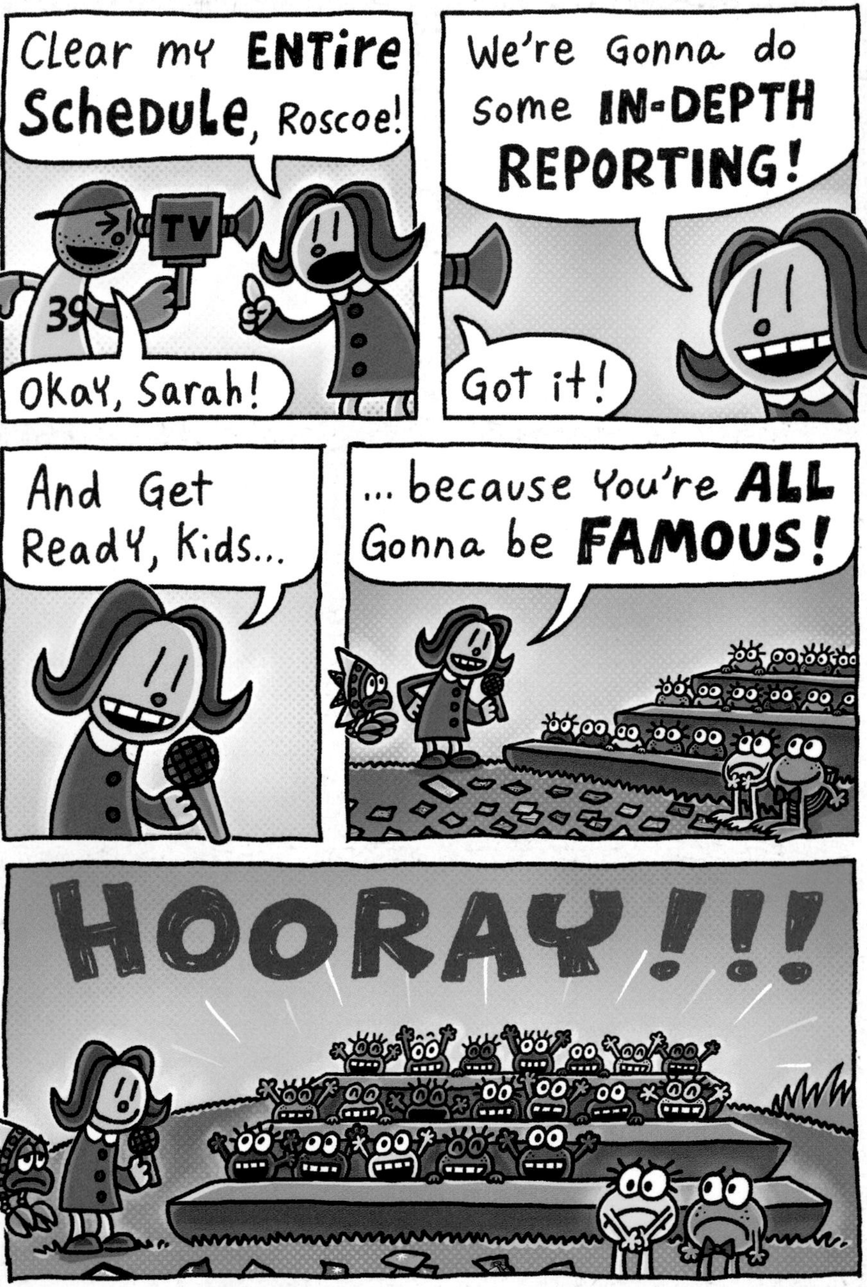
Clear my ENTire SchedULe, Roscoe!
OKaY, Sarah!
We're Gonna do some IN-DEPTH REPORTING!
Got it!
And Get ReadY, Kids...
... because You're ALL Gonna be FAMOUS!
TV
39
HOORAY!!!

CHAPTER 7

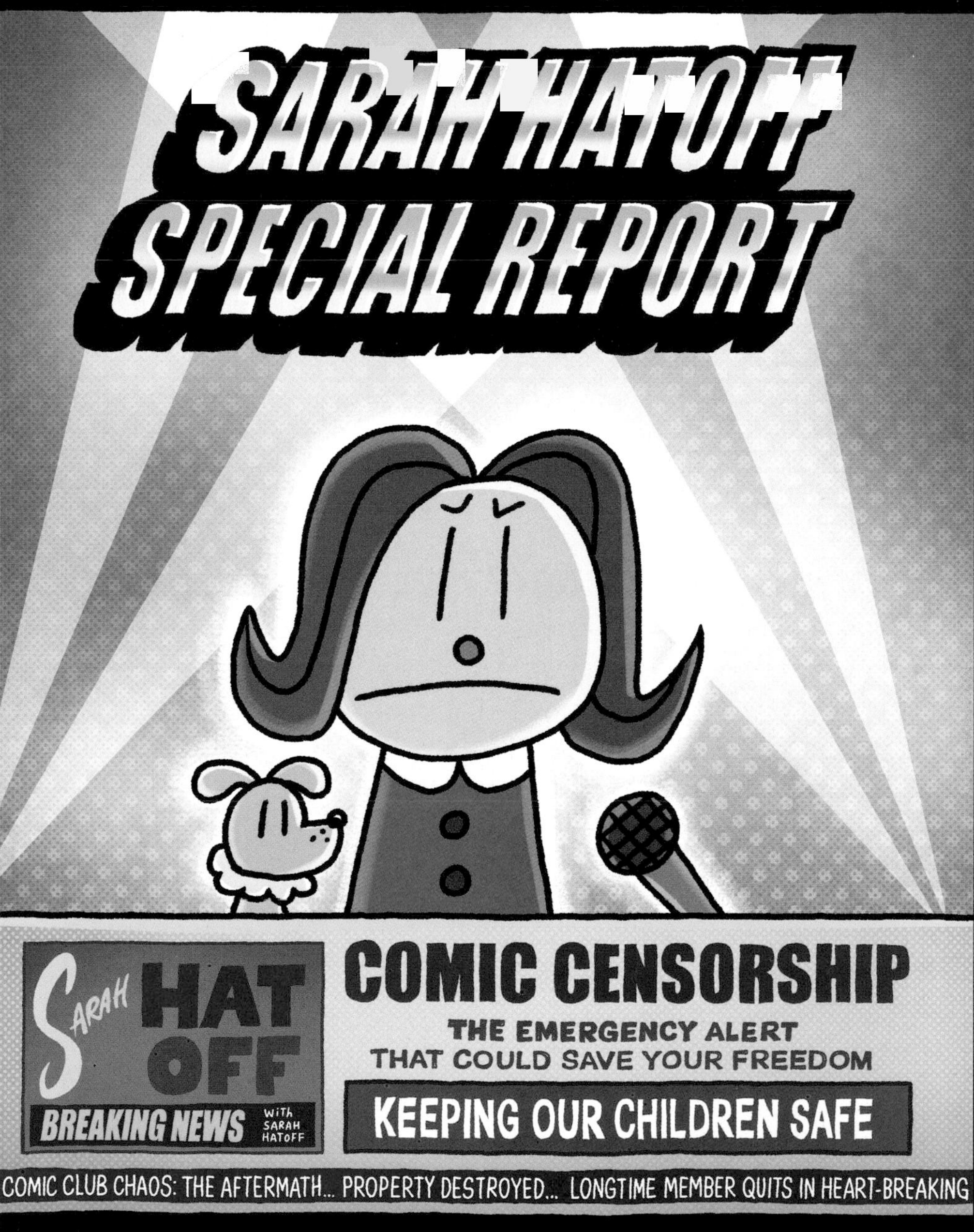

SARAH HATOFF SPECIAL REPORT
SARAH HAT OFF
BREAKING NEWS
WITH SARAH HATOFF
COMIC CENSORSHIP
THE EMERGENCY ALERT THAT COULD SAVE YOUR FREEDOM
KEEPING OUR CHILDREN SAFE
COMIC CLUB CHAOS: THE AFTERMATH... PROPERTY DESTROYED... LONGTIME MEMBER QUITS IN HEART-BREAKING

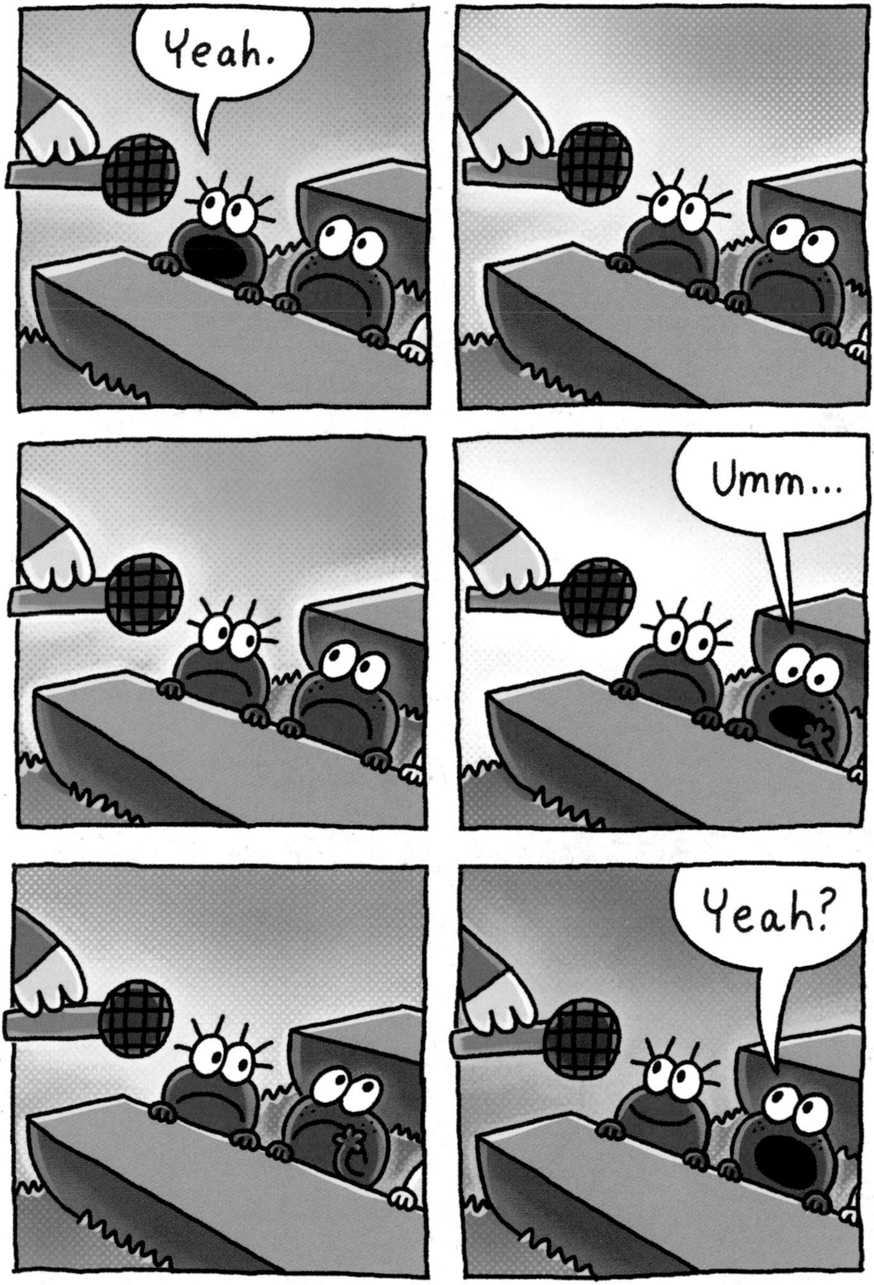

Yeah.
Umm...
Yeah?

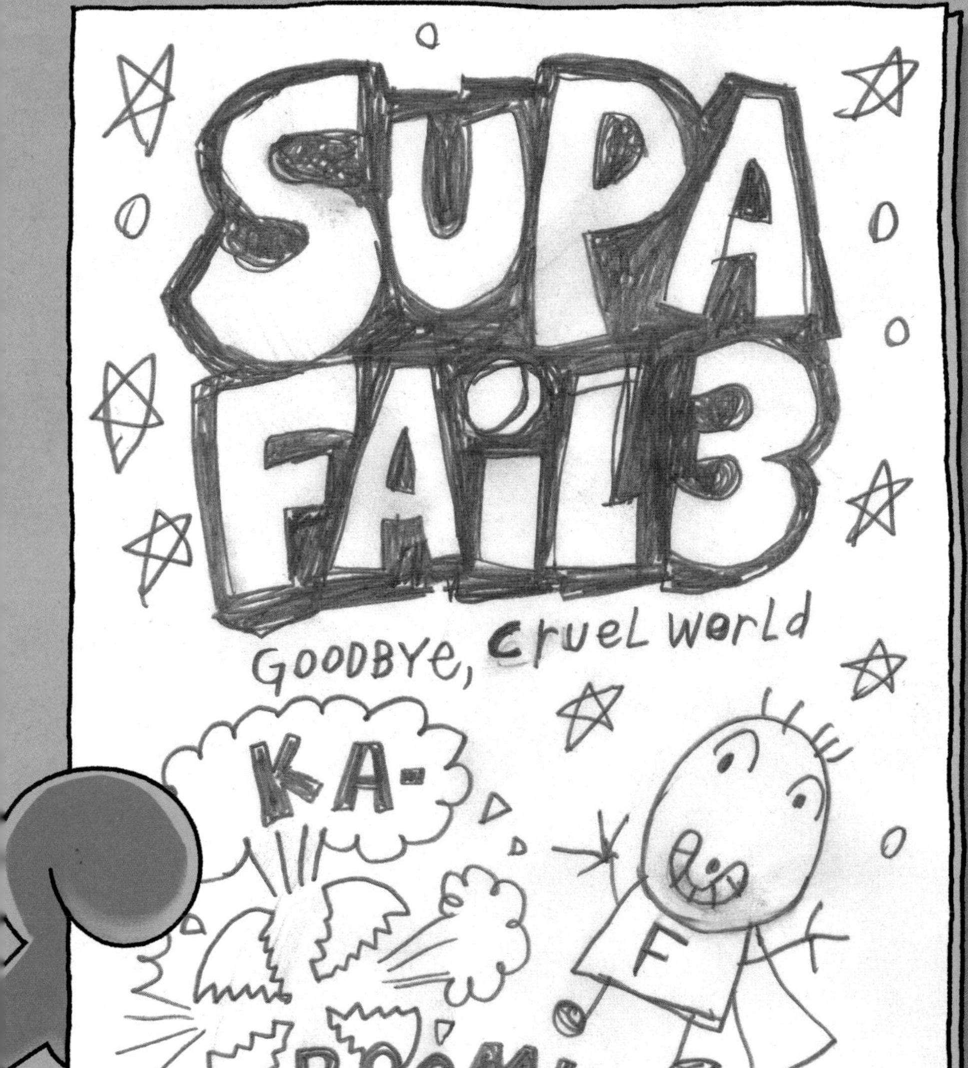
SUPA FAIL 3
GOODBYE, Cruel World
KA-
BOOM!
F
BY K.T., Kip, and Curly

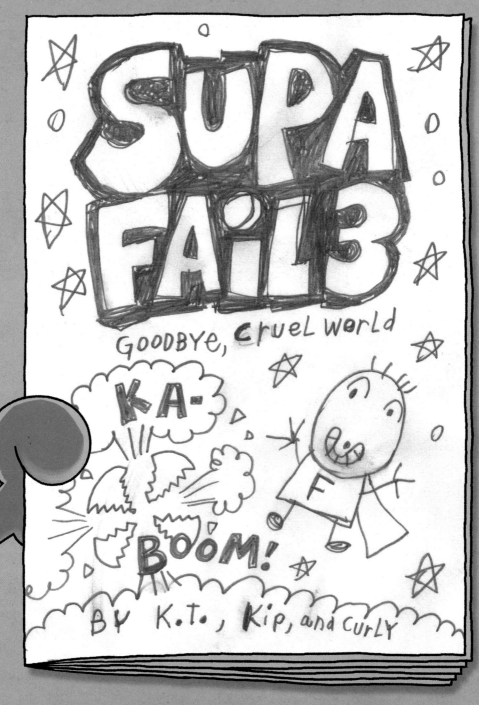

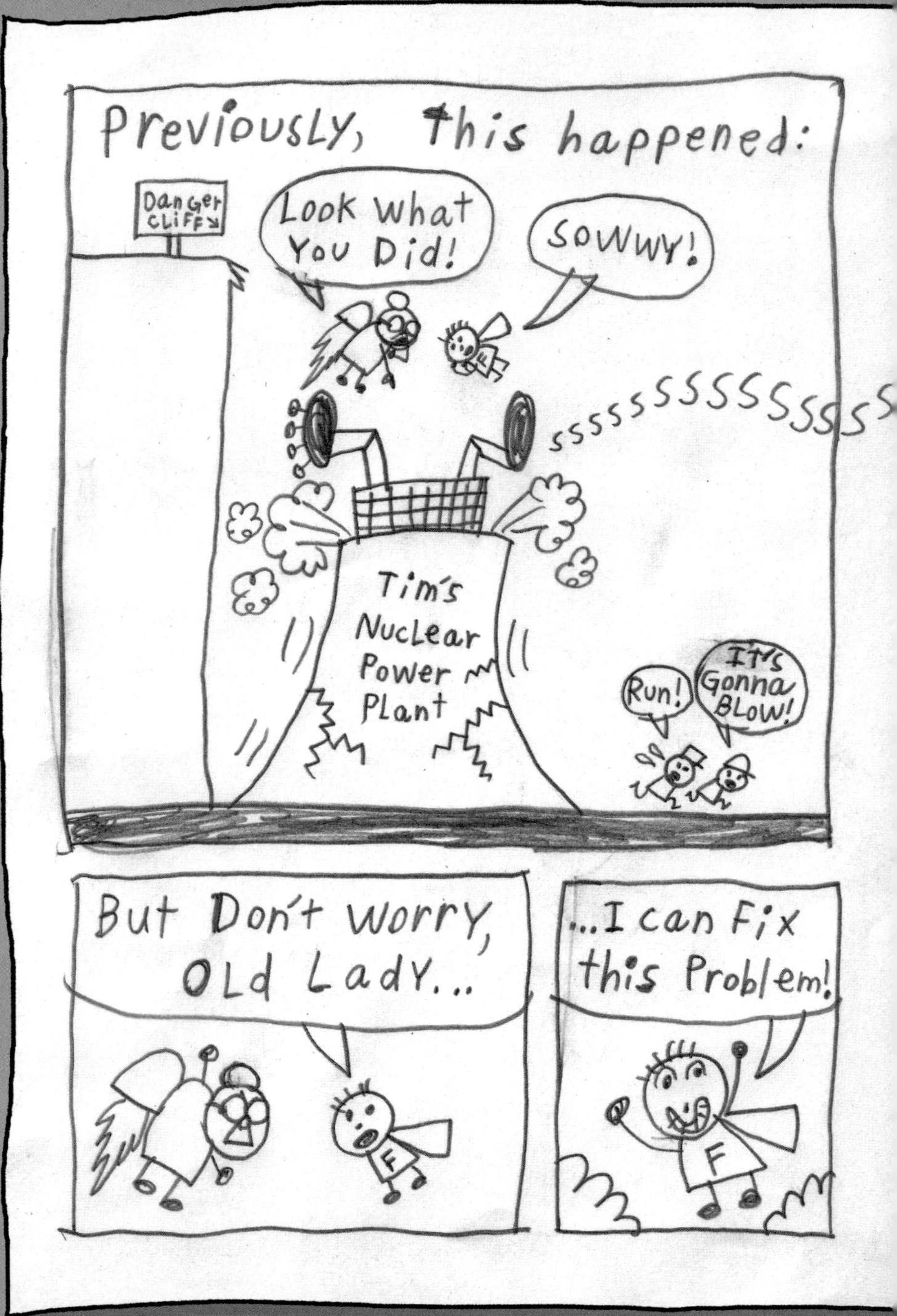
Previously, this happened:
Danger CLIFF
Look What You Did!
SOWWY!
SSSSSSSSSSSSSSS
Tim's Nuclear Power Plant
Run!
It's Gonna BLOW!
But Don't worry, Old Lady...
...I can Fix this Problem!

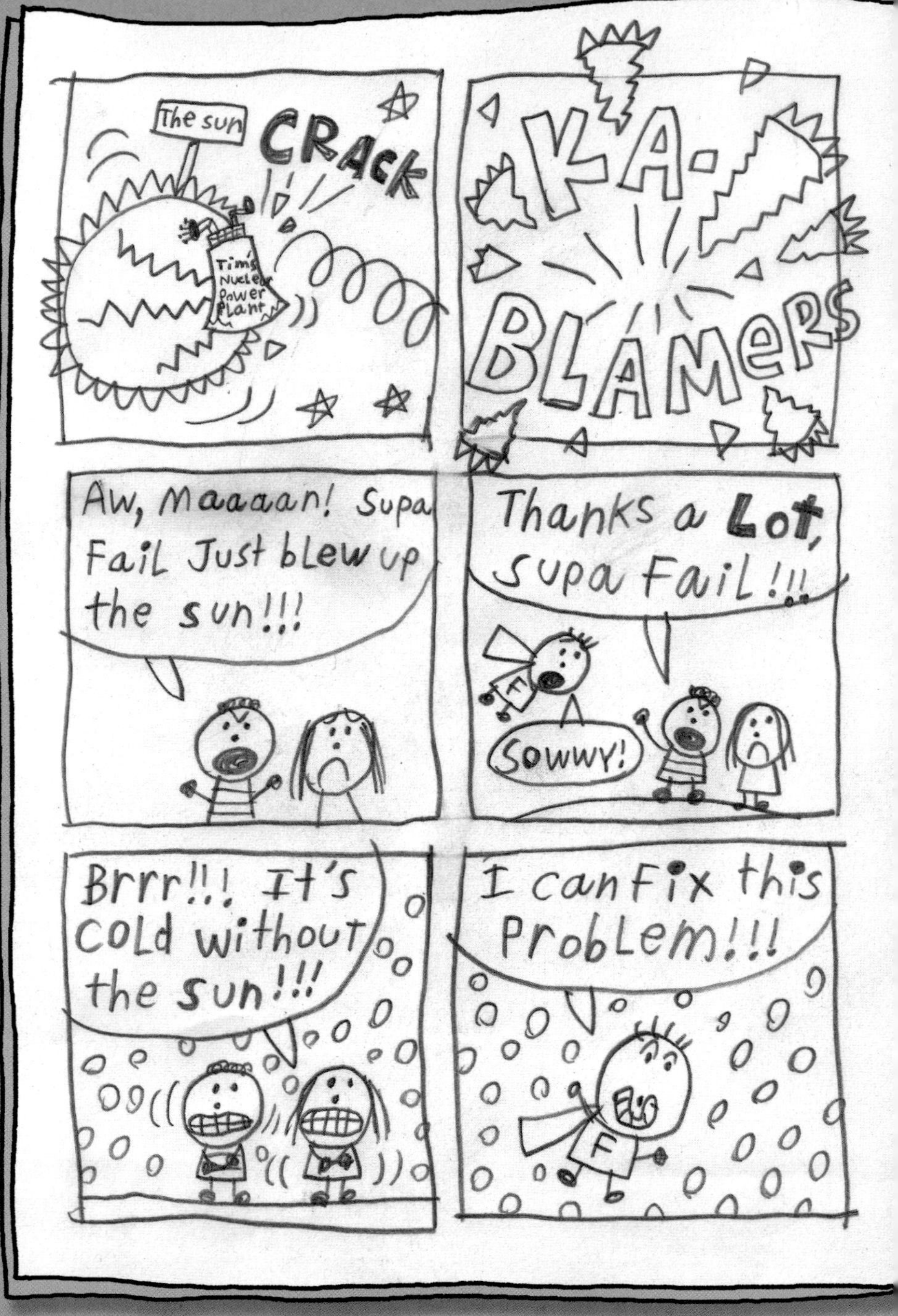
The sun
CRACK
Tim's Nuclear Power Plant
KA-BLAMERS
Aw, Maaaan! Supa Fail Just blew up the sun!!!
Thanks a Lot, Supa Fail!!!
SOWWY!
Brrr!!! It's COLd without the sun!!!
I can Fix this ProbLem!!!

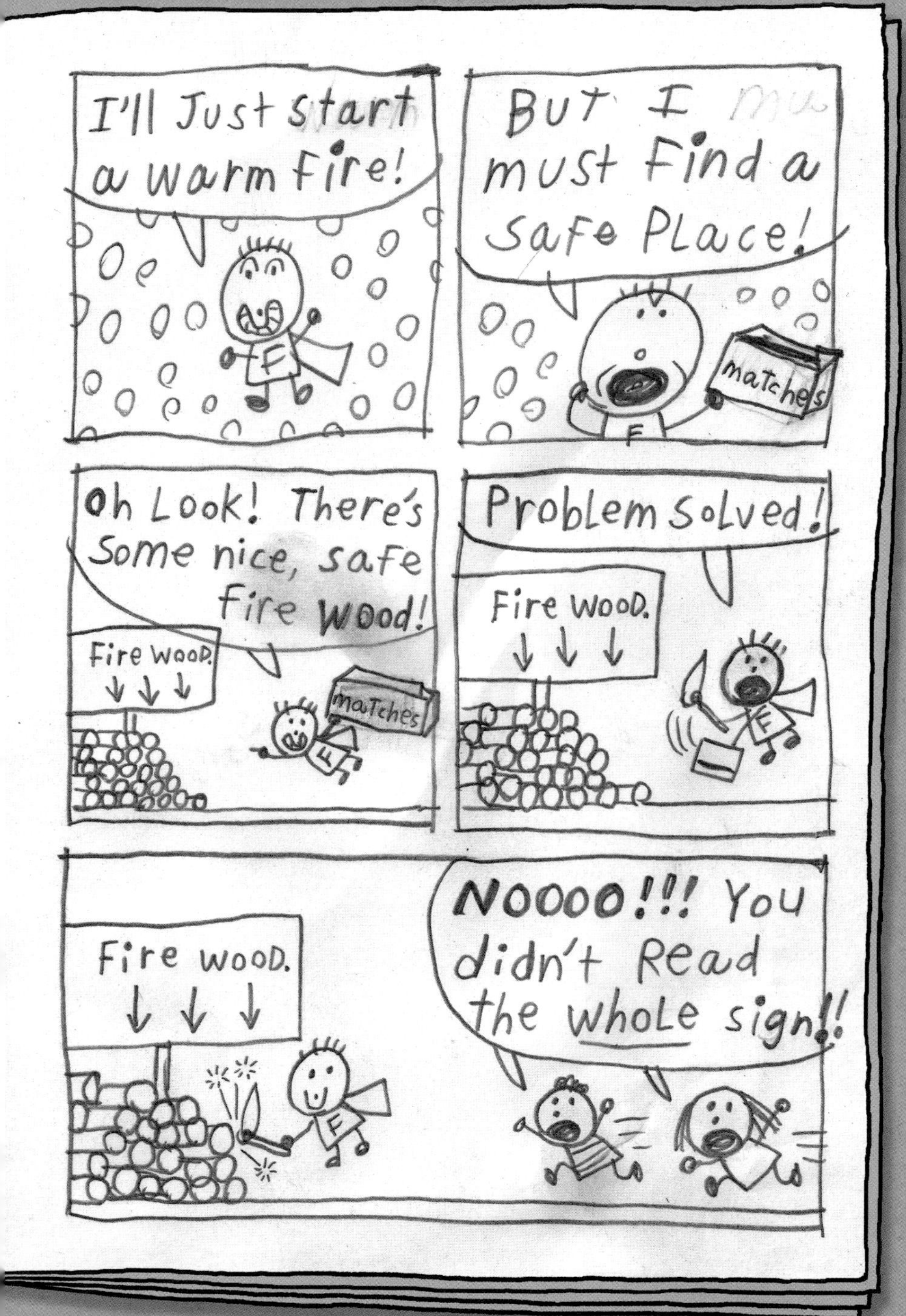
I'll Just start a warm Fire!
But I must Find a safe Place!
matches
Oh Look! There's Some nice, safe fire wood!
Fire WOOD.
matches
Problem Solved!
Fire WOOD.
Fire WOOD.
NOOOO!!! You didn't Read the whole sign!!

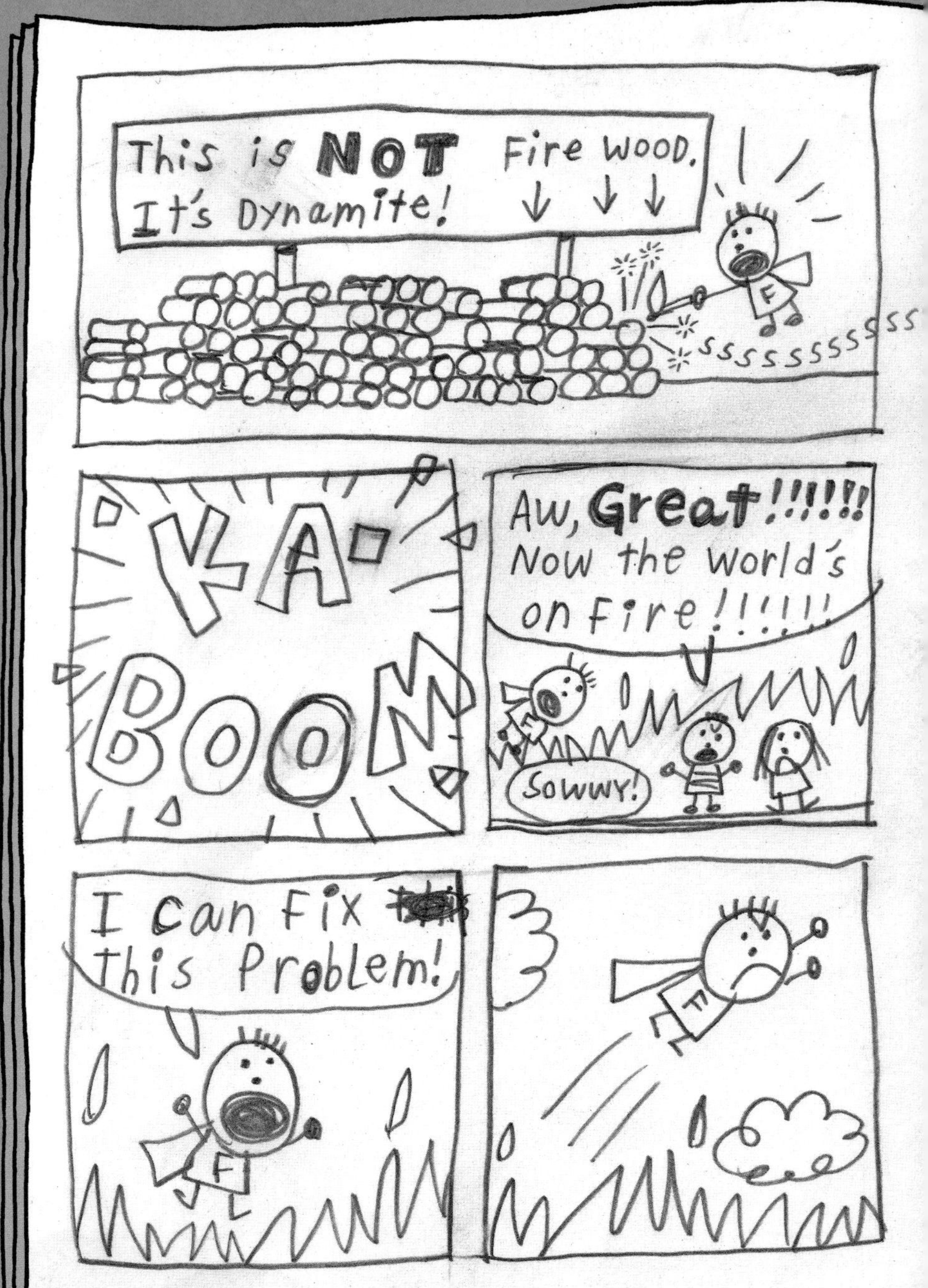

This is NOT Fire wood.
It's Dynamite!
sssssssssssss
KA-BOOM
Aw, Great!!!!!!
Now the world's on Fire!!!!!!
Sowwy!
I can Fix this Problem!

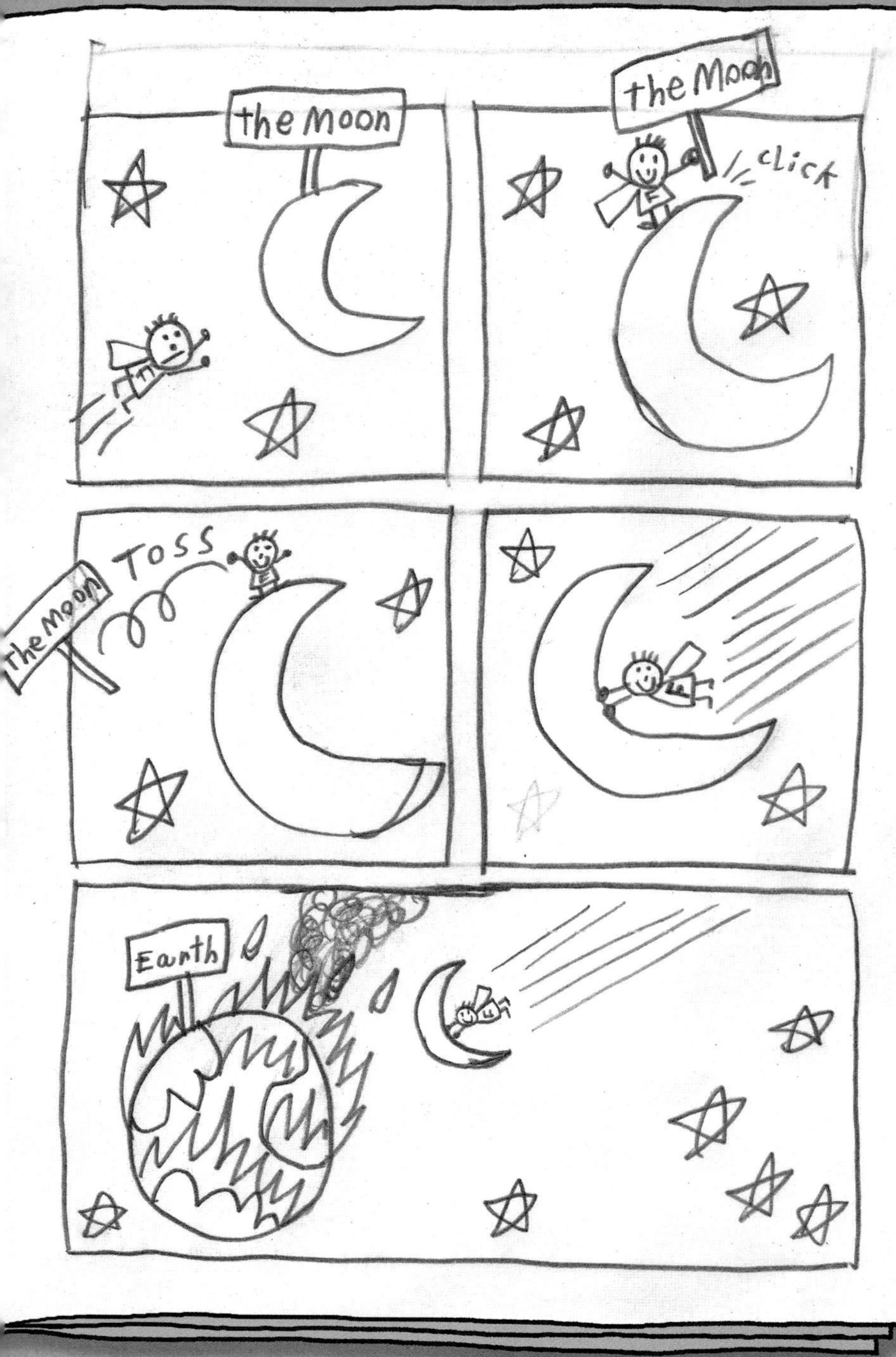
the Moon
the Moon
click
the Moon
TOSS
Earth

98

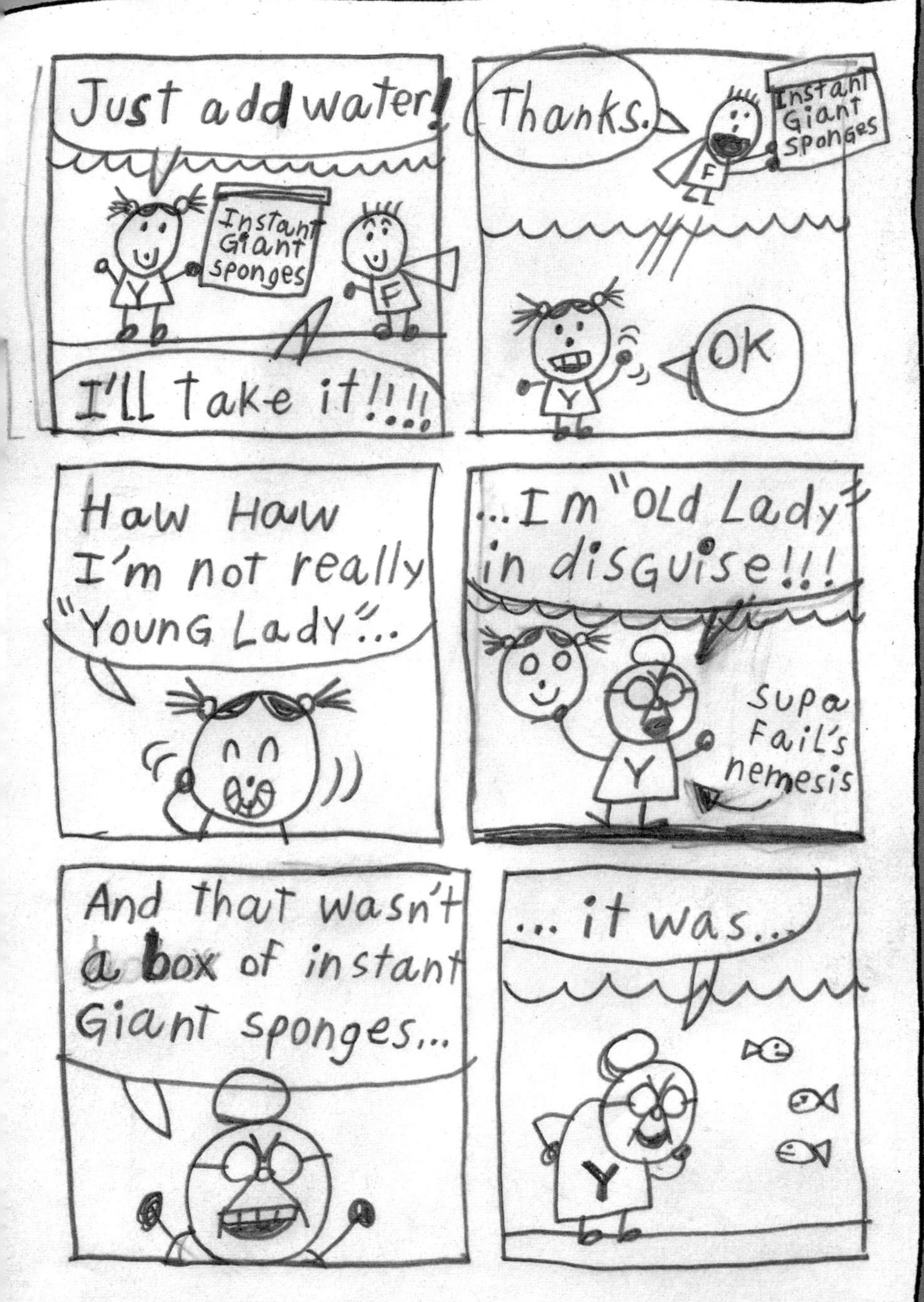

Just add water!
Instant Giant sponges
I'll take it!!!!
Thanks.
Instant Giant Sponges
OK
Haw Haw I'm not really "Young Lady"...
...I'm "Old Lady" in disguise!!!
Supa Fail's nemesis
And that wasn't a box of instant Giant sponges...
... it was...

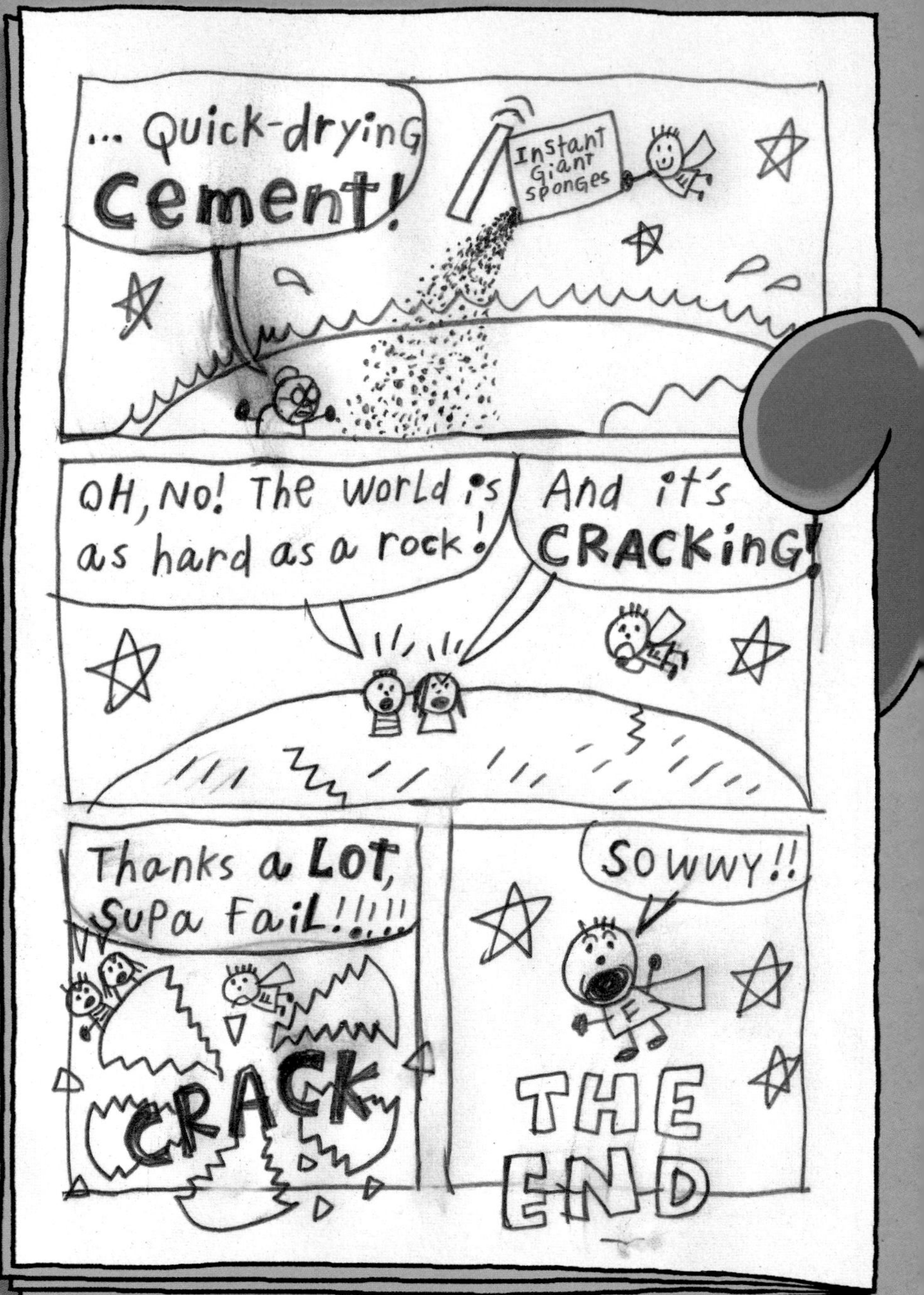
... Quick-drying
cement!
Instant Giant sponges
OH, No! The world is as hard as a rock!
And it's CRACKinG!
Thanks a LOT, SuPa FaiL!!!!!!
CRACK
SOWWY!!
THE END

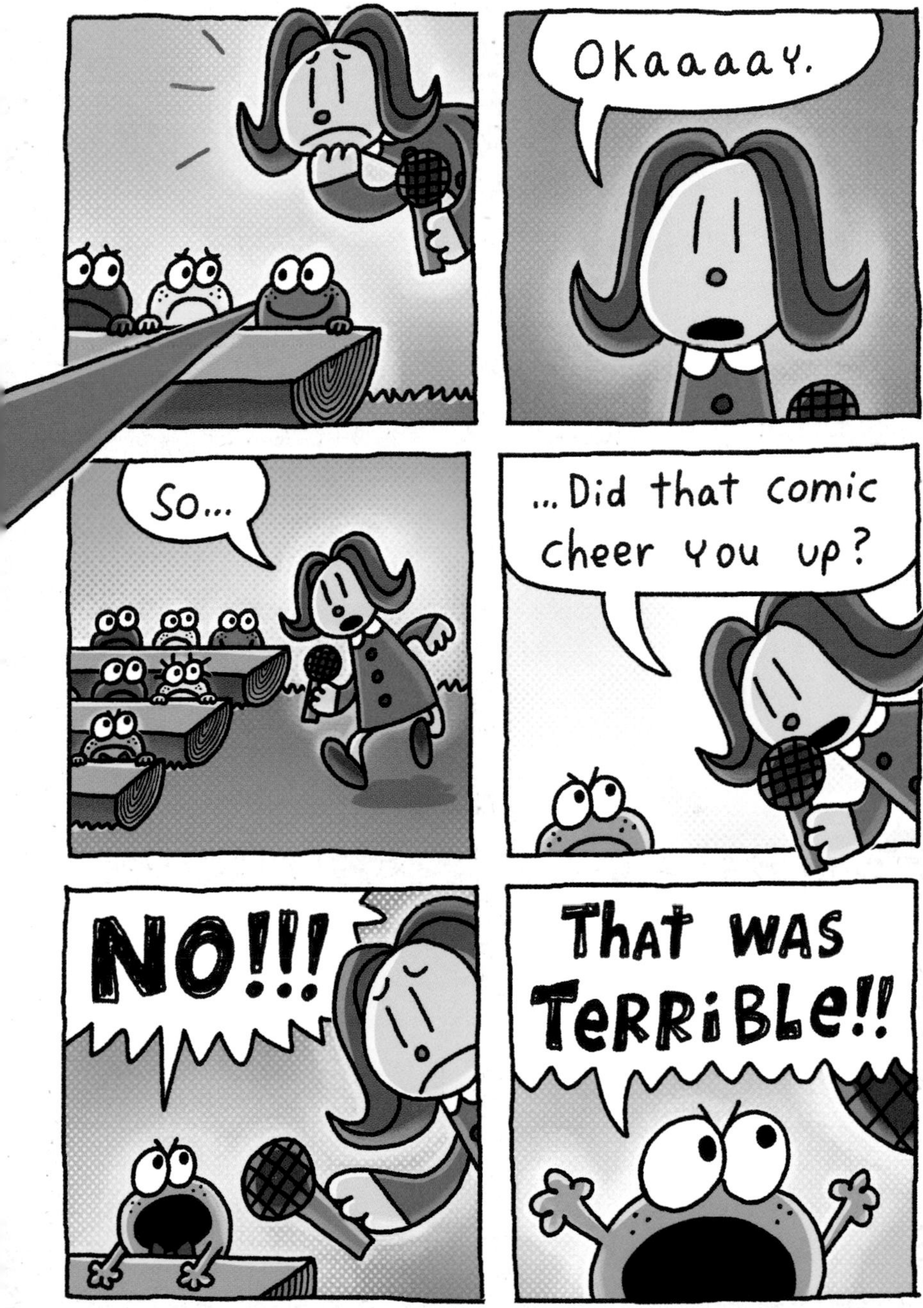
Okaaaay.
So...
...Did that comic cheer you up?
NO!!!
That WAS TeRRiBLe!!

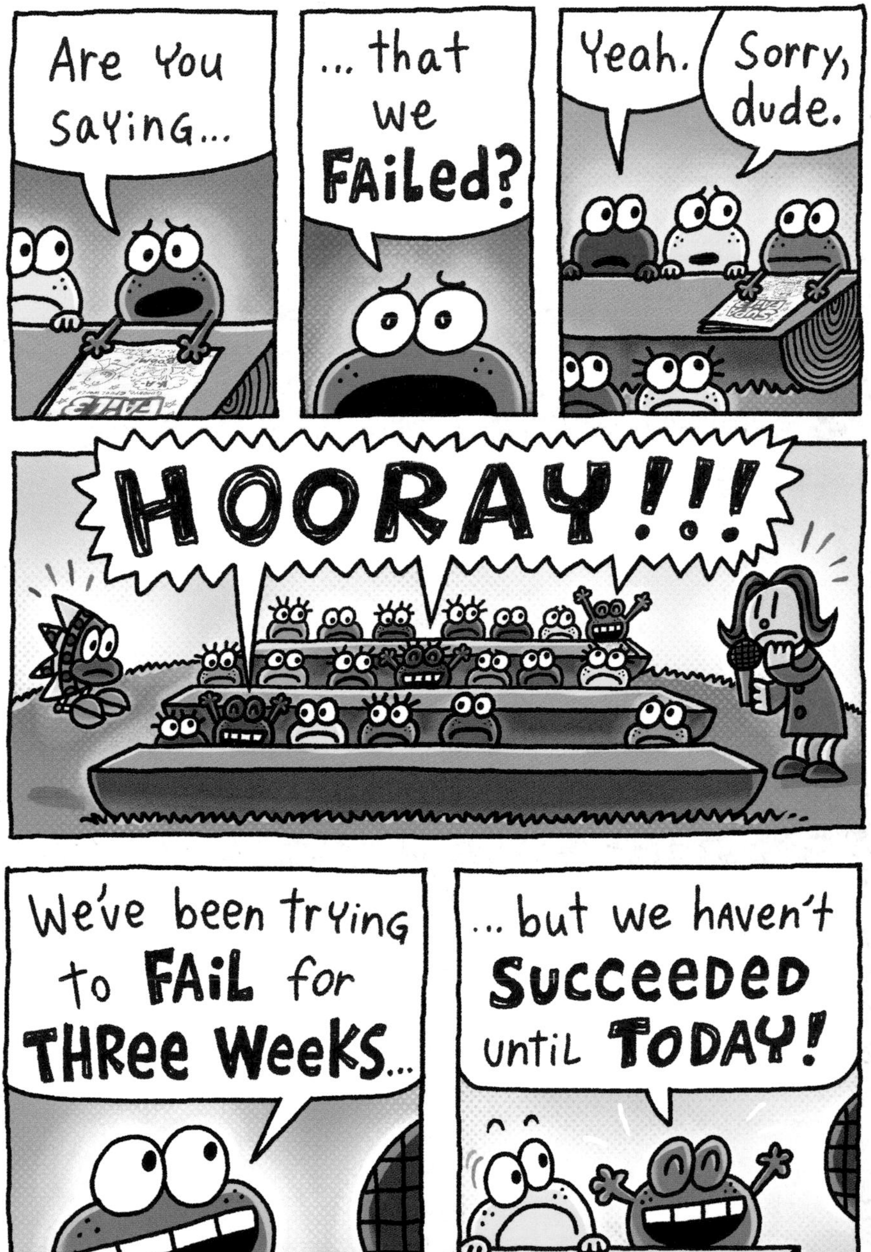

Are you saying...
... that we FAILED?
Yeah.
Sorry, dude.
HOORAY!!!
We've been trying to FAIL for THREE WEEKS...
... but we haven't SUCCEEDED until TODAY!

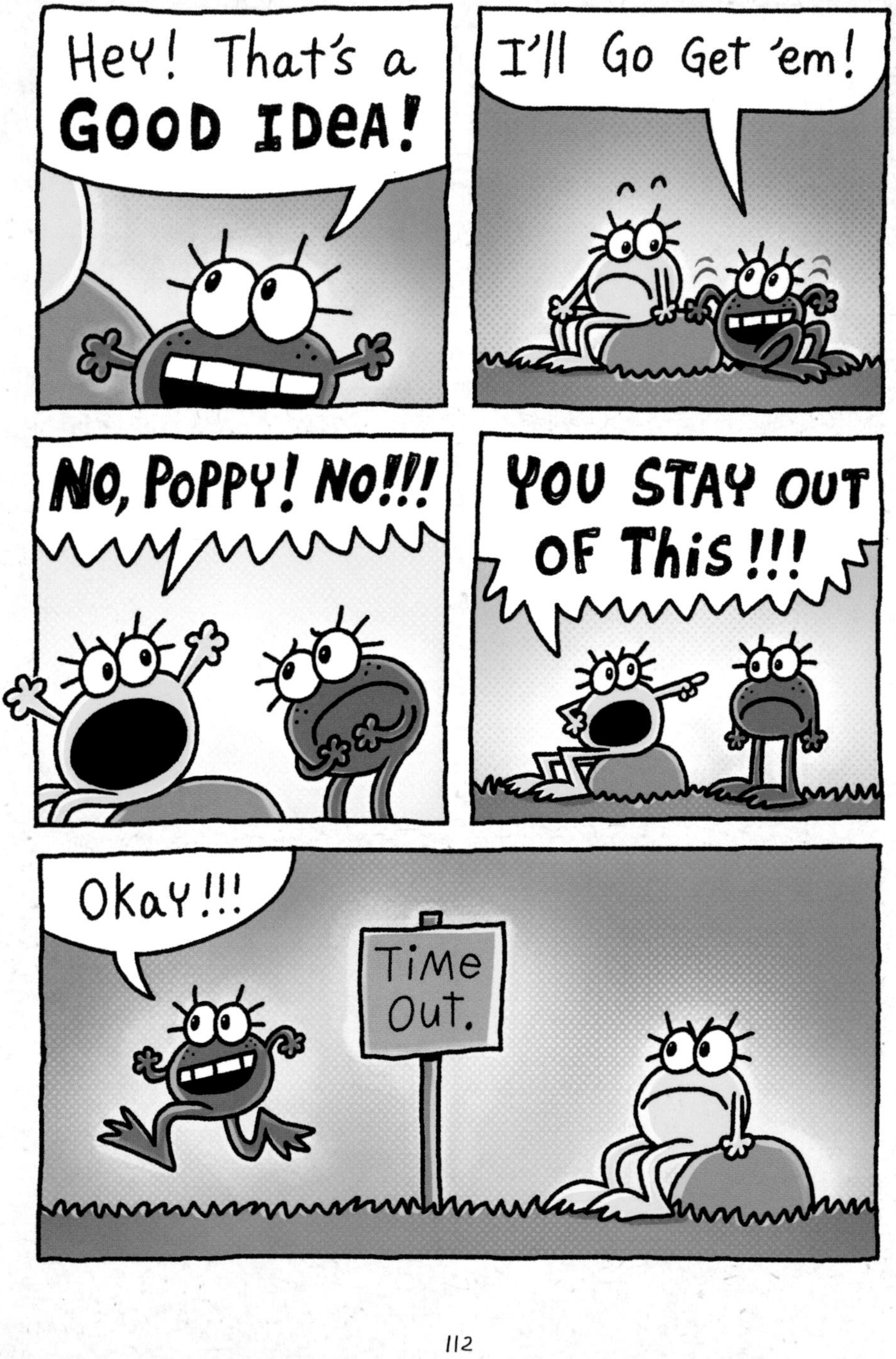
Hey! That's a GOOD IDEA!
I'll Go Get 'em!
NO, POPPY! NO!!!
YOU STAY OUT OF This!!!
Okay!!!
Time Out.

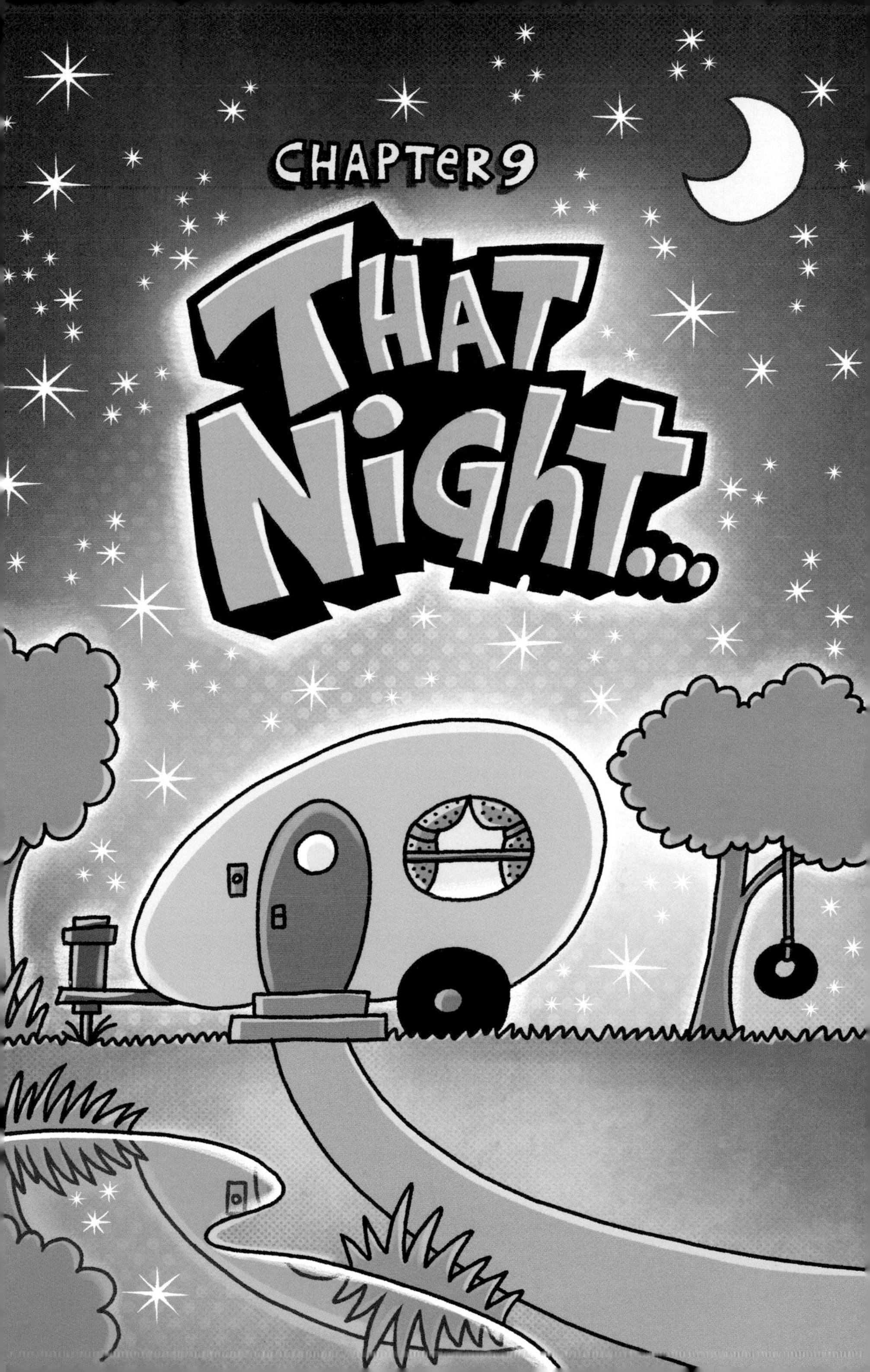
CHAPTER 9
THAT NIGHT...

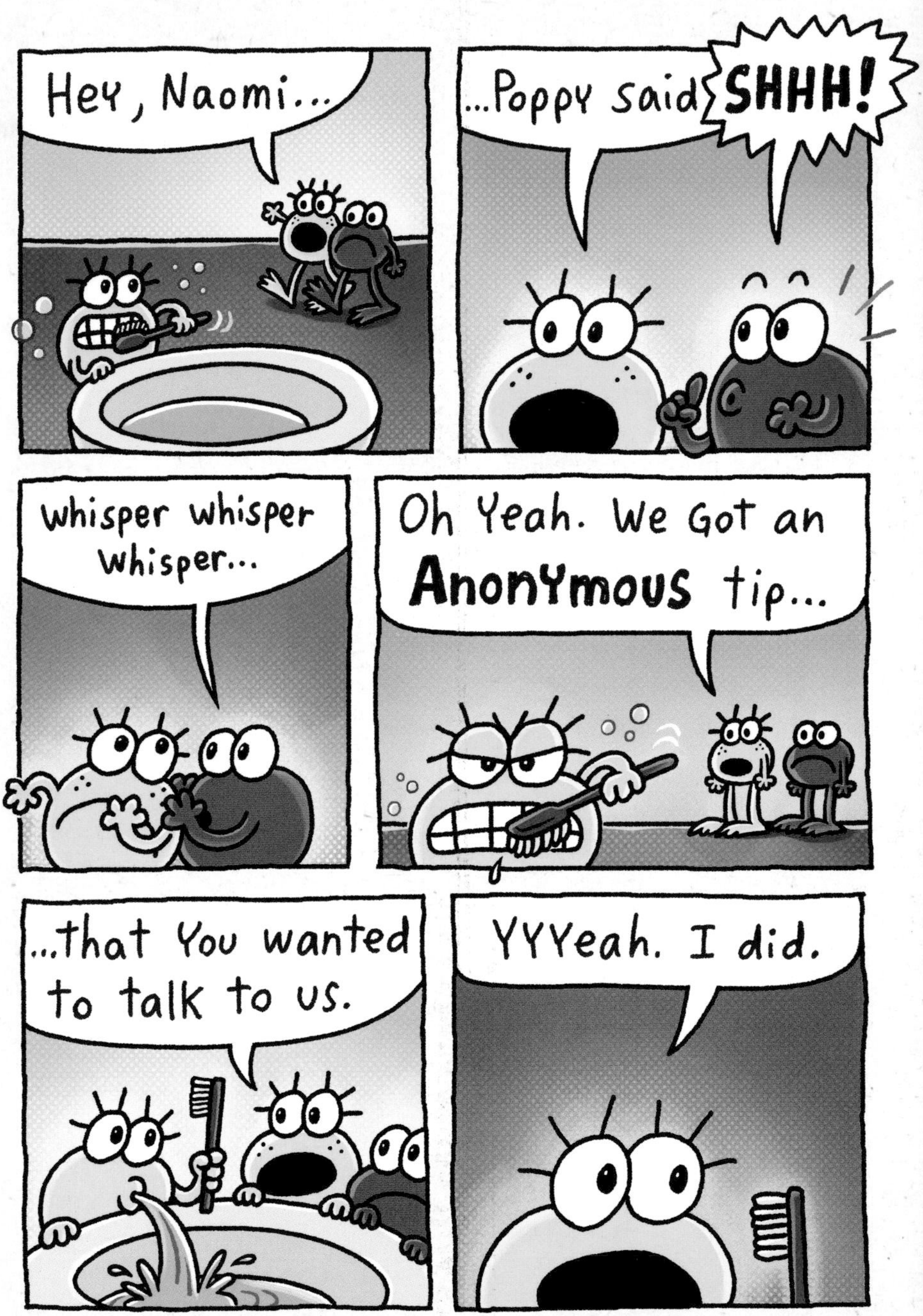
Hey, Naomi...
...Poppy said
SHHH!
whisper whisper whisper...
Oh Yeah. We Got an ANONYMOUS tip...
...that You wanted to talk to us.
YYYeah. I did.

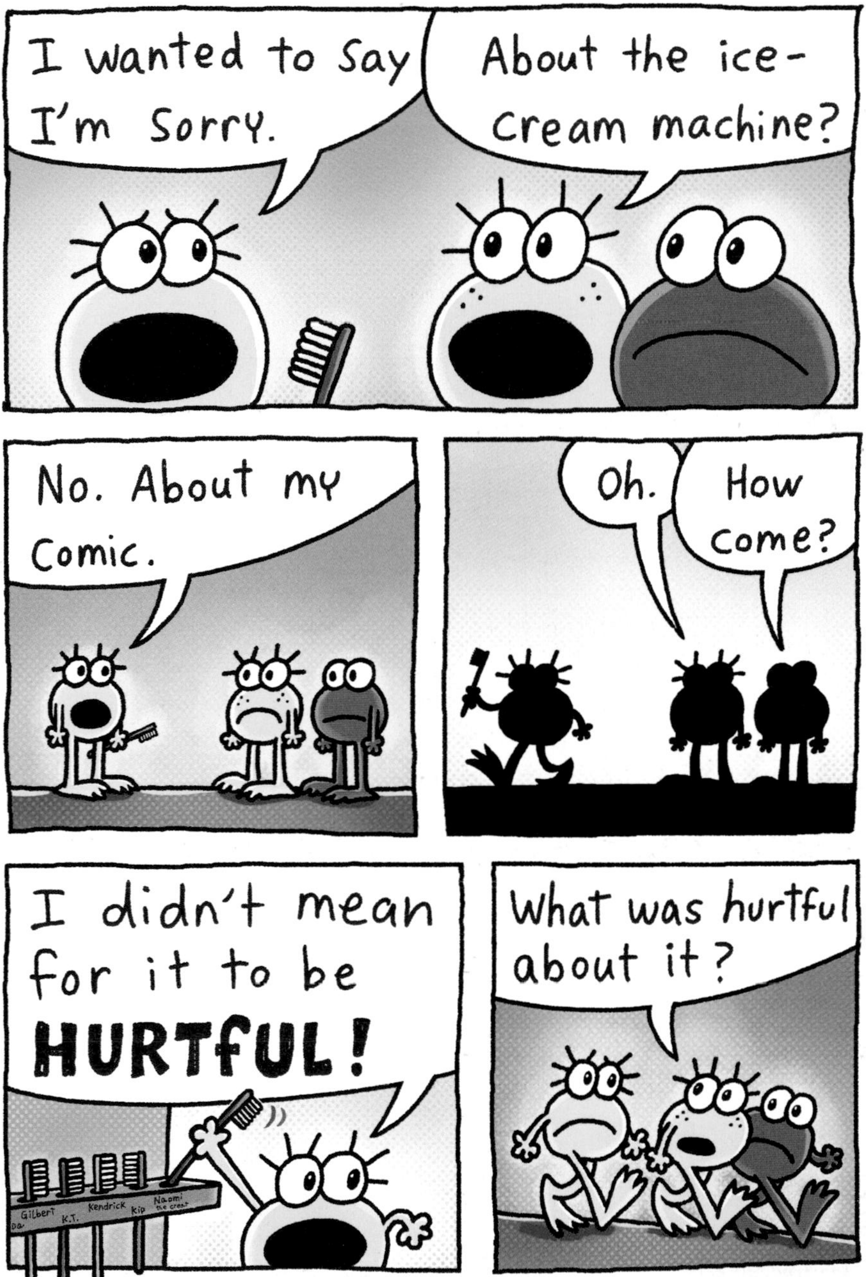
I wanted to say I'm sorry.
About the ice-cream machine?
No. About my comic.
Oh.
How come?
I didn't mean for it to be **HURTFUL!**
Da
Gilbert
K.T.
Kendrick
Kip
Naomi the great
What was hurtful about it?

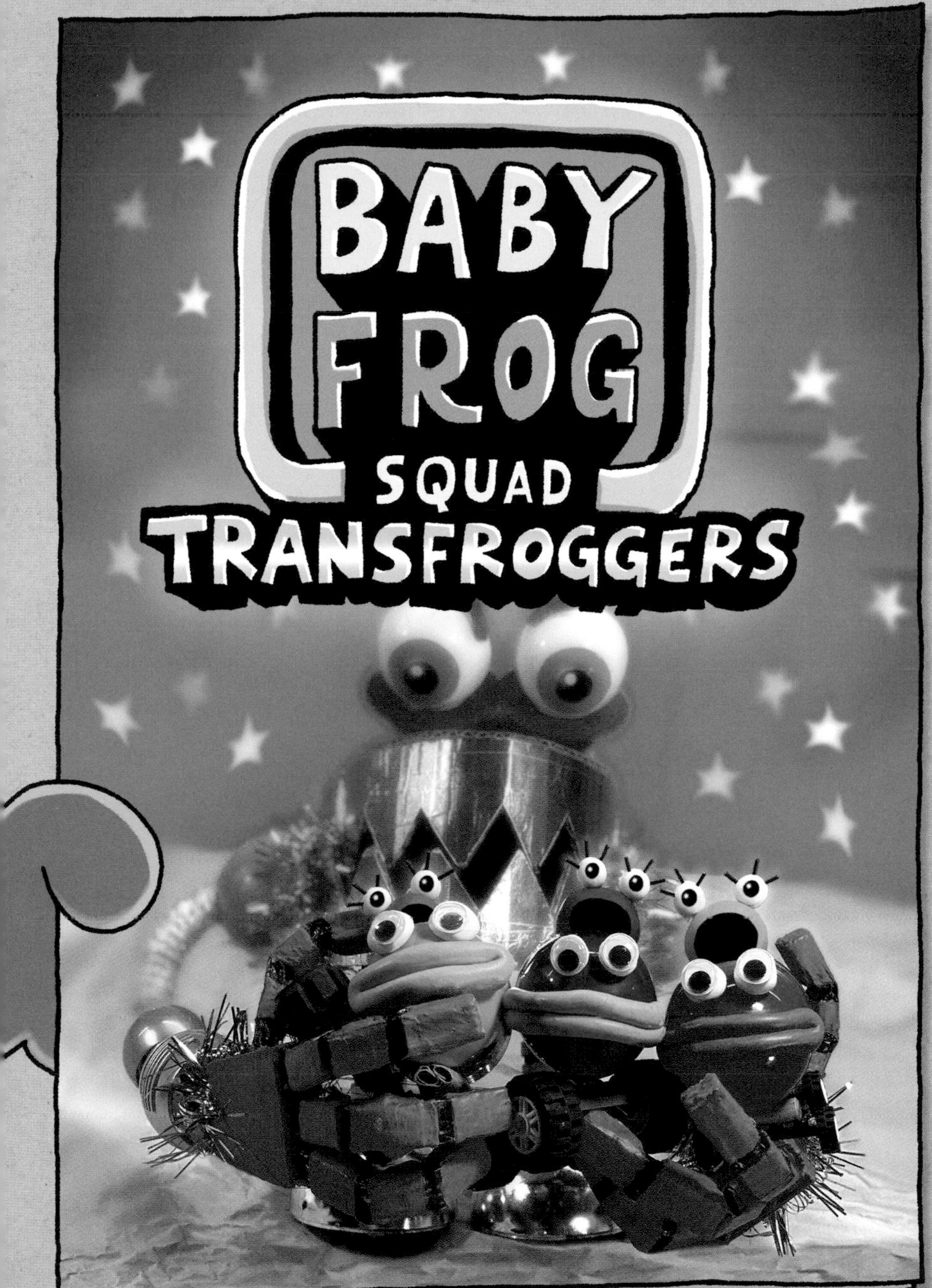
BABY FROG
SQUAD
TRANSFROGGERS

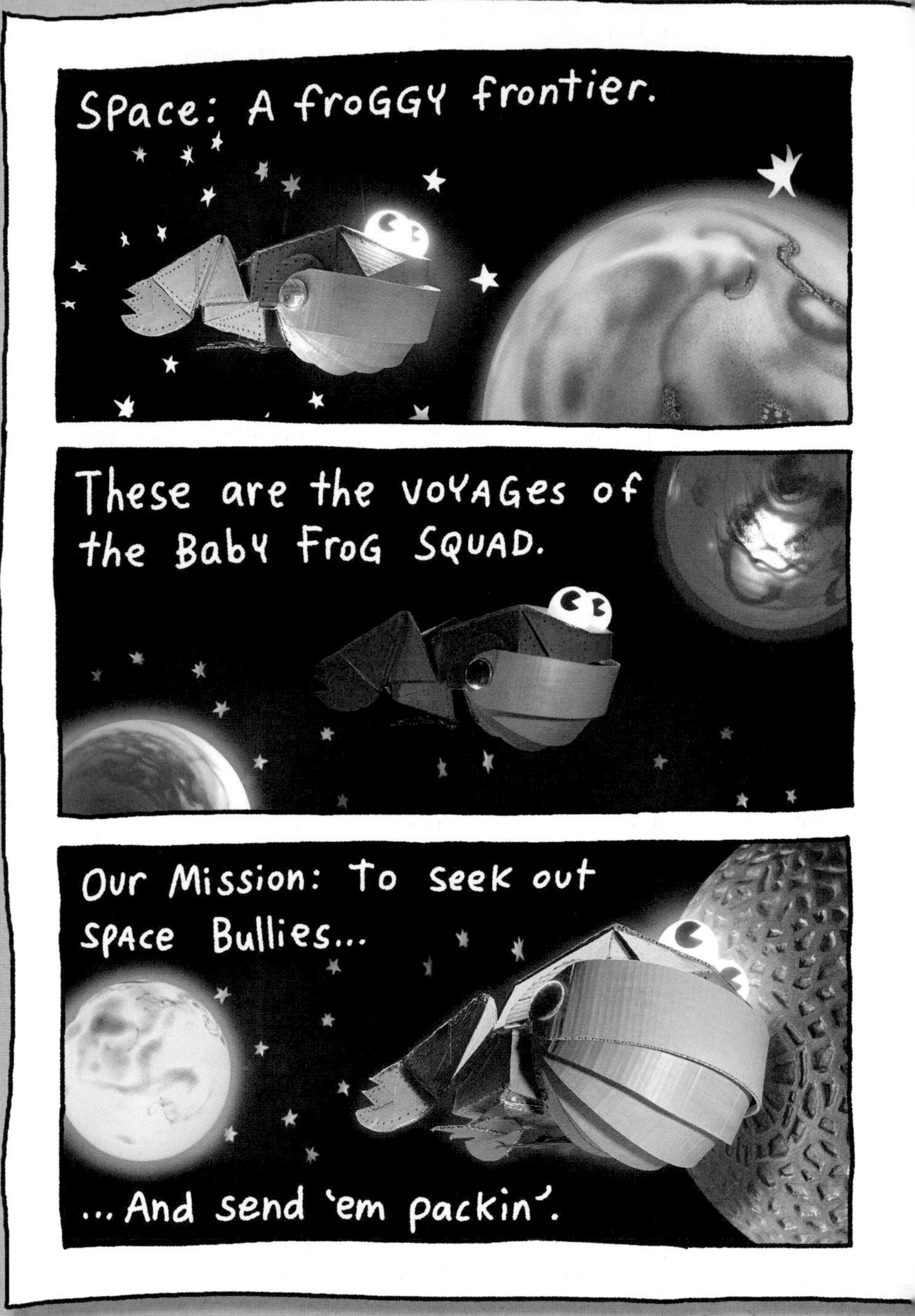
Space: A froggy frontier.
These are the voyages of the Baby Frog Squad.
Our Mission: To seek out space Bullies...
...And send 'em packin'.

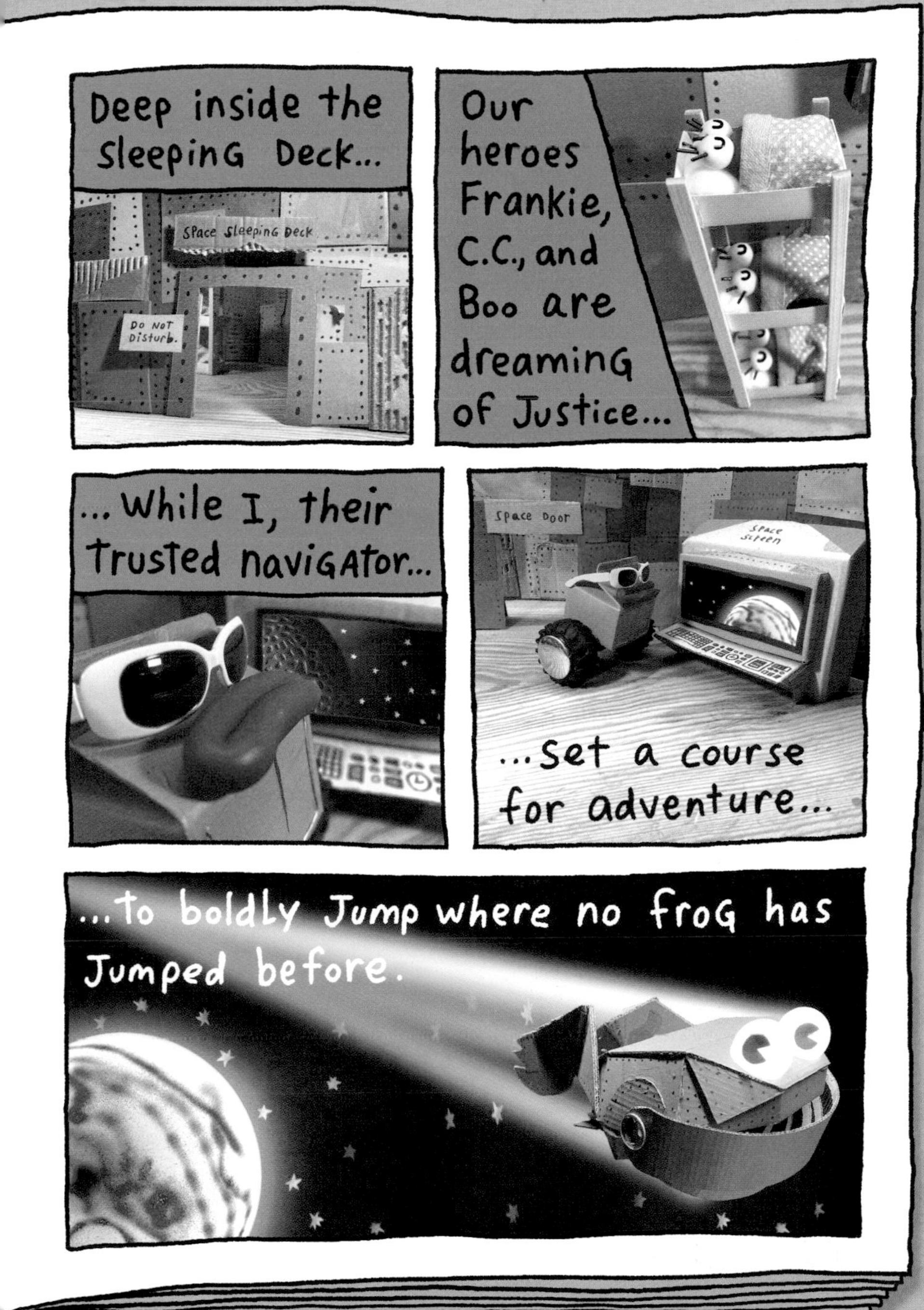
Deep inside the Sleeping Deck...
Space Sleeping Deck
Do Not Disturb.
Our heroes Frankie, C.C., and Boo are dreaming of Justice...
...While I, their trusted navigator...
Space Door
Space Screen
...set a course for adventure...
...to boldly jump where no frog has jumped before.

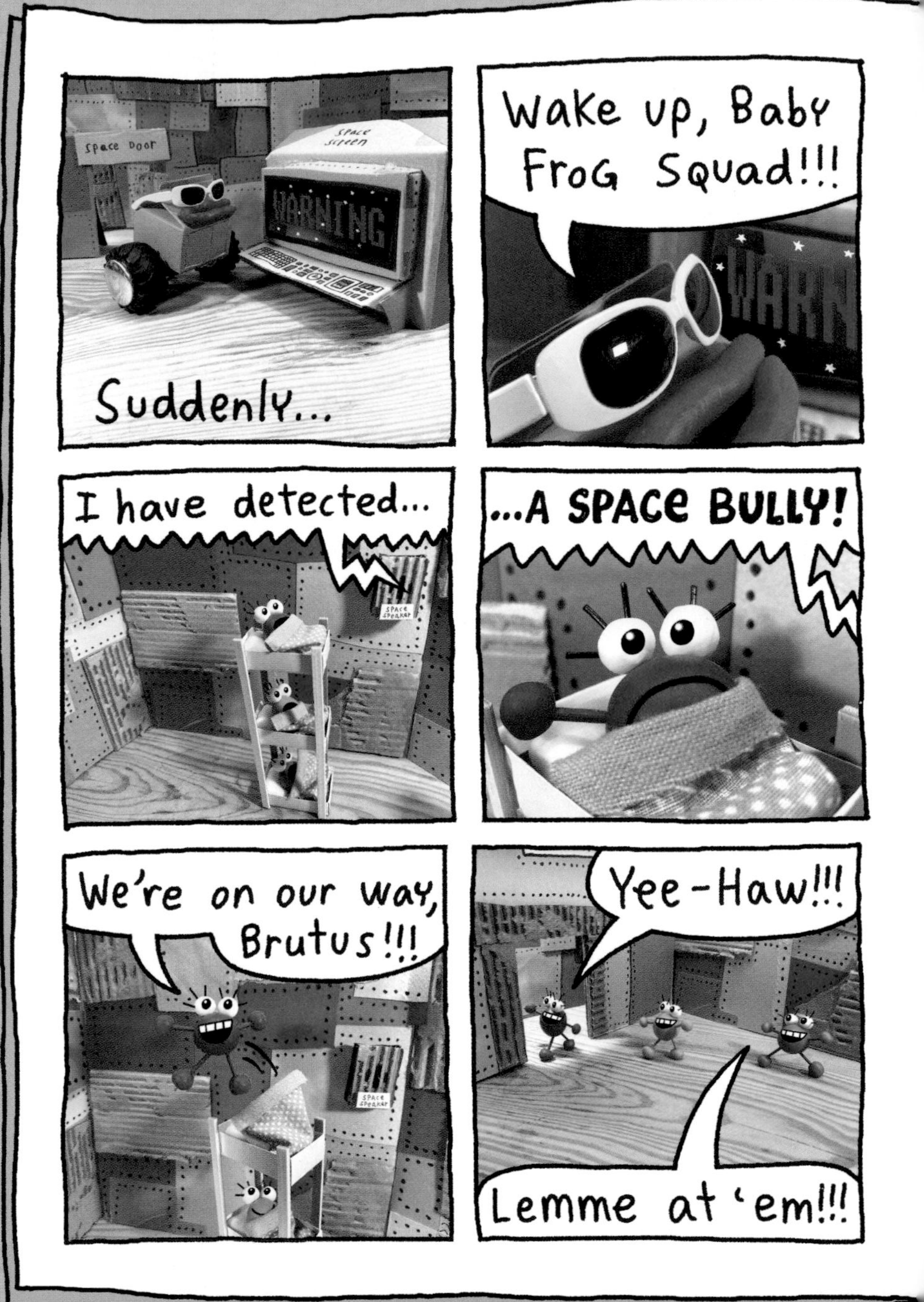

Space Door
Space Screen
WARNING
Suddenly...
Wake up, Baby Frog Squad!!!
I have detected...
SPACE SPEAKER
...A SPACE BULLY!
We're on our way, Brutus!!!
SPACE SPEAKER
Yee-Haw!!!
Lemme at 'em!!!

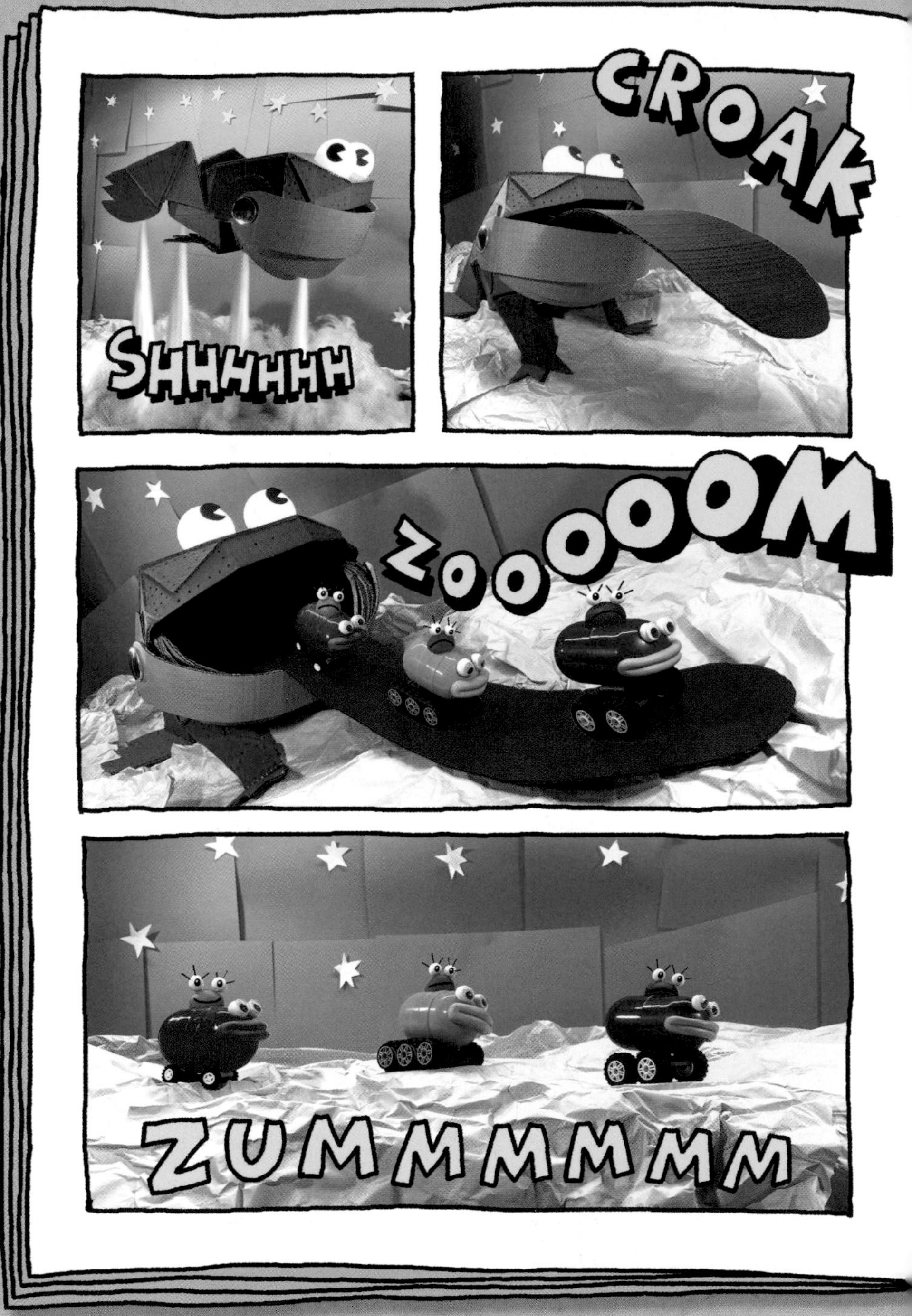
SHHHHHH
CROAK
ZOOOOOOM
ZUMMMMMM

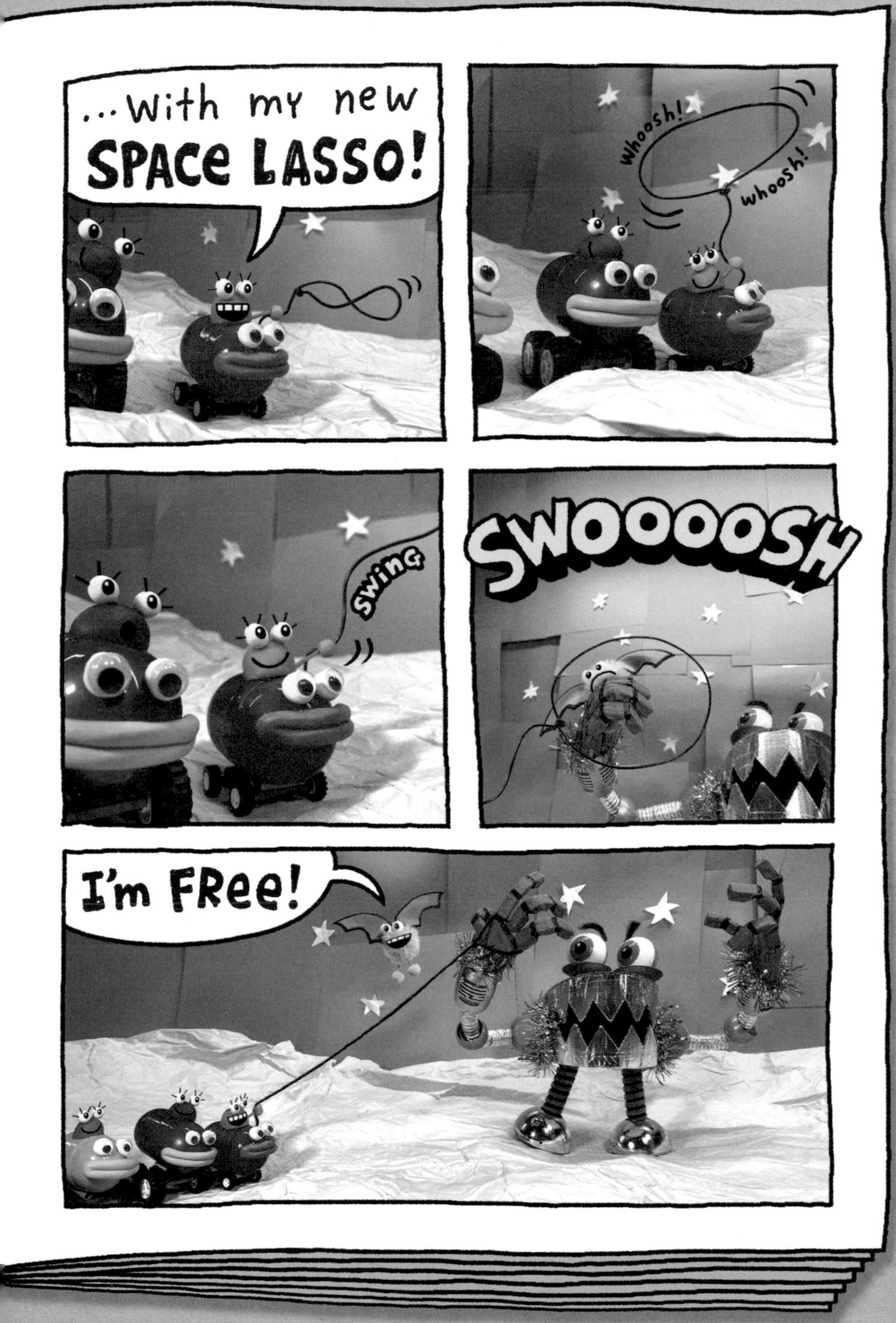
...With my new SPACE LASSO!
Whoosh!
Whoosh!
SWING
SWOOOOSH
I'm FRee!

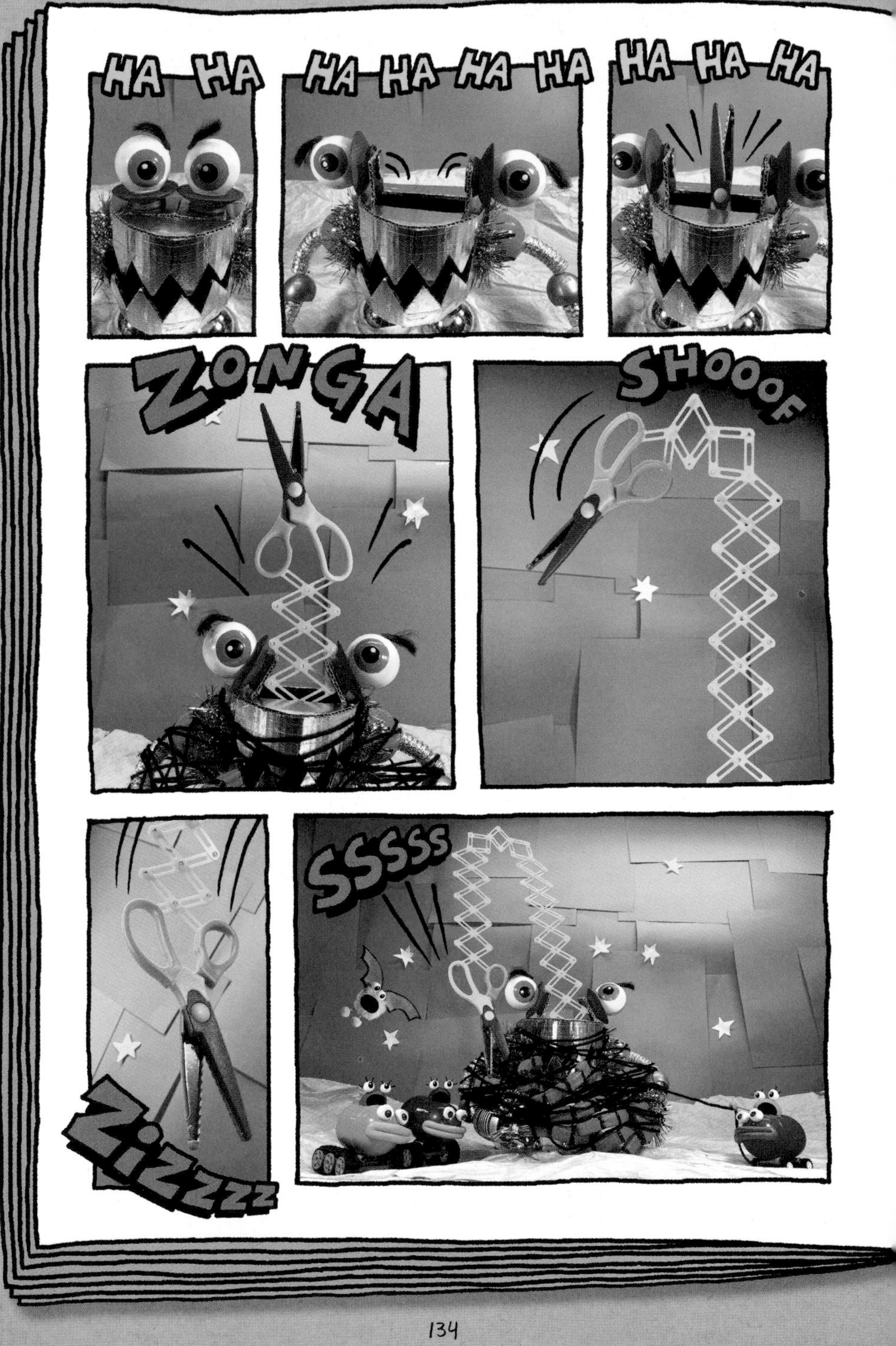
HA HA
HA HA HA HA
HA HA HA
ZONGA
SHOOOF
ZiZZZZ
SSSSS

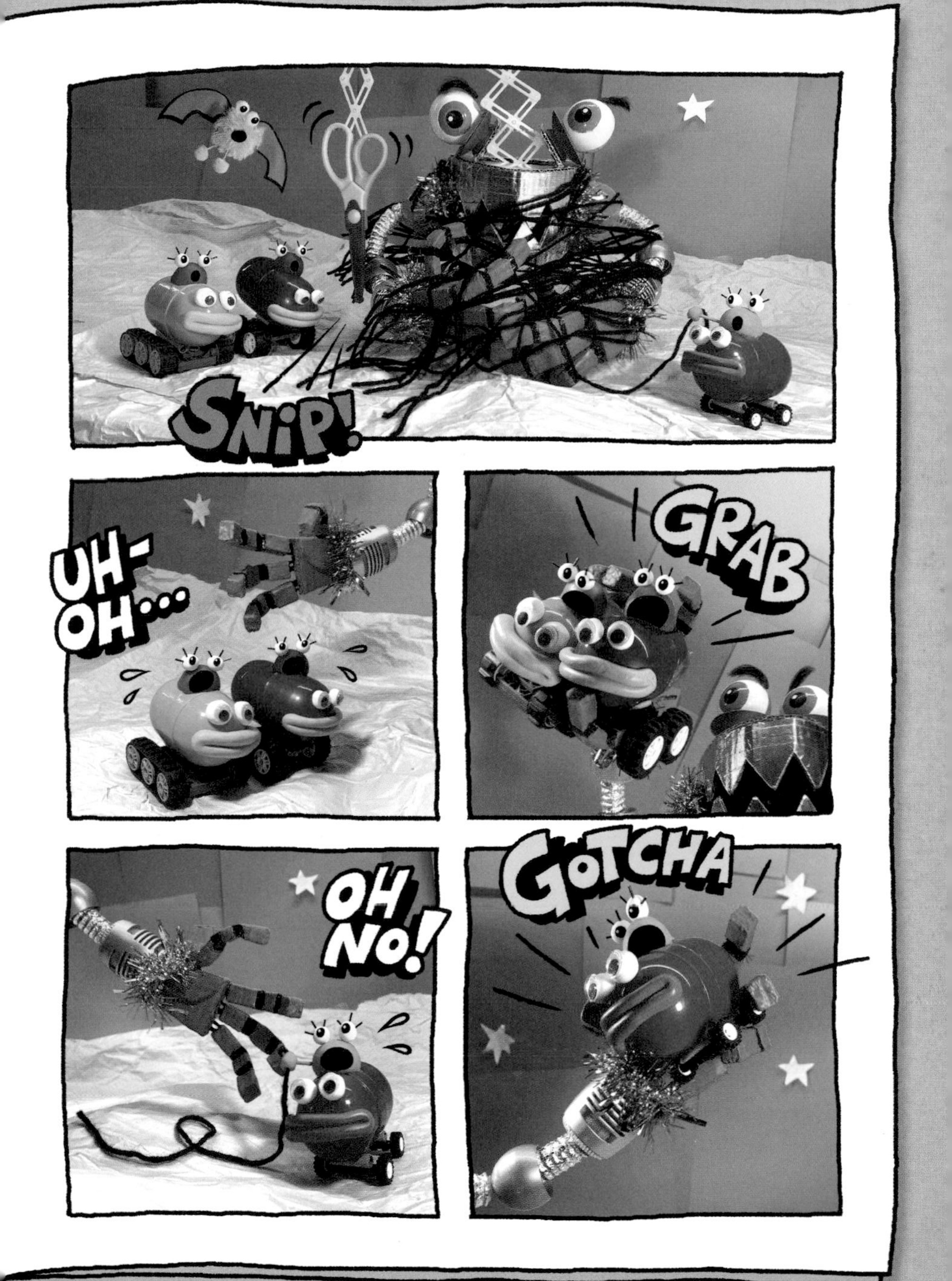
SNIP!
UH-OH...
GRAB
OH NO!
GOTCHA

140

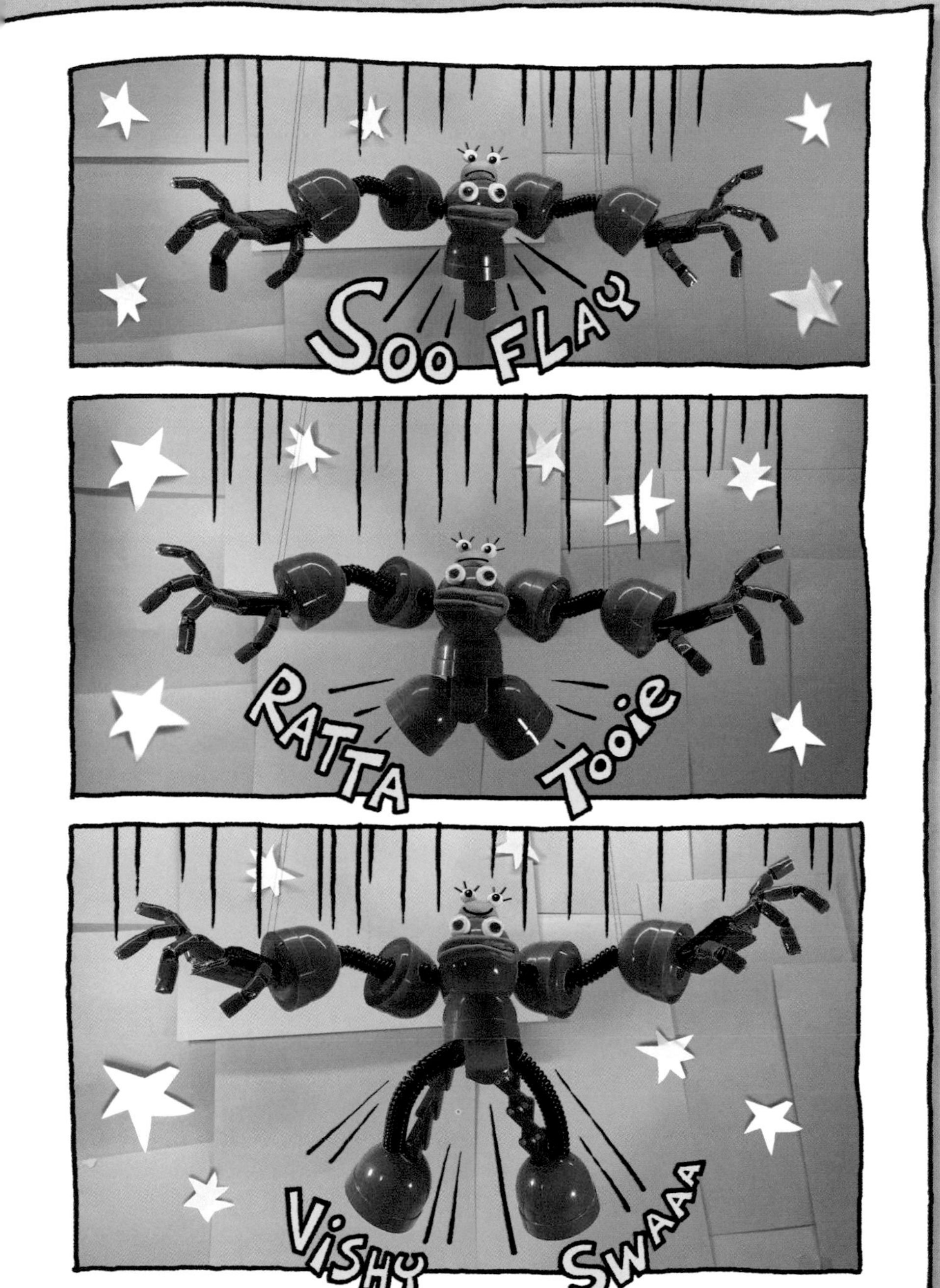
SOO FLAY
RATTA TOOIE
VISHY SWAAA

142

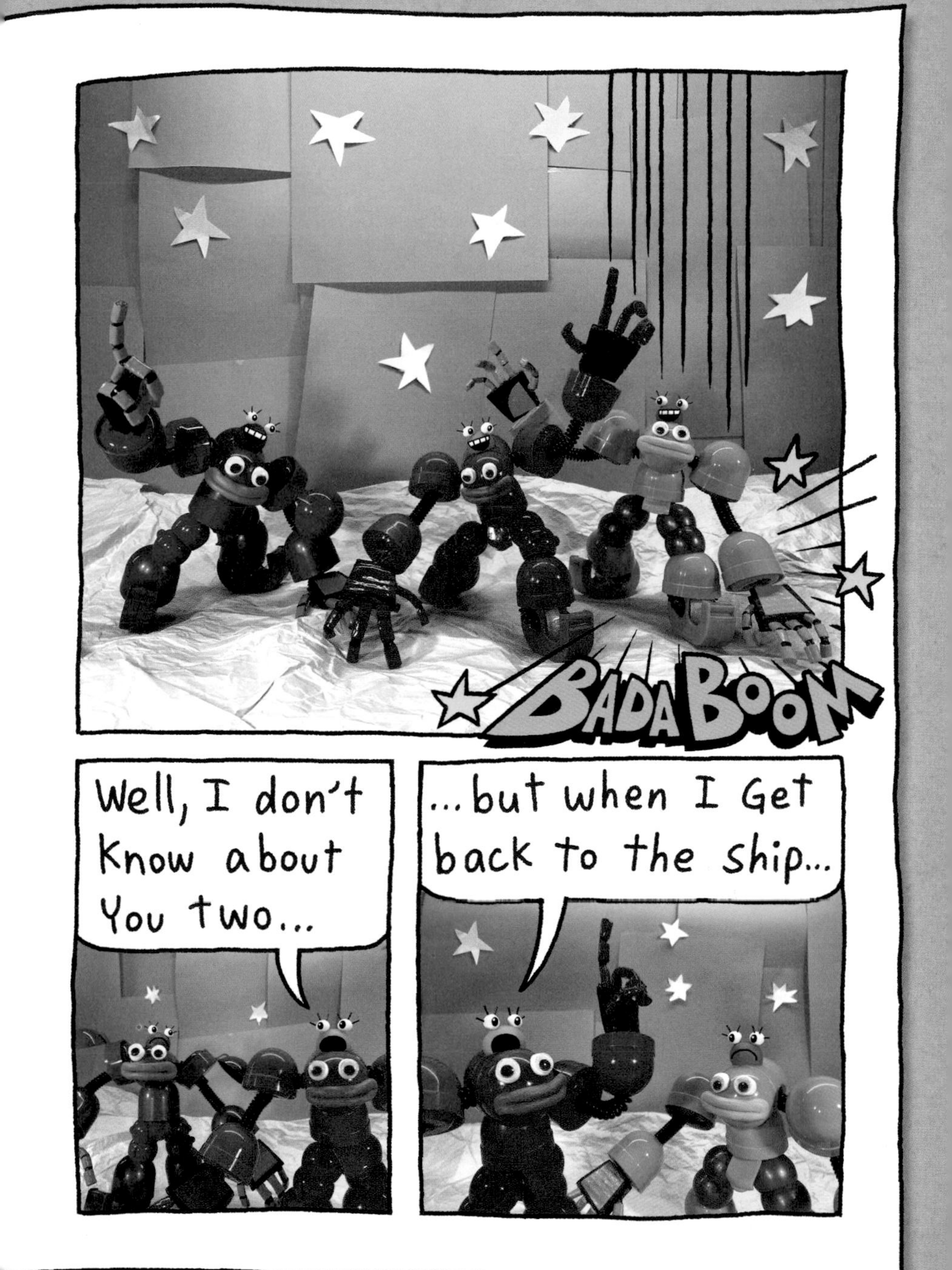
BADABOOM
Well, I don't Know about You two...
...but when I Get back to the ship...

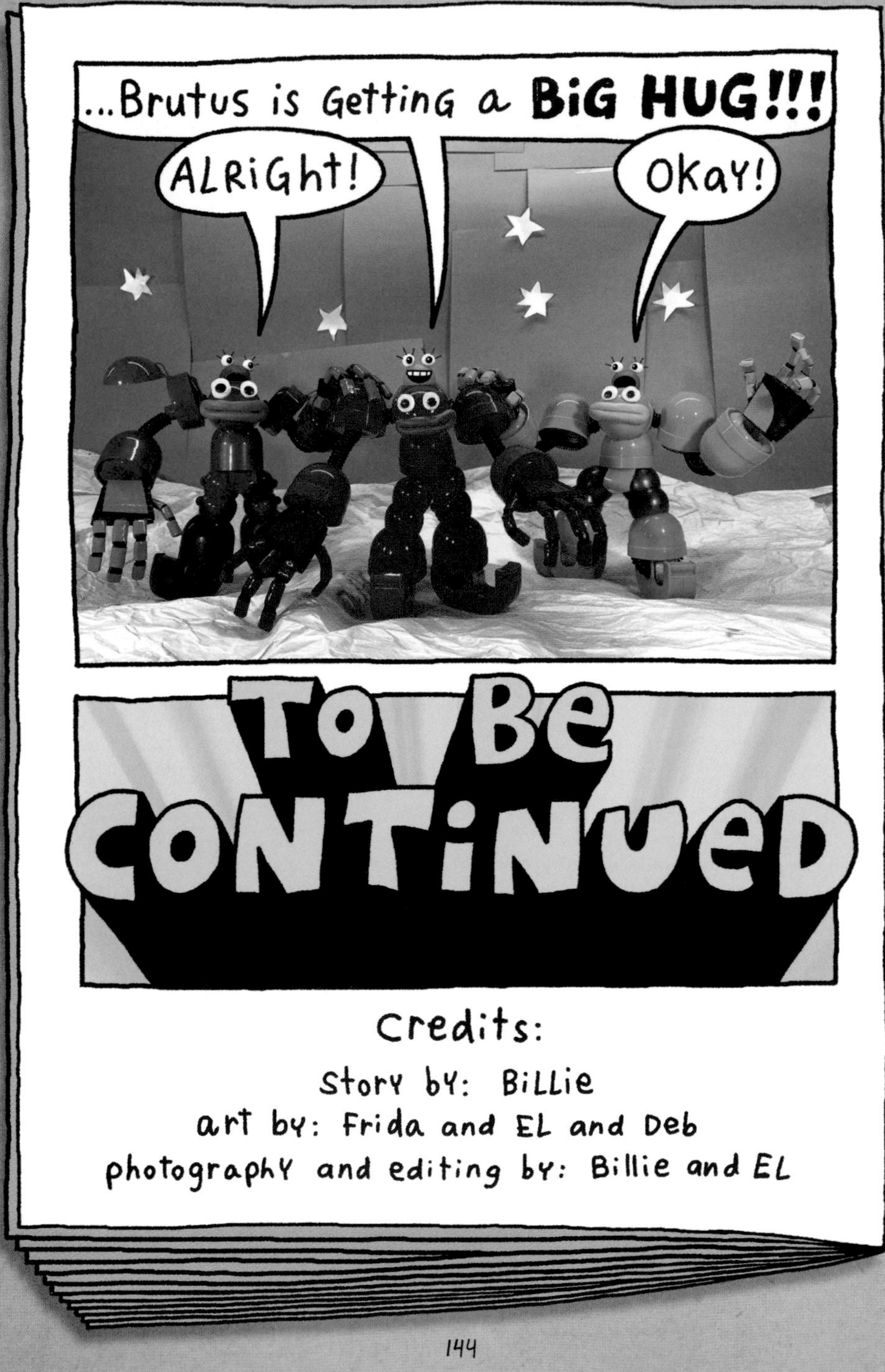
...Brutus is Getting a **BiG HUG!!!**
ALRiGht!
OKaY!
To Be Continued
credits:
Story by: BiLLie
art by: Frida and EL and Deb
photography and editing by: Billie and EL

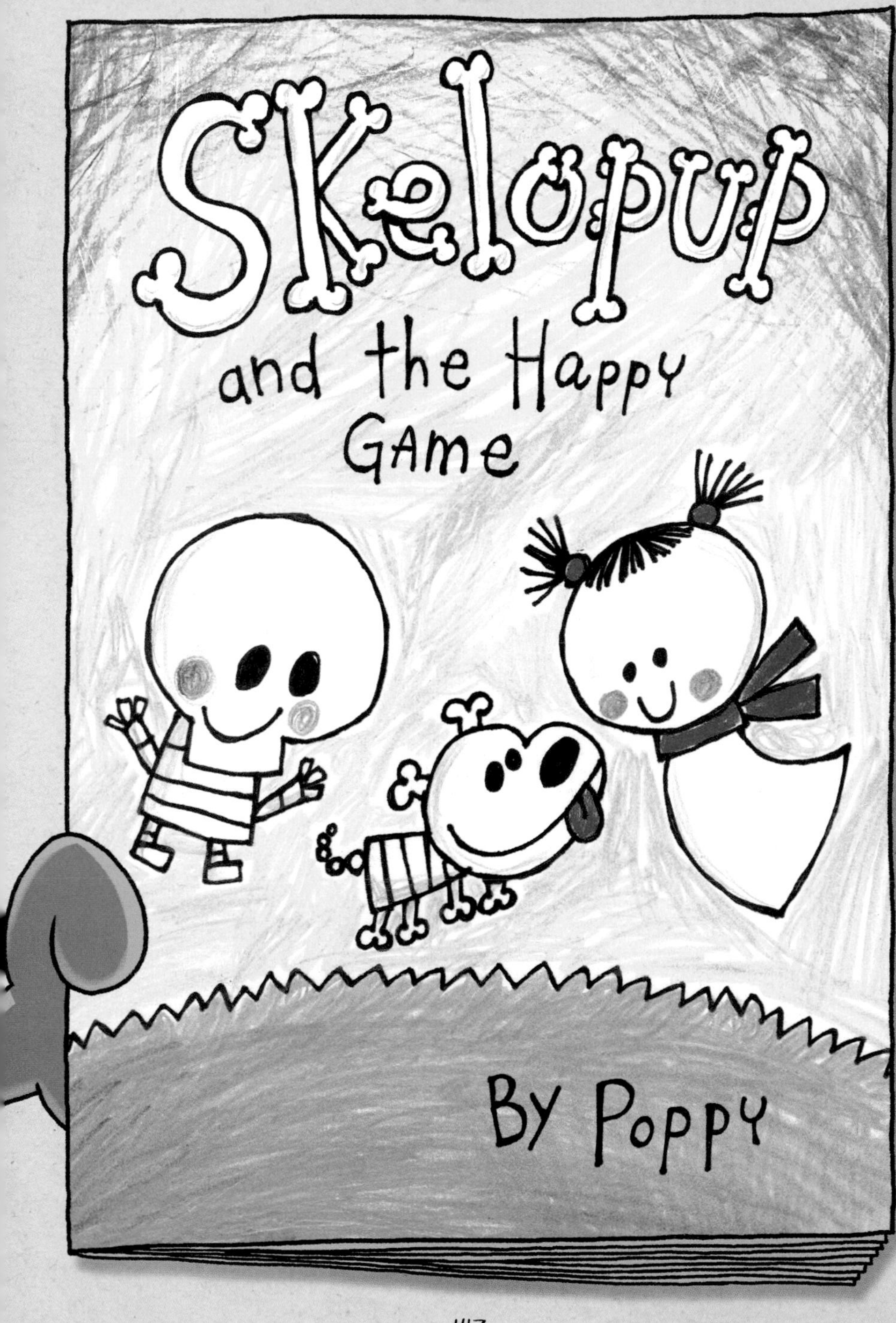
Skelopup
and the Happy Game
By Poppy

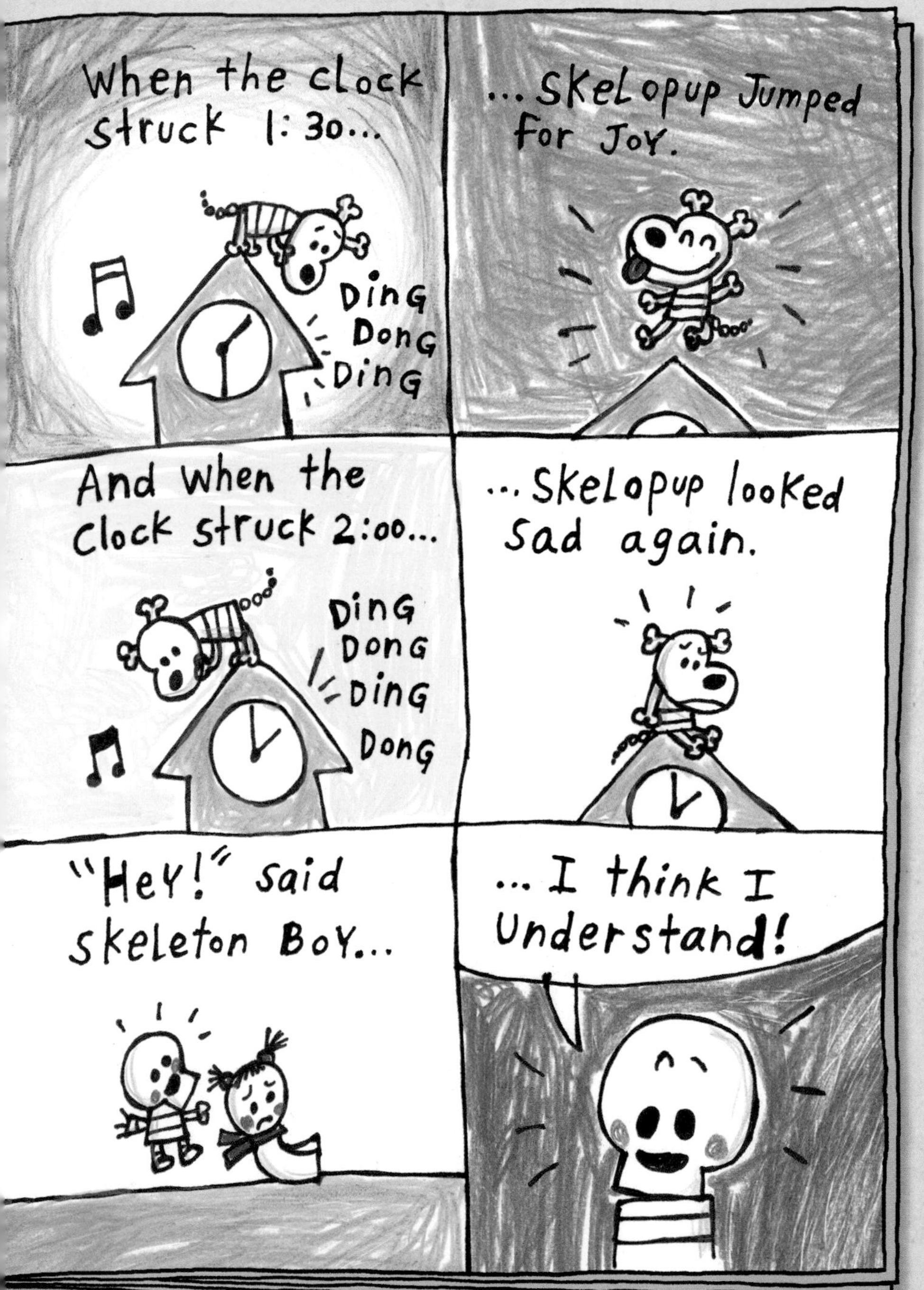
When the clock struck 1:30...
DING
DONG
DING
...SKeLopup Jumped for Joy.
And when the clock struck 2:00...
DING
DONG
DING
DONG
...SKeLopup looked sad again.
"Hey!" said skeleton Boy...
...I think I Understand!

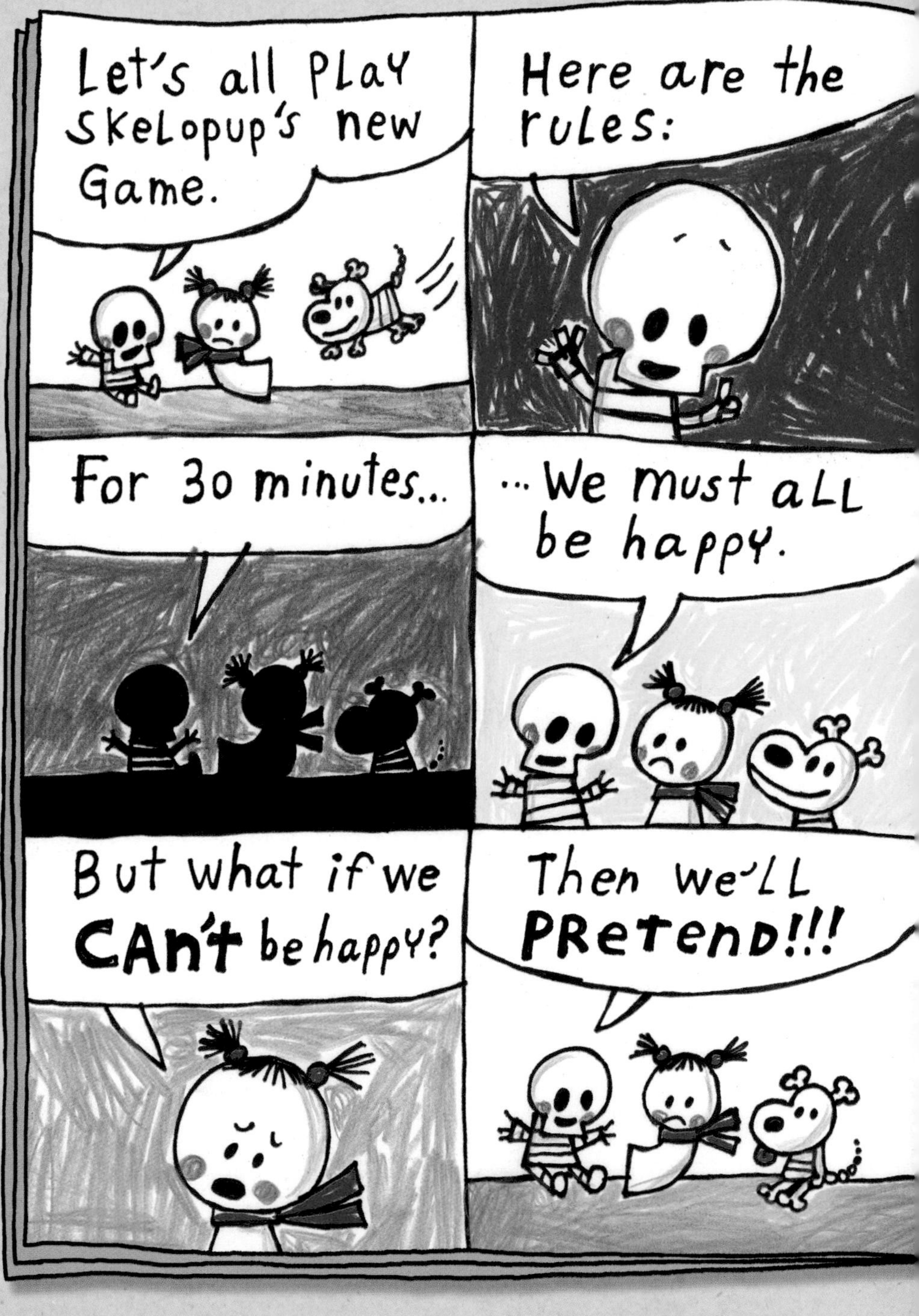
Let's all play Skelopup's new Game.
Here are the rules:
For 30 minutes...
...We must all be happy.
But what if we CAN'T be happy?
Then we'll PRETEND!!!

153

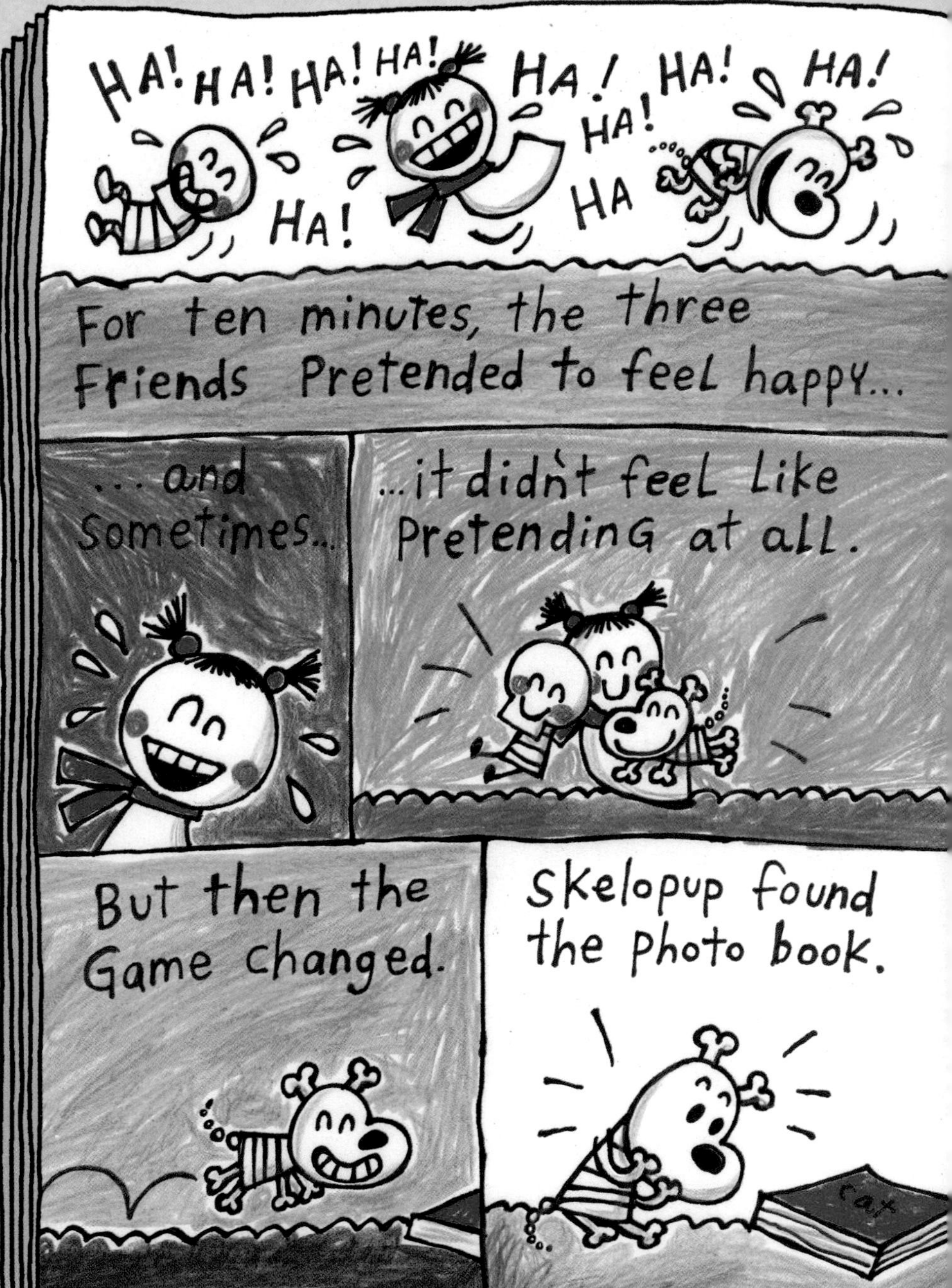
HA! HA! HA! HA!
HA!
HA! HA! HA!
HA!
HA
For ten minutes, the three friends pretended to feel happy...
... and sometimes...
...it didn't feel like pretending at all.
But then the game changed.
Skelopup found the photo book.
cat

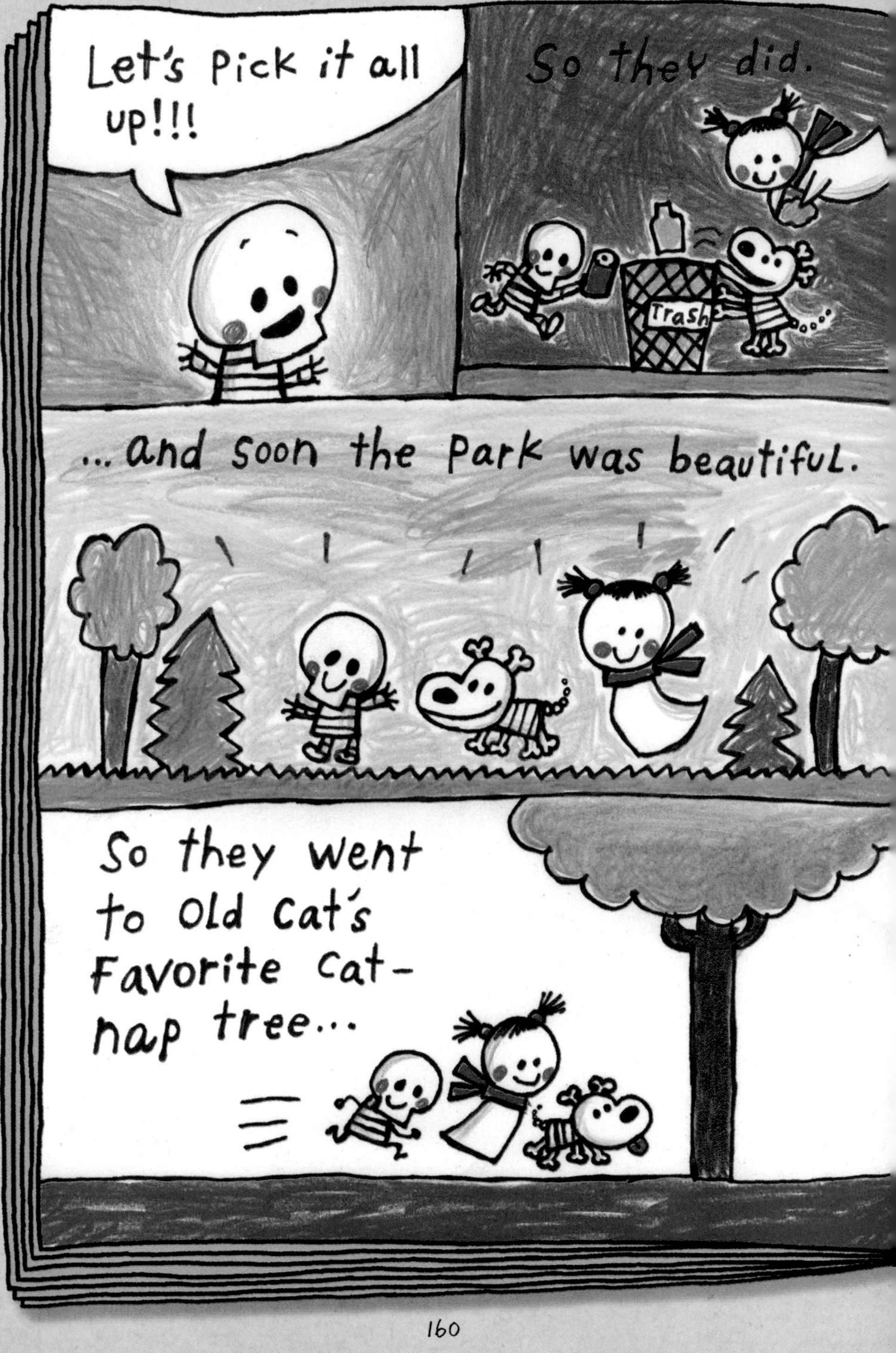
Let's pick it all up!!!
So they did.
Trash
...and soon the park was beautiful.
So they went to Old Cat's favorite cat-nap tree...

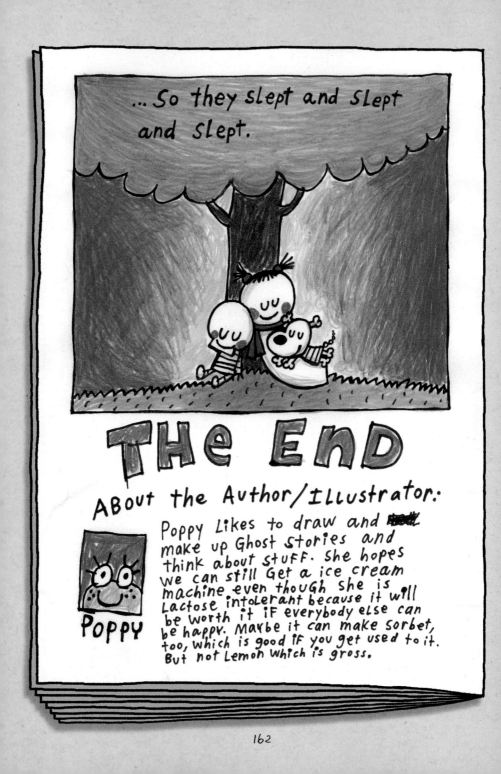

...So they slept and slept and slept.

THE END

About the Author/Illustrator:

Poppy likes to draw and ~~tell~~ make up ghost stories and think about stuff. She hopes we can still get a ice cream machine even though she is lactose intolerant because it will be worth it if everybody else can be happy. Maybe it can make sorbet, too, which is good if you get used to it. But not lemon which is gross.

POPPY

CHAPTER 11

Melvin's Awesome Idea

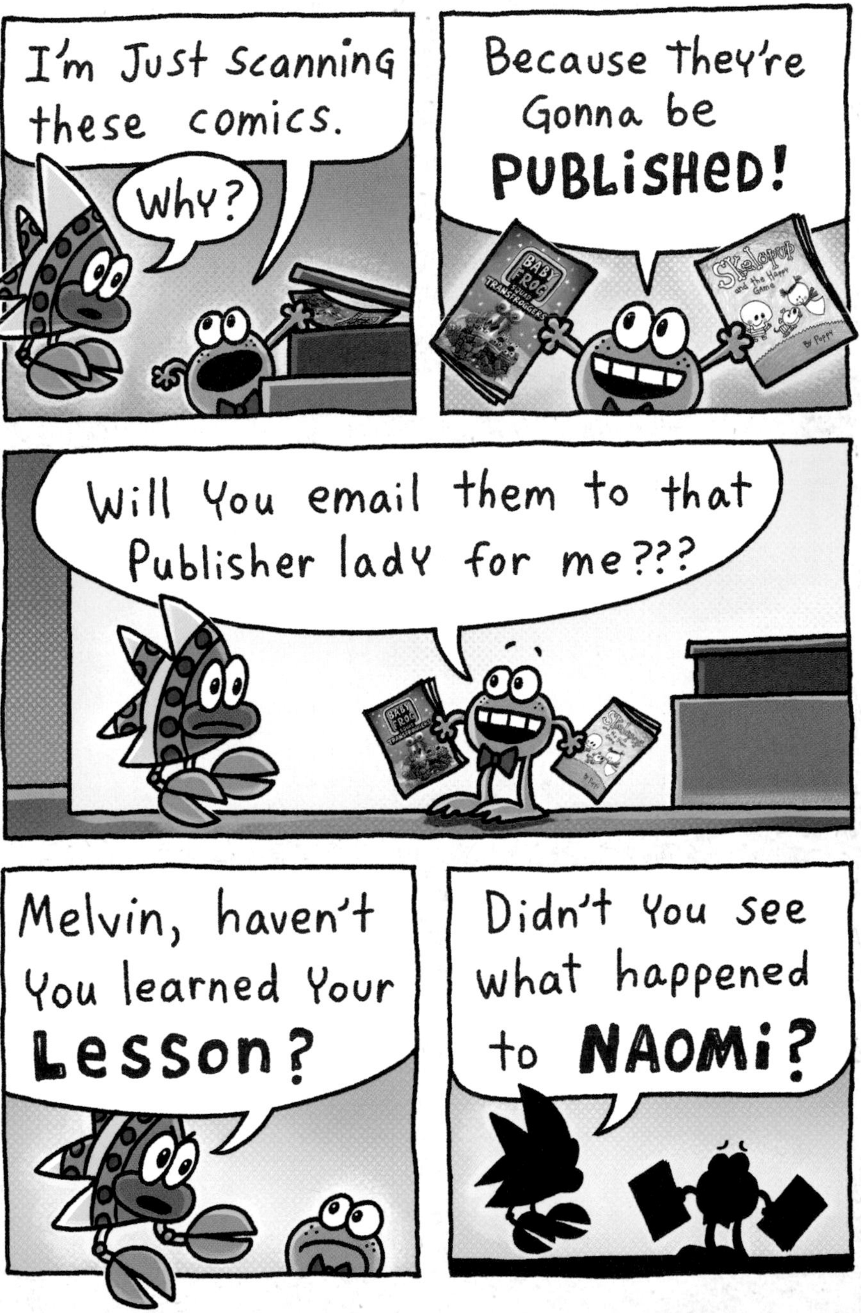
I'm Just Scanning these comics.
Why?
Because they're Gonna be PUBLISHED!
Will You email them to that Publisher lady for me???
Melvin, haven't You learned Your Lesson?
Didn't You see what happened to NAOMI?

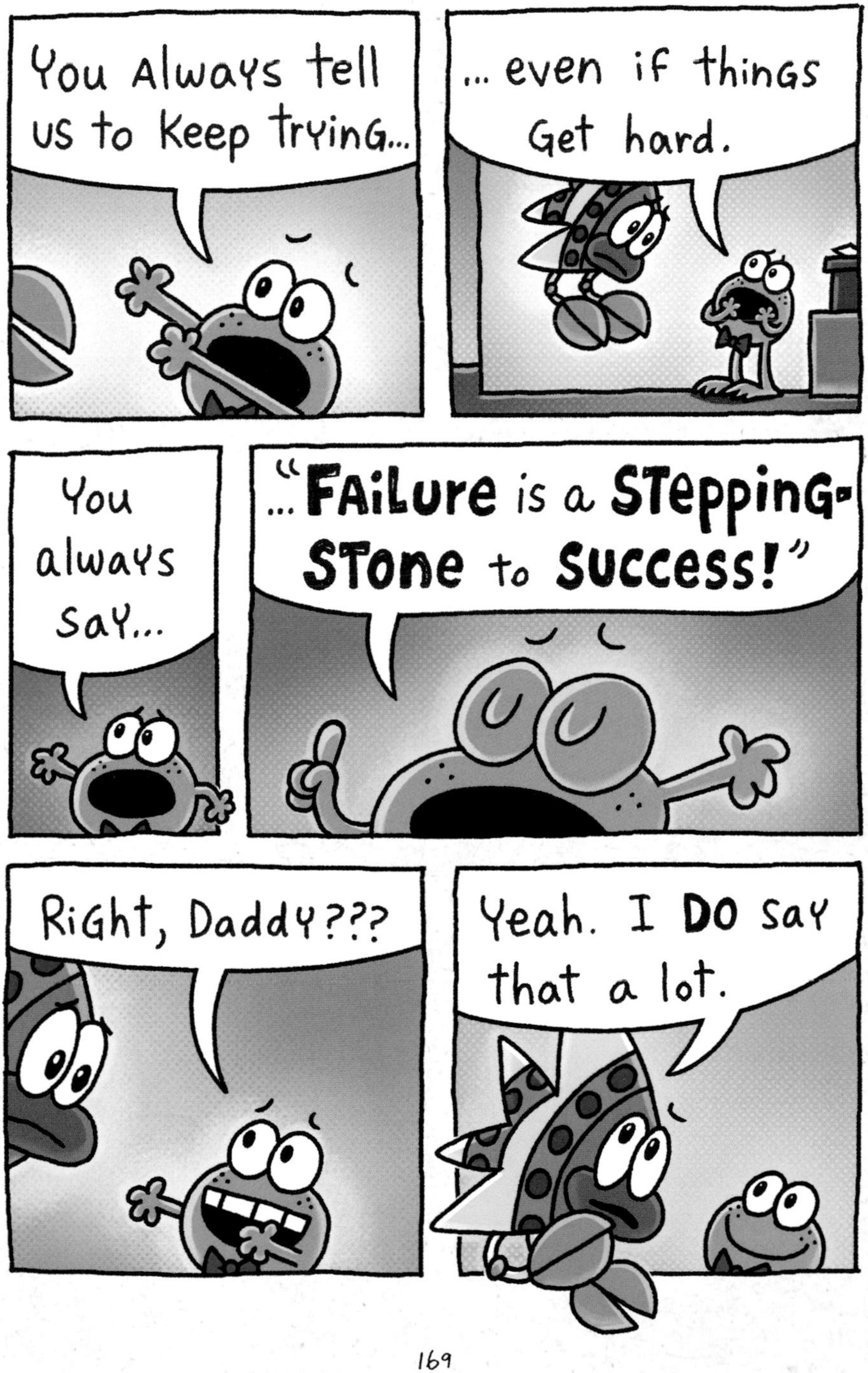
You Always tell us to keep trying...
... even if things Get hard.
You always say...
..."FAILURE is a STEPPING-STONE to SUCCESS!"
Right, Daddy???
Yeah. I DO say that a lot.

CHAPTER 12

New Comic, Old Problem

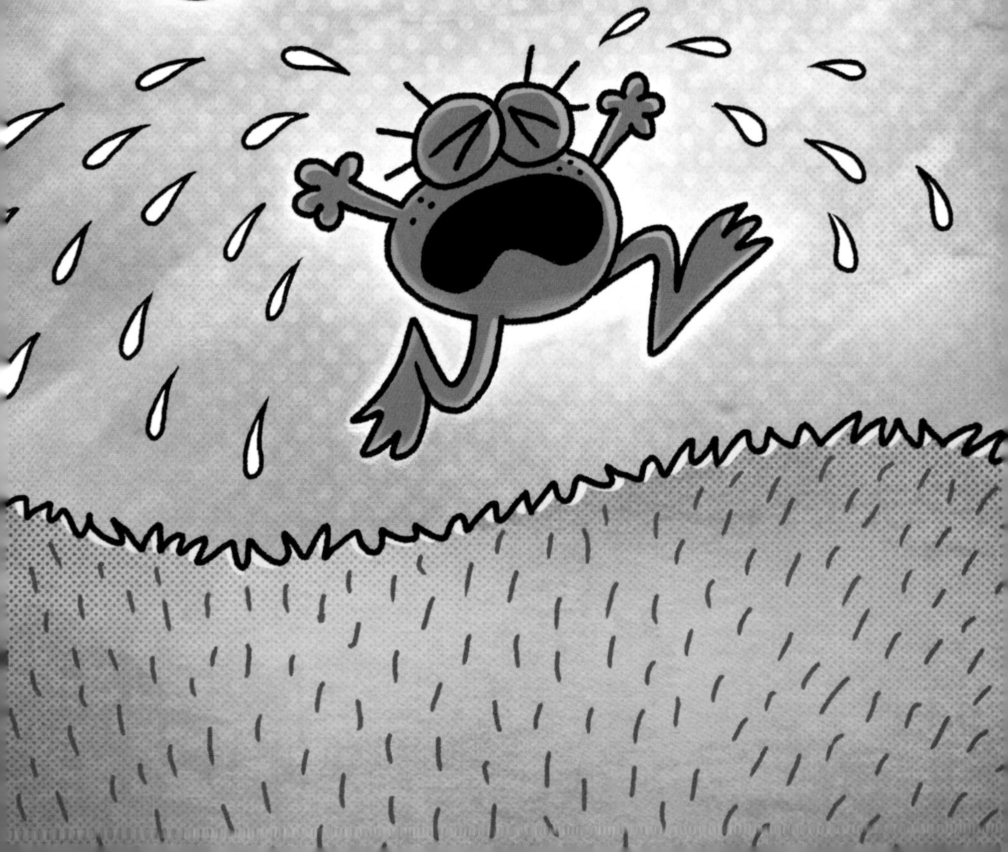

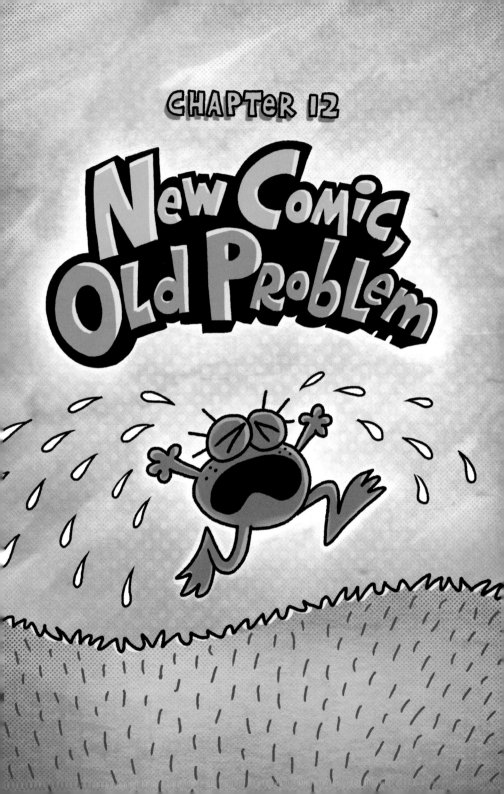

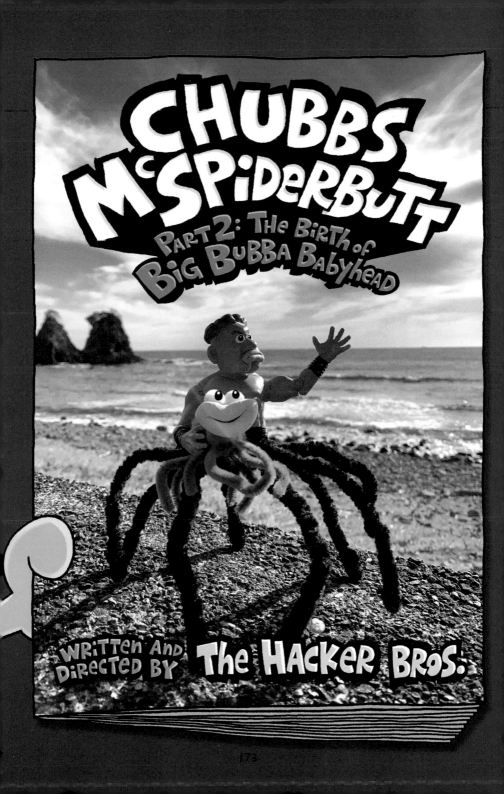

Well he said your gym shorts and dress shoes look silly together.

No he didn't!

Shhh!

Oh, he **Did**, did he?

So Chubbs McSpiderbutt thinks he can insult MY Fashion Sense...

...and Get AWAY with it ?????

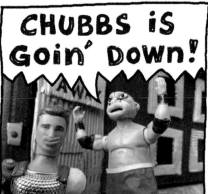

CHUBBS iS Goin' DOWN!

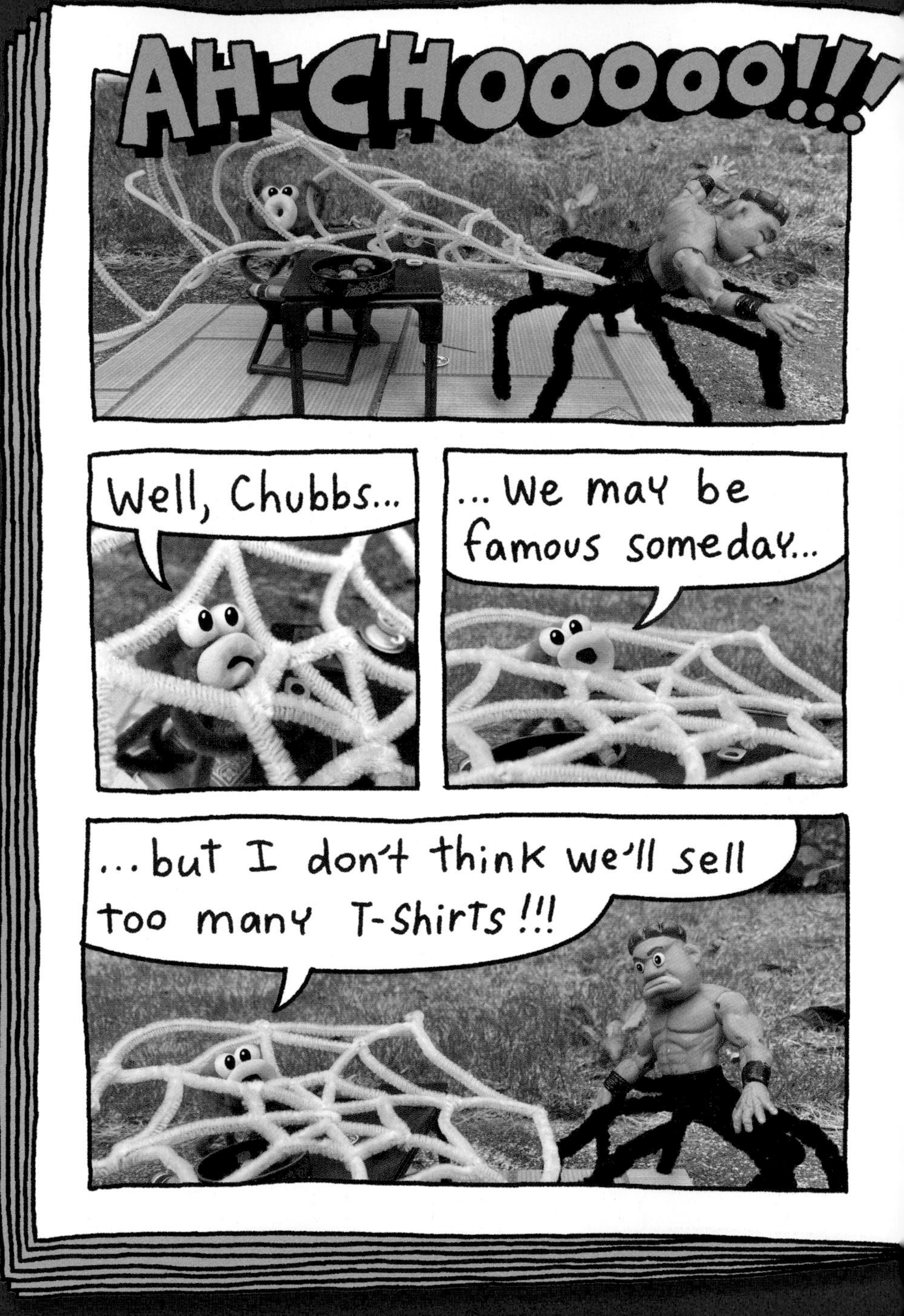
AH-CHOOOOO!!!
Well, Chubbs...
...We may be famous someday...
...but I don't think we'll sell too many T-Shirts!!!

193

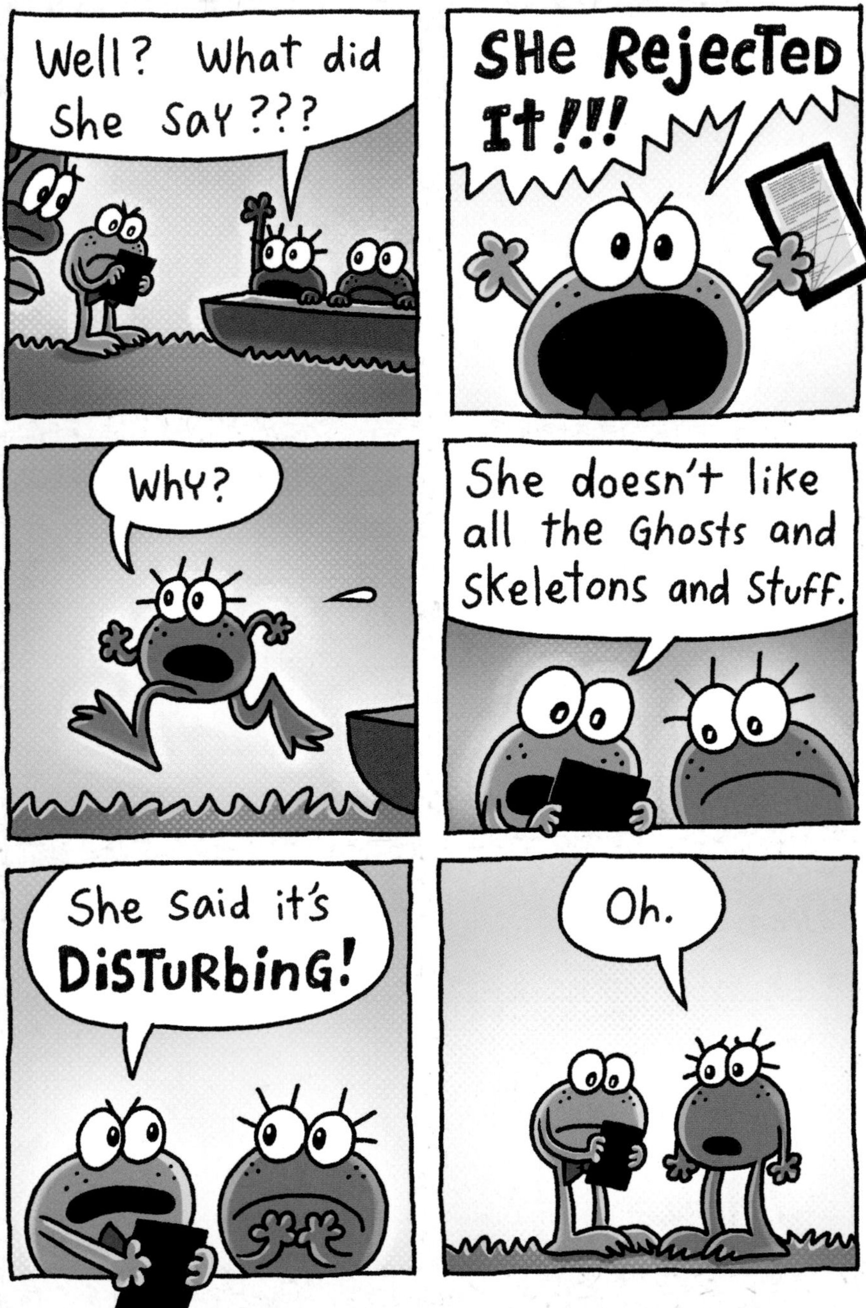
Well? What did she say???
SHE REJECTED IT!!!
WHY?
She doesn't like all the Ghosts and Skeletons and Stuff.
She said it's DISTURBING!
Oh.

CHAPTER 13

Just be You

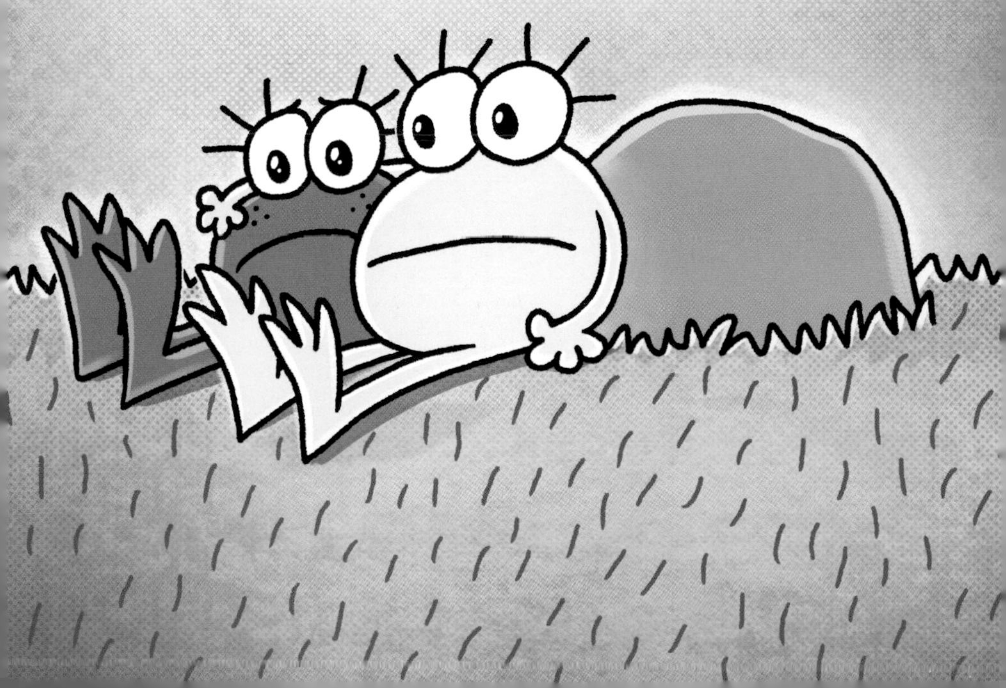

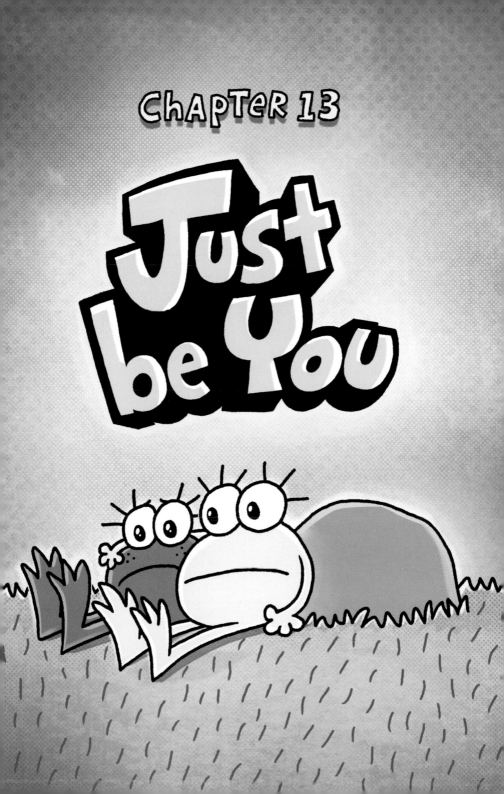

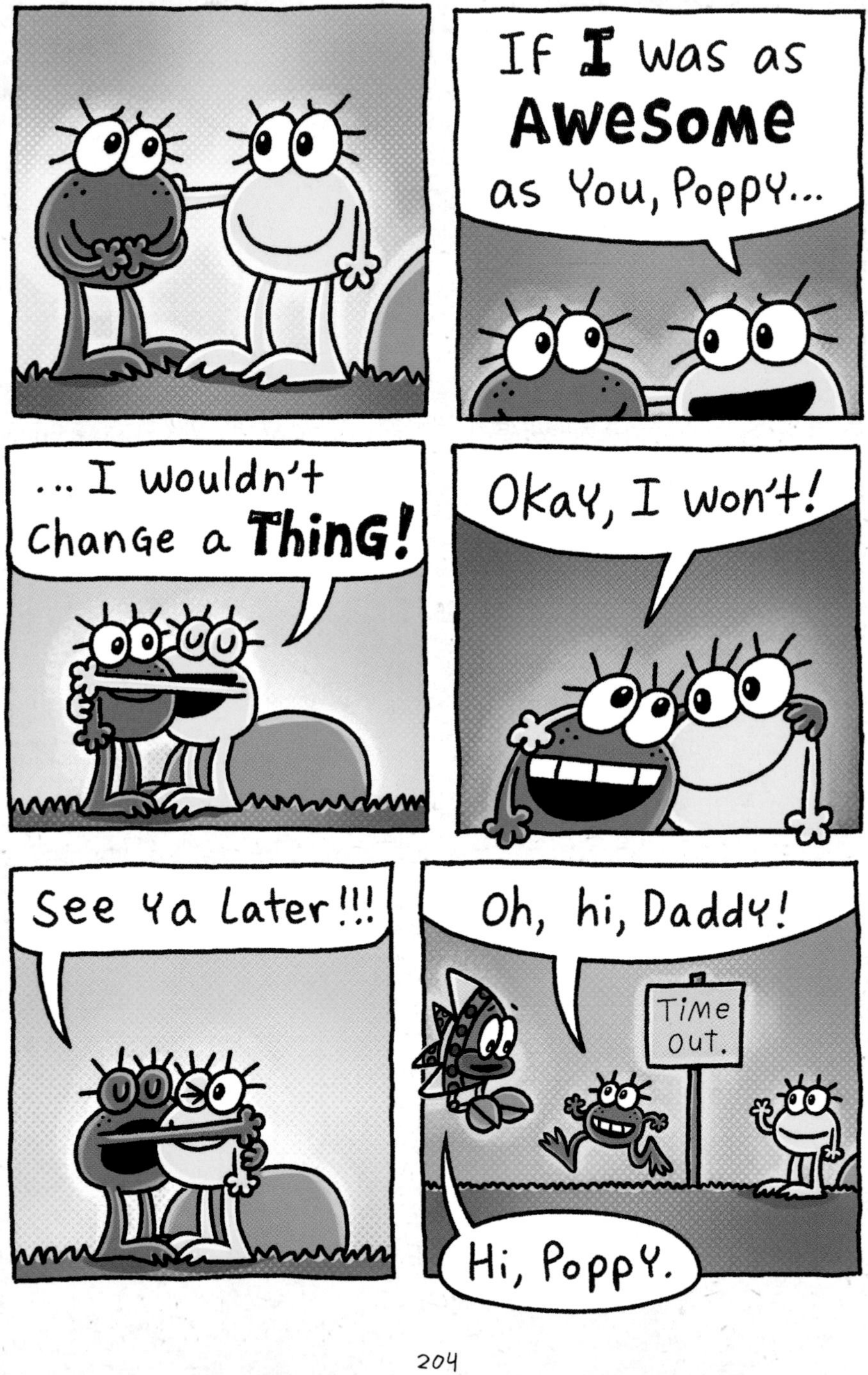
If I was as AWESOME as You, Poppy...
... I wouldn't change a ThinG!
Okay, I won't!
See ya Later!!!
Oh, hi, Daddy!
Time out.
Hi, Poppy.

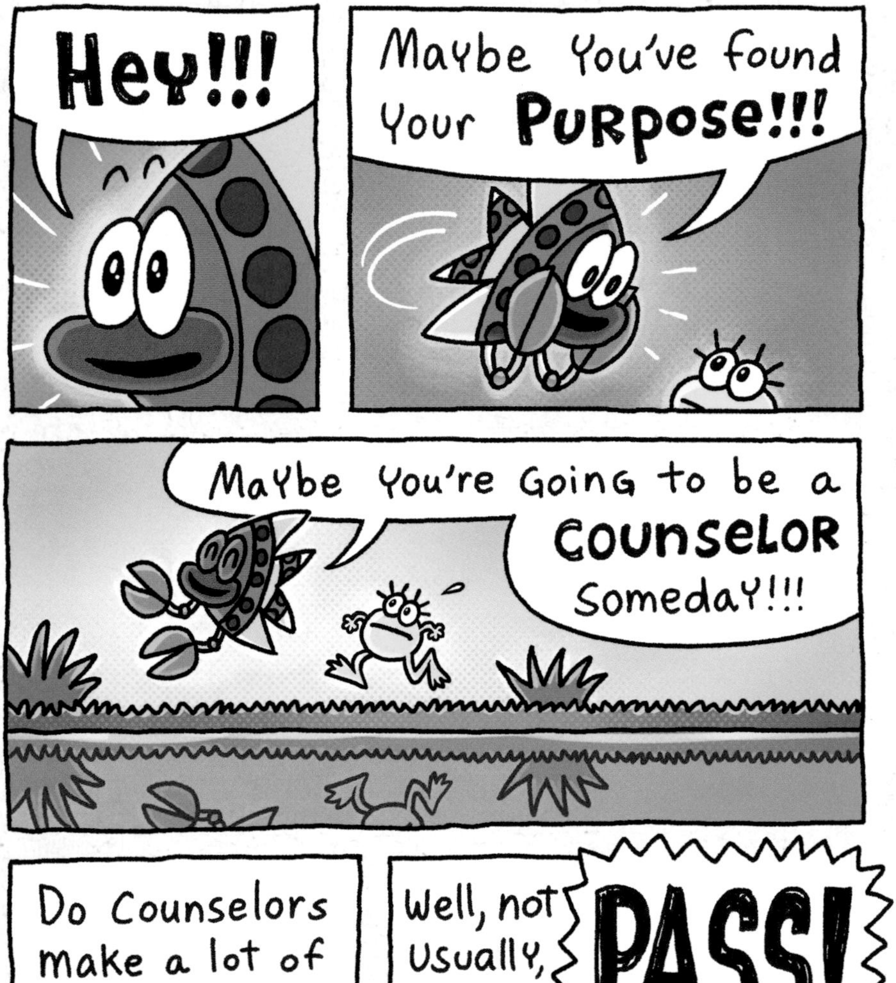
Hey!!!
Maybe You've found Your PURPOSE!!!
Maybe You're Going to be a COUNSELOR Someday!!!
Do Counselors make a lot of money?
Well, not Usually, but they
PASS!

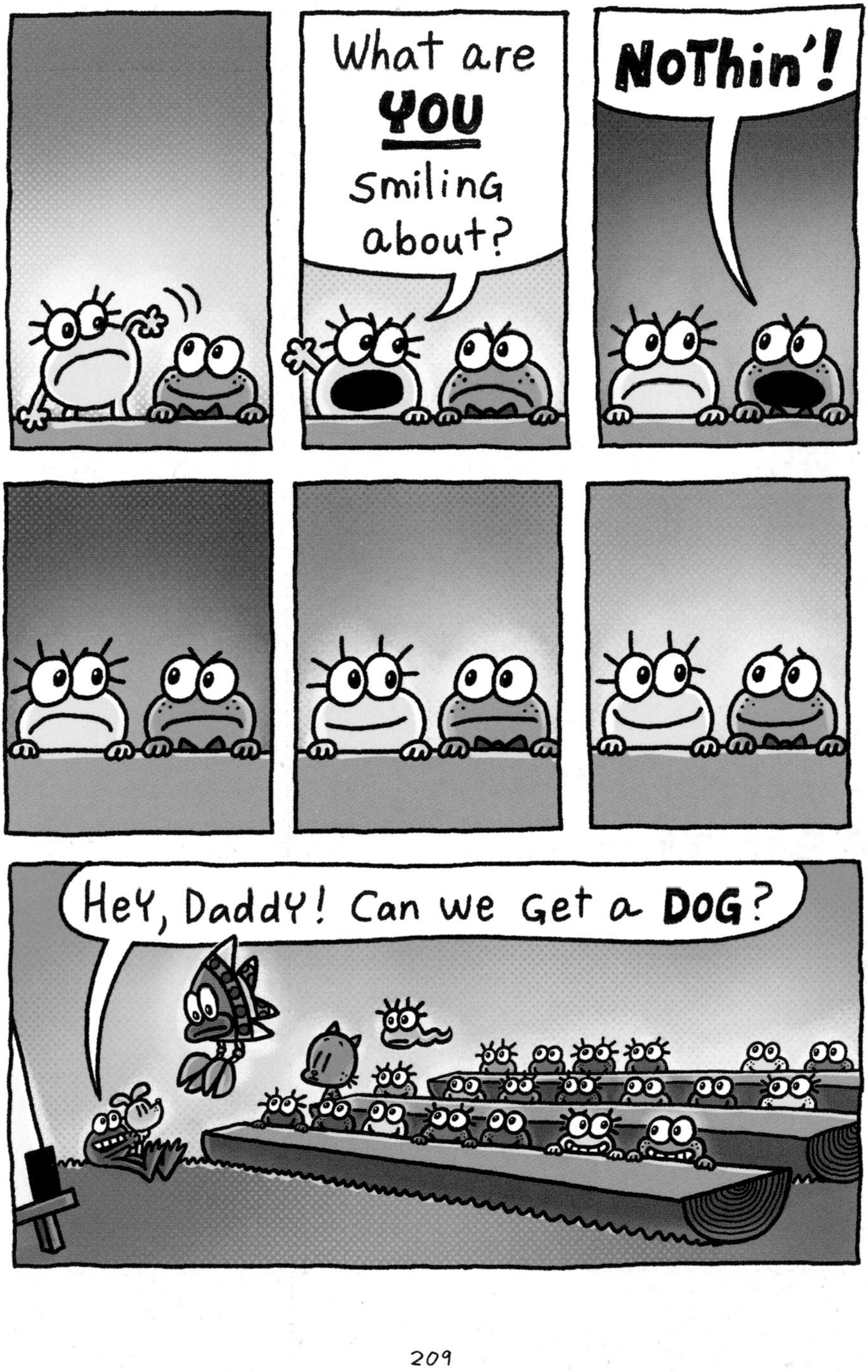
What are YOU smiling about?
NOThin'!
HeY, DaddY! Can we Get a DOG?

220

NOTES & FUN FACTS

★ The cover artwork for this book was made from cardboard, wire, crumpled-up construction paper, putty, acrylic paints, glue, and a small sheet of fake grass.

★ Most of the planets in BABY FROG SQUAD are balloons, airbrushed with markers, that were photographed in front of a light bulb. The planet that looks like a melon is a close-up photo of the plastic lid of a fruit cup.

★ The Baby Frog Squad's bunk beds were made out of matchboxes glued to bamboo shish-kebab skewers.

★ Over 2,000 photographs were taken for the Chubbs McSpiderbutt mini comic, but only 111 were used.

★ Chubbs is correct on page 182. Spiders DO produce webs from their spinnerets, located at the tips of their abdomens (their butts). Most spiders don't "shoot" webs, but a few do. The Darwin's bark spider can "shoot" a web up to 82 feet (25 meters) long. Sweeeet!!!

★ Big Bubba Babyhead's gym shorts came from a 1972 action figure called "Big Jim." This action figure also inspired a character in the Dog Man series.

★ The Ethel Merman Disco Album really DOES exist, although it is rarely used to frighten baby frogs.

★ Melvin's words on page 169 were inspired by the following quote:

> "Discouragement and failure are two of the surest stepping-stones to success."
>
> —Dale Carnegie

KEEP READING WITH DAV PILKEY!

The epic musical adventure is now available from Broadway Records!

Go to planetpilkey.com to read chapters, make comics, watch videos, play games, and download supa fun stuff!

ABOUT THE
AUTHOR-ILLUSTRATOR

When Dav Pilkey was a kid, he was diagnosed with ADHD and dyslexia. Dav was so disruptive in class that his teachers made him sit out in the hallway every day. Luckily, Dav loved to draw and make up stories. He spent his time in the hallway creating his own original comic books — the very first adventures of Dog Man and Captain Underpants.

In college, Dav met a teacher who encouraged him to write and illustrate for kids. He took her advice and created his first book, WORLD WAR WON, which won a national competition in 1986. Dav made many other books before being awarded the California Young Reader Medal for DOG BREATH (1994) and the Caldecott Honor for THE PAPERBOY (1996).

In 2002, Dav published his first full-length graphic novel for kids, called THE ADVENTURES OF SUPER DIAPER BABY. It was both a USA Today and New York Times bestseller. Since then, he has published more than a dozen full-length graphic novels for kids, including the bestselling Dog Man and Cat Kid Comic Club series.

Dav's stories are semi-autobiographical and explore universal themes that celebrate friendship, empathy, and the triumph of the good-hearted.

When he is not making books for kids, Dav loves to kayak with his wife in the Pacific Northwest.

Learn more at Pilkey.com.